GIRLS
FROM
DA HOOD

GIRLS FROM DA HOOD

**Nikki Turner
Roy Glenn
Chunichi**

URBAN BOOKS LLC
www.urbanbooks.net

Urban Books LLC
10 Brennan Place
Deer Park, NY 11729

ISBN 1-893196-50-X

First printing September 2006
Printed in the United States of America

10   9   8   7   6   5   4   3

Distributed by Kensington Publishing
850 Third Ave.
New York, NY 10022
For store orders call 1 (800) 221-2647 ext 527

Printed in the United States of America

ACKNOWLEDGMENTS

Nikki Turner

Thank You, God, for giving me the strength to endure in the midst of every situation in my life. Thank You, God, for opening up doors that no man can shut. Thank You, Father, for giving me peripheral vision to see through those who meant me no good, and placing angels in my path to comfort me, encourage me, and keep me lifted up in prayer. Thank You for giving me the words, wisdom and knowledge to give the literary world yet another classic.

My Timmond and Kennisha, as I reflect, go through and endure the pains, struggles, the storms and feeling like I can't do this anymore, it is you two that breathe motivation, victory and triumph into me. Hearing you tell me I am the best whether I am writing or making you dinner, it is you that keeps me going when I feel like I can go no further. Thanks for being my strength and inspiration. I love you soooo much!

My mother, thanks for your unconditional love.

As I raise my own children, I am able to truly understand your struggle of being mother and father. Nothing material could ever show my appreciation. Uncle Sonny, thanks for constantly pulling my coat and schooling me to the game called life. Uncle Byron, thanks for always assisting me in ventures I was clueless about—cars, TV, shopping, etc.

To my devoted fans, thank you for the undying love that you've given me from day one. Even with all the typos that were in my previous books, never have you turned your back on me. You always knew that I am just a writer, not a publisher or editor. Thank you big time!!! I love you from the depths of my belly!

I have been soooo blessed and fortunate to have so many people in my life who have held me afloat at times when I felt like I was drowning. DeAudrey, please don't ever think that I don't appreciate you, because I do. Angie, for being my ride or die friend and our lunches at Hooters are always the main reason why I have cheated on my "diets," but anything for you! So much love to you, cousin Cha, for always having something super fly to say out your mouth at the right time. Brenda Thomas, you keep it sooo real. Thanks for being you all the time! Jemise, thanks for being just a phone call away no matter which estate or coast you were living on. B. Lawson and Diaamah, thanks for being so genuine. Sharissa, you have become such a dear sistergirl, the laughs and heart to heart, I love you and wish you the absolute best in every one of your endeavours. Patrice C, thanks for keeping me abreast on life and being nothing less than a friend. To my beloved sistah, Wahida, thanks for such a unique sisterhood that we share. I wish you could have been on this project, but we're gonna Thelma and Louise the next one. To my bother Jerron, thanks so much for your insight in my work and my life. Craig, there are no words for the astronomical love you have given me over so many years. Always know that it's truly reciprocated. My dear Wayne, this is bulletproof, baby. Zane, thanks for giving me the best-kept secrets of this game and embracing me. Rakeem W, the sky is the limit, baby!! To the world's champ and my 3-way bandit, keep knockin' 'em out, baby. Joi, you never cease to amaze me how you hold me down. Kwan, you are still my Clyde. Tracy Brown, for not turning your back on me when so many others did. To VA's finest: Mocha, Ghost, Blunt, Jewel, Tonya Blount, we are really putting VA on the map. Kedy, for always holding me down with whatever drama is brewing. Lazette Carter, you are truly a woman of virtue. God sees the good work you do. Sandra West, thank you! Thank you! Thank you! Bill Adkins, I love you and you could never know how much I appreciate you. Thanks! Tamia Washington, they say we look just alike and could be sisters. I love you as a sister. Thanks! Pam (The Ritz), thanks so much for sharing when you didn't even know me and since then we have become such good friends. My secretary and friend, Nicey B, you have been there for me through it all. Eternal love! Melissa, thanks for making my life a lot easier.

Carl Weber, thank you for believing in me and my work, giving me the opportunity to do this project and all the support and laughs. To Martha, my editor, thanks so much for all your hard work. Marc, the super agent, thanks so much for all your encouragement and for the big deal. You promised me the zeros and guess what? You got them. Earl Cox, for assisting me in any way you can. I know I don't say much, but thank you sooo much. I think I have broken your rest early in the a.m. so much that you are now a.m. person. Pat MacCally, girl, why are you the best? I feel like I may have been your sister in another life. Thanks for really wanting the best for my career. Gary Raskin, for being my bridge over troubled water. Pam Crockette, the flyest attorney, who has always kept it real and gave me encouragement when I thought I was all cried out. Earl B, for all you do. Special, special thanks to the Urban Books and Random House families for welcoming me with open arms!

To the First Union Baptist Church and all of the folks who were supportive to me and my family as we dealt with the loss of my grandmother. You all were nothing but a blessing to us. Thank you!

If I have forgotten anyone, please forgive me . . . charge it to my head, not my heart!

Last and definitely leastly, to the haters: Every time you strike at me, it just builds me back up.

MESSAGE TO THE READER

I have been told by so many of my readers to take it straight to the gutter, and that's what I have done this go 'round. By no means does my story apply to every girl from the hood. However, I feel that it is my job to bring to light the tricks, scams and low-life scandals that the best of the gutter-snipes try to dish out. Somewhere within every hood across the world lies a certified hoodrat. Most of them cannot be seen with the naked eye, for they don't have a distinguishing look. Some roll alone while others may travel in twos, threes or bunches, and you can hear them coming before they are even seen. Others keep a low profile, moving in complete silence. It is my hope that once you take this journey with me through the sewers and gutters, you'll be able spot a hoodrat a mile away. Thank you so much for your undying support. I'll keep my ear to the streets, listening and hearing them talk, so I can bring the stories to you!

Eternal Love,
Nikki T.

Unique

JUST PART OF THE GAME

Riiiiiiing.

Unique knew automatically that it was her man, Took, calling from jail. This was the call she had been waiting for, praying for. She had been through hell with gasoline drawers just to be able to get this call. The phone company had cut off the phone two days before, but Unique schemed and hustled up the three hundred dollars to pay to have the service reconnected so she wouldn't miss Took's calls.

Before Took went to jail, three hundred dollars was play money to Unique. She used to practically throw away three hundred dollars on meaningless things like a bottle of Cristal or dinner for her and her girl, Strolla, at one of Richmond's most exquisite restaurants, but to gather up three hundred dollars nowadays, especially for a phone bill, was surely a difficult task. If she never respected Took for all the work he put in on the streets trying to make a better life for them, she did now.

The past few months without him, truly made her feel a newfound love and respect for him.

She answered the phone. "Hallllooo!"

"Hello," replied an automated operator. "This is Bell Atlantic with a collect call from . . ."

"Took." Unique heard Took's voice as he spoke his name. Boy, did he sound good.

The automated voice continued. "If you do not wish to accept this call, please hang up now. To accept this call, press zero now."

Without any hesitation, Unique pushed the button to accept the call. The automated voice responded. "Your call is being connected. Thank you for using Bell Atlantic."

"Hello," Took said with a sigh of relief.

"Hey, boo," she gushed when she heard his voice. The sound soothed her soul. Now, everything she had gone through to get the phone back on suddenly felt well worth it. The anguish, frustration and humiliation was all erased from her memory.

"I was tryin' to call and I couldn't get through," Took complained.

"I know, boo. They cut the phone off."

"Damn, I thought Shawn was gonna give you the money to pay the bill."

"Well, he didn't."

"Damn, I can't believe that nigga."

"I know, boo, but don't get upset 'bout it."

"Well, did Fat Tee ever give you dat money he owes me?"

"Nope."

"Call that nigga on the three-way."

"Boo, I'm tired of calling him. He doesn't answer the phone when he sees my number. Then when I walked around the street the other day to see if I saw him, it was like he had the lookout guys looking out for me, like I was the police. Every time I go around there they say he ain't out there. Now, when have you known Fat Tee to even leave the projects?" Unique asked.

"I swear to God, I'm gonna take care of that fat, twelve-sandwich-eatin' ma'fucka when I get home."

"Boo, don't worry 'bout it. I'm gonna get a job." She transferred the phone from her right hand to her left then rubbed her itching nose.

"Where you gonna get a job at?" Took asked.

"I don't know yet, but I gotta do something. As hard as times are right now, I'll take a job anywhere."

"Oh, hell naw. You ain't working nowhere either."

"Boo, for real, I've gotta be able to hold these bills down until you get back out here. I mean, I know Train got my back 'cause he did give me a hundred towards the phone bill, but I can't be depending on him to come through for me all the time. He got his own life, not to mention a slew of baby mommas and hoes always begging. I mean, I gotta make sure I got a plan for me, just in case he gets locked the hell up too. Baby, I know you don't want me to work, and I know if you were here, I wouldn't have to. But, boo, I gotta do what I gotta do. I can't be going through this. I can't be going through what I went through yesterday tryin' to get this phone on, and last week when I didn't even have gas money to come and see you."

This was game she had falling out of her mouth. Unique wasn't really thinking about getting any job to hold the bills down. As far as she was concerned, she shouldn't be paying any bills anyway.

She knew there were plenty of suckers dying for a lick, and with so many suckers on the streets of Richmond, her bills would get paid one way or another. Still, she had to fake like she was so responsible, holding the fort down while Took was gone, so she could keep him under control. He couldn't know the real reason she was going out to get a job. She was going to a real players' ball, where all the renowned players, pimps and dons from all over the country would be, and she needed the money to buy just the right outfit to catch a man who would pick up exactly where Took left off.

She was only telling Took what she knew would sound good to him. "I gotta keep the phone on so I can talk to you, baby. Not to mention the other li'l household bills—lights, gas, and water." She rolled a blunt while she was pouring the game on Took.

"Plus I gotta keep a li'l food in the refrigerator. I mean, I know this place is paid for, but remember I got a second mortgage on this house to pay the lawyer for your appeal, so I gotta make sure I keep up those payments or I ain't gonna have nowhere to live." Unique knew that laying a guilt trip on Took was always a good way to keep him under control and off her back.

"I hate you living in that raggedy-ass, sugar shack any fucking way." Took sucked his teeth.

"Well, if you wouldn'a had Black Mike and all them coming over to our house talking 'bout they yo' right hands, then we would still have our house. But the state got that now. I ain't complainin', though." She put the blunt to her lips and lit it.

"You right," Took said quickly, not wanting the

conversation to go where she was trying to take it. "But, boo, I hate the fact that you gotta live in the spot that I used to have as my crap house, and it's right across the street from them raggedy-ass projects too."

"Me too. I'm just grateful that it was paid for and the folks ain't take this too. Otherwise, my ass would be right on the streets and your lawyer wouldn't be paid. So look on the bright side, boo." She inhaled a hit off her blunt.

Took was mad as hell but trying not to reveal his frustrations to her. "A'ight," he said, "but just make sure you get some hours so I can be able to talk to you."

"You know you ain't even gotta say that."

She wasn't deaf. She could hear his frustration and anger. The reality was he was no madder than she was. She had accepted the fact that "out of sight, out of mind" was exactly how the dudes who owed Took thousands of dollars felt. They wouldn't be giving up any money to her while Took was away. It wasn't anything out of the ordinary; it was simply a part of the game. Unique wasn't worried about it, though. Even though Took was sentenced to nine years, he could get about eighteen months off his sentence for good behavior if he did what he had to do. It wouldn't be long before he would be back on the bricks, and as sure as his name was Took, he'd take care of each and every thug who owed him and shitted on him.

Took was one of the most well known and also one of the most feared guys around the streets of Richmond. A hell of a hustler, getting money was never a problem for him. He had a heart of gold and went to the ends of the earth for his friends, but to the other big-head hustlers and especially his foes—well, that was another story.

It was his own enemies who gave him the unusual name Took because that's exactly what he did. He rolled up to a crap game and never shot the dice; he just "took" the money. He owned plenty of corners and crack houses in the 321, 359 and 643 areas. Still, at any given time the crack houses and corners that belonged to his foes became his just on GP (general principle). He would roll up on the corners, lay the dealers down and "took" everything from them, down to the shoes on their feet. The crack houses were the same. He would roll up in there and "took" all the drugs and money out of there, holding every soul at gunpoint. It didn't matter to him if they were men or women; he didn't discriminate. He would make them strip down to their boxers, panties, and bras. They all knew better than to disobey his directions, for if they did, they would without a doubt be the next ones biting the dust.

Most of the time Took rolled with a legion of tickbirds, but he never actually needed an entourage. If he happened to be by himself and ran into some clown who needed to be dealt with, he could hold his own.

Ironically, Took didn't have the look of the average hustler. He could pass for a young adolescent, barely weighing in at a hundred and twenty-five pounds and standing five feet six inches tall. There was no hair on his baby face, and his close haircut didn't help him look any older. He always wore thin, wire-framed Versace or Fendi glasses, which, along with a backpack containing a couple of bogus textbooks, gave him the nerdy look of a young, innocent schoolboy.

For a long time, his appearance led the police to overlook him, mistaking him for a studious boy stuck living in the hood. After years of manipulating police intelligence, he was finally taken in, but even then he was taken in as a juvenile. Took was the perfect example of the idea that you should never judge a book by its cover.

Took might have looked like a little boy, but he was very much a grown man, especially where it counted. Some folks say it's not the size of the ship, it's the motion of the ocean that matters. Well, if Took's manhood were to be classified as a ship, it would be a cruise ship. As far as his motions in the ocean, it was no secret that Took knew how to rock his boat in a way that made women fall to his feet. This fact made Took so confident in his sex game that he wasn't worried in the least about Unique giving it up to another man while he was away. Besides, she had made Took wait three months to get his first taste of that coochie, and the average brother on the streets wasn't going to wait three weeks, let alone three months. There was too much easy coochie out there on the streets of Richmond for them to be waiting on Unique. Maybe a corporate dude working a 9-5 would wait three months to get a piece, but Unique wasn't the type of woman for a dude trying to get ahead in the business world anyway.

Without a doubt she was beautiful. She had long, flowing, sandy brown hair and cat-like hazel eyes. Her skin was flawless, and she had a distinctive mole near her lip, just like the one that made supermodel Cindy Crawford famous. Standing five feet four inches, her body was a perfect ten—firm, C-cup breasts, a big, badooka butt, and gorgeous hips curving out from her small waist. No matter what Unique wore, whether she had paid twenty dollars for it or convinced some sucker to pay two hundred, she made it look like a million.

Unique was definitely easy on the eyes, but she had little to no book sense. This was the one flaw that Took believed would make her unworthy of the 9-5 dudes who might desire her. When she did go to school, it was only if she had something new to wear. After she met Took, he provided her with so much money that she started spending her days shopping, then waiting on the couch in sexy lingerie for Took to come home and make love to her. With the lavish lifestyle Took was able to give her, school seemed like more of a burden than anything. She dropped out completely by the time she was in tenth grade.

Took was happy to provide Unique, with her pretty face and banging hourglass figure, with everything she ever dreamed of. What he didn't know, though, was that at the end of the day, the love of his life would turn out to be a bonafide hood rat. Took had been snatched off the streets to do a lengthy bid thanks to his once-upon-a-time homeboys turned snitches. What he needed now was a Ride-or-Die chick—one who had some goals and dreams beyond lying on the couch, waiting for him to bring home some more money. He needed someone who at least had a job or saved some of that fast money for a rainy day. Someone who might open her own business so that they could have peace of mind while he was lying down, doing his bid. At the very least, he needed someone who wasn't spending recklessly while her man was on trial, letting forty-five grand slip through her fingers like water.

When Took was on trial, Unique was too busy shopping to stop and think *What if he doesn't beat his charges?* She failed to realize that her man was being charged in a Commonwealth state, not to mention the capital of the Confederacy, and he could be facing a twenty to thirty year sentence. It didn't even cross her mind to do research on crimes in Virginia like the one he had been accused of. She had no book smarts and even less common sense, so while Took stood trial, she continued on with life as usual, living by the motto "You gotta use what you got to get what you want." Now she was suffering the consequences, scrounging for three hundred dollars to get the phone turned on. And Took was sitting in jail, unaware that his girl, the one he had chosen to be on his team, was beautiful on the outside but had no soul.

DESPERATE TIMES CALL FOR DESPERATE MEASURES

Two days earlier

The refrigerator was so empty that Unique could see damn near up to Mechanicsville Turnpike. There was one cracked-up egg, a corner of grape Kool-Aid in a Tupperware pitcher, and a box of baking soda to keep the empty refrigerator fresh.

While Unique looked at the sad sight inside the fridge, her friend, Strolla, walked into the kitchen. "Girl, cook us something to eat. I'm hungrier than a ma'fucka."

"Girl, it ain't nothing to cook."

"You don't have no food stamps left?"

"Shoot, they only give me a hundred twenty-one dollars since I don't have no kids. I got groceries at the beginning of the month when I first got those, so they good and gone."

Food stamps were one of Unique's little hustles. Although they had lived together for three years, she never let Took know that she was receiving stamps from the government. Instead, she asked him every month for $50, claiming she knew a girl named Tonya who would sell her $100 worth of stamps at half price. Unique would pocket the $50, with Took believing all the while that she had spent it on stamps. Unique didn't really need the stamps anyway, since Took already bought hundreds of dollars of stamps every month. Took just gave her the money to buy the stamps from her "friend" Tonya because he believed they could never have too many food stamps. The way he saw it, they would always need food to survive. He had no idea that the stamps meant more than that to Unique. When he was standing trial and money ran low, Unique went to her stash of stamps and started selling them off for cash. Now she was standing in front of her barren refrigerator wishing she had some of those damn stamps for some real food.

"Is it some Kool-Aid in there so I can at least take my medicine?" Strolla asked.

"Nope, girl, it ain't nothing but a corner left. You just gonna have to get some water out of the sink and take your medicine."

"Girl, how much money you got?"

" 'Bout a dollar twenty." As she spoke the words, Unique couldn't believe how bad things had become for her.

"Damn, girl, you got me beat. I think I just got some change in my pocketbook. We got to do something."

"You ain't lyin'." Unique slumped onto the chair in the kitchen, wondering how she was going to get out of this situation and back to her life of luxury.

Unique and Strolla spent the afternoon trying to come up with a plan to make some money, but neither was motivated enough to get serious. Neither one liked the idea of actually going out and finding a job to handle their troubles. Instead, they just complained about the situation until they both fell asleep on the living room couches. It was after sunset when Unique awoke to the sound of her pager vibrating against the wooden coffee table. She rubbed her eyes to adjust to the darkened room, then she rolled over and checked the pager. It was Teddy, a dude she went to school with. She had run into Teddy at the club a week before.

Teddy was a suave dude. He could dress his butt off and had diamonds like Liberace. He was a classy guy who had never touched or sold a drug a day in his life, but one would never know that, because he dressed and drove a Benz that made him look just like all the big time drug dealers. Teddy was a spoiled brat who came from a wealthy family with a chain of lucrative convenient stores around Richmond and surrounding counties. His family gave him everything he could ever want in the hope that it would prevent him from falling victim to the lure of easy money from the streets. So, Teddy had it all—a bank account so he could splurge exactly like the hustlers did, and his own place filled with the finest of everything.

Seeing Teddy's number on her pager made her smile. She was already forming a plan to get some money for her and Strolla. Teddy had just been placed in a special category: official victim of Unique.

Unique picked up her cordless phone, eager to call Teddy. However, she was greeted by total silence. She knew she had left the phone off the charger for too long, so she ran to use the other phone, but found another dead line. She couldn't believe the damn phone company had disconnected her service.

"Them ma'fuckas!" she shouted. "Don't you know they cut my shit off?" she roared to Strolla. "Gimme that change you got."

Strolla gave her what little change she had. Unique grabbed her keys, threw on some flip-flops and made her way to the payphone behind the projects. Strolla tagged along. Unique went to use the phone around the back of the 643 projects, hoping that the chicks around the projects wouldn't see her using it. They would all know her phone was cut off. Unique surely didn't want everyone knowing that she didn't have it together the way she used to.

First she called the phone company. A representative explained that since she hadn't made her arranged payment of $75 the week before they interrupted her service. Now, instead of paying the $75, which would have kept the service on, she had to pay the whole past due amount of $326. Unique had no idea where she was going to get the money from, as broke as she was. For a split second she thought about returning one of the outfits she had bought when she was still splurging, running through Took's forty-five Gs. She had already worn them all, though, and didn't think she could pull off returning them.

Her next plan was to check in with Took's homeboy, Train, to see if he could help her out. Train was a young dude who was loyal to Took ever since the day Took helped him out with his momma's drunk-ass boyfriend. The boyfriend had Train's momma in the middle of the street, beating her buck-ass naked behind. Train was only fifteen years old, but he went out there trying to help his momma. The boyfriend turned on Train and started beating him like he was a grown man. Took came through the cut and couldn't believe his eyes when he saw the child being beaten unmercifully by this big man. Without hesitation, he shot the boyfriend. Ever since that day, Train looked up to Took.

As the years passed, Train moved to the city's south side and learned to pimp the streets for all they were worth. When word of Took's arrest reached Train, he dropped Took a letter to let him know he had his back. He was ready to repay his debt to Took from so many years ago. Sure enough, Train came through time and time again with sizable money orders, booty pictures of stripper broads, and all the numbers he could be reached at when Took needed him. Took didn't smother Train by blowing him up on the phone tip, but every Sunday evening they talked. Before long, Took knew pretty much everything going on in Train's life and became his mentor from inside the can. After a while, when his other so-called friends had deserted him, Took felt that Train was the only true soldier he had left. Many acted the part and surely wanted the respect that came with being a part of Took's army, but at the end of the day, Train was the only one who was real to the cause.

Unique knew that Train was loyal to her man and he would do anything for Took. She was ready to call in a favor. She paged Train and put in her

pager number so that he could page her back with
a phone number where he could be reached. She
knew it wouldn't be long before he called back, because anything having to do with Took, including
a call from his better half, and Train was always
prompt and diligent.

In a matter of minutes Unique received a page
from Train, and she dialed his phone number in a
hurry. When he answered, she explained the situation with the phone company and asked him what
he could do to help her out. Train explained that
he had plenty of drugs but not much cash on
hand. He could give her $100 toward the phone
bill. They agreed on a place to meet in an hour,
and Unique hung up the phone feeling relieved.
Then she called Teddy, knowing he would be the
best way to get the rest of what she needed.

"Hey, Teddy. This Unique," she said in her most
sultry voice. She didn't want him to have any
doubt about what she was calling for.

"What's the deal, baby?"

"Nothin' at all."

"And why is that?"

"Broke as hell, that's all."

"Damn, as pretty as you are, you don't have no
reason to be broke. I know if you was my girl, you
wouldn't be broke."

"I hear you talking. Shoot, don't talk about it, be
about it." She turned to Strolla and smiled, letting
her know everything was working out as they had
hoped.

"Come over then, and make sure you don't have
on no drawers either. I'm gonna look out for you
once you get here. I'll put a li'l change in your
pocket."

That last comment was like music to her ears. She didn't know how much money he was talking about, but as broke as she was, anything was better than what she had. Plus, whatever his contribution was, it would put her closer to getting her phone back on so she would be able to talk to Took.

She had been to Teddy's house before, but he still gave her the address. As many chicks as had been running in and out of his bedroom, he had probably forgotten Unique had ever been there. If his bedroom walls could talk, oh, what stories they would tell.

On the walk back to the house, Strolla and Unique mapped out the game plan for the night. First they had to head over to the south side to meet Train, who never came across the James River to the 643. This was an unspoken rule for the south side boys. They were always beefing with the neighborhoods across the water, whether it was the 321 (the north side), the 643 (the east end/Church Hill), or the 359 (the west end). The south side boys always stayed in a beef with at least one or all of these hoods across the water. If the south side boys were caught in one of those neighborhoods, they went back across the water in a body bag or with multiple gunshot wounds, and the same went for anybody from the 643, 359 or 321 coming across the river. Nobody left their own territory unless they were going with carloads and were strapped with plenty of ammunition to assure that they'd make it back to their hood.

In order to stay on schedule, Strolla and Unique would need to put some pep in their step to get the money from Train, then get back to see Teddy in the west end.

Strolla hollered from in front of the almost empty

linen closet while Unique was ironing, "Girl, I need a towel! It ain't no towels in the closet."

With no shame at all, Unique answered, "Use the one you had from yesterday because it ain't no more. All the towels are dirty. We need to wash clothes bad. Hopefully I'll be able to grind up enough money to wash the clothes."

Strolla didn't comment. She was just as trifling as Unique. She was on her second day of taking penicillin for the gonorrhea she had contracted from one of two or three guys. She had narrowed down the list of possible suspects, but wasn't sure because she was too embarrassed to mention to any of them that she had an STD. She just knew that she couldn't ever sleep with any of the dudes without a condom again.

Trifling habits were not the only way that Strolla and Unique were alike. In fact, they looked so much alike that they could have passed for sisters. Strolla had the same cat-like hazel eyes and long, sandy brown hair as Unique. The only difference was that Strolla was a tad bit taller and a few shades lighter, making her light, bright, and damn near white. Whenever it would help them, they lied, claiming they were first cousins. On this night, like every other, Strolla was willing to play whatever part Unique told her to play to get what they needed.

Strolla felt like she owed Unique, who had welcomed her into the apartment with open arms a few days earlier, after she had been evicted from her own Section 8 housing. She had been having a beef with some chick who finally called the rental office and reported to them that Strolla didn't really have any kids. Strolla had used her niece's name on her application, claiming the child was

hers in order to get the $34 a month apartment.
Once the rental office investigated and discovered
the child didn't actually live there, they gave Strolla
ten days to evacuate the premises. That was when
she headed over to live with Unique.

When Strolla first got to Unique's place, there
was not a stick of furniture. Everything Unique
had financed while she was busy running through
Took's money, had just been repossessed. Strolla
saw this as a perfect opportunity to show her appreciation to her dearest friend. She called Rent-
A-Center and ordered a whole house full of new
stuff: a big screen television, a beautiful butter-
scotch oversized leather sectional, end tables and
lamps to match, an area rug, and even a large
African painting. Strolla gave the salesman four
references, all different aliases with phone and
pager numbers that belonged to her and Unique.
When Rent-A-Center called for a reference, the
women disguised their voices and gave an impressive recommendation.

Strolla had the stuff delivered to her old address,
the now-vacant apartment. As soon as the delivery
truck left, a U-Haul truck pulled up and some dudes
loaded the rented furniture to take it all over to
Unique's house. Strolla and Unique had a house
full of new furniture and Rent-A-Center would never
know where to look for it. Now Strolla was pumped
to help Unique with another scam involving Teddy.

After they got dressed, Strolla and Unique hopped
in Unique's white 7 Series BMW and headed to
Richmond's south side.

Train got out of his Cadillac when he saw the girls
pull up. He gave Unique a hug and asked, "How

much gas you got in this car?" He was sure the meter was on E.

"I got a li'l bit," Unique answered, although the indicator light was on.

Train shook his head and told her, "Look, follow me up the street so I can get you some gas."

Whenever Train and Unique met up he would take her to the station to fill her tank. He also faithfully paid her car note every month. At first he was just giving her cash to make the payments, but Unique finally confessed to Took that the car note was three months behind. Train stepped in and caught up on the payments, then he stopped giving her the cash and personally made the loan and insurance payments for her so she could keep the car.

No one—not Took, Train or even Strolla—ever fully understood why Unique got the car. She had no need for a new car. Took had purchased her a brand new 5 Series BMW three years earlier, and the car was paid in full. At the time she traded it in, it only had 56,000 miles on it. Anybody who knows anything about cars knows that BMWs haven't even been broken in at 56,000 miles. When Took questioned her about why she chose to get a gas-guzzler 7 Series and take on a hefty car payment each month when she had a perfectly good car already, Unique knew just how to shut him up.

"Took, I got it for you, baby," she told him. "They're gonna be shipping you soon, and they'll move you far away in the damn boondocks somewhere. It could be East Hell as far as I know, but I don't care if it's Bum Fuck, Egypt. I'm coming to see you, and I'm gonna need a dependable car;

one that's not gonna leave me stranded on the highway. I mean, I got at least seven years to travel the highway by myself, putting all those miles on my car, so I needed to get a new one."

Just like everything else that came out of Unique's mouth, Took fell for it. Took, who had so much street sense in every other situation, could usually see bullshit coming from miles away, but he was blinded by Unique's love. He fell for it every time. At twenty-one years old, six years his junior, there was simply something about Unique that made him weak. She had a way of manipulating Took's heart and making him feel like her stupid and careless actions were acceptable. So now Unique had her new, very expensive car, no questions asked, and she wasn't paying a dime on it. This girl just knew how to get what she wanted.

Once Unique got the money and a full tank of gas from Train, she and Strolla headed to the west end to see Teddy. Strolla ducked down in the car while Unique went to the door and knocked. Teddy greeted her in his boxers. Unique looked at him in only a way that a bonafide hoodrat could look at man—a look that said *Nigga, I am about to tear yo' ass up!*

Teddy didn't waste any time. He led her straight to the bedroom then took the big bankroll from the dresser and handed it to Unique. She removed the Coach backpack from her back and placed the money in without even counting it. Teddy sat back on the bed and looked at her with his long, skinny joystick in his hand.

"What you got to drink in this house?" she asked him.

"Go in the kitchen and look. And while you're in there, bring me a Heineken too."

"A'ight." She headed to the kitchen and looked in his refrigerator. "You don't have no bottled water?"

"Nope. Just get it out the faucet," he called out to her.

"Oh, okay." She smiled and turned on the faucet full blast. She left it running while she went to unlock the front door and flash the porch light twice to signal Strolla.

Unique went back into the bedroom with the Heineken in one hand and her glass of water in the other. While Teddy drank his Heineken, Unique turned Power 92 on his stereo system. When she heard "It's a Booty Call," she placed her glass of water on the dresser and began to shake a little bit, popping her butt and hips in slow motion. Unique knew these moves were enough to drive any man wild, and Teddy was no exception. She locked eyes with Teddy in a seductive stare as he watched her lick her finger and play in her hair. She flowed with the music until she knew she had his attention, then she raised her skirt to reveal the fact that she wasn't wearing any panties. It was written all over Teddy's face—he was turned on and ready for some penetration. Unique knew what he wanted, and she had no mercy on him. She sat on Teddy's lap and teased him with an expert lap dance until he looked like he was in "La-La Land," then she slipped his manhood into her wet canal and rode him like a jockey on a racehorse. Before she knew it, he was busting a nut.

* * *

Teddy lay on the bed trying to catch his breath while she grabbed her backpack and went into the bathroom to wash up. She let his juices run down her leg while she pulled out the bankroll Teddy had given her and started counting. She wanted to make sure the money was right. To her surprise, Teddy had pulled the "okie-doke" on her, a common stunt among hustlers, but one she didn't expect Teddy would try to pull on her. Now she realized he was more of a hustler than she had thought. He had given her a stack of thirty ones with a twenty on top.

I can't believe this ma'fucka had the nerve to give me a damn gypsy bankroll. It's all good. That nigga gonna get his.

She smiled. She wasn't mad, because she was sure Strolla had gotten him for more than fifty dollars worth of his food out of the deep freezer. While the music was playing and Unique was riding Teddy like the Lone Ranger, Strolla had been going through the rest of the house, helping herself to whatever they needed. Even if Teddy thought he had just gotten over on Unique, he would find out soon enough that the joke was on him.

Unique looked at the nice towels he had in the bathroom cabinet. *Damn, these some nice-ass towels. Ralph Lauren, huh? Teddy ain't so cheap after all—just when he's buying pussy. It's all good.*

As she looked at the tag she thought, *I'll take two of these for me and Strolla, and let me get these two washcloths, being all of ours are dirty anyway, and this nigga ain't even giving me enough money to wash clothes. Umm, I'll take one of these eight packs of soap too.*

Unique stuffed all that would fit into her backpack without making it too obvious. Suddenly, another bright idea popped into her head. She remembered that Teddy's sister, Kim, was living with him ever since her boyfriend put her ass out. Unique had never liked Kim's stuck-up ass, ever since she had tried to holla at Took when he and Unique first hooked up. Unique was about to capitalize off that too.

She smeared lotion all over her skirt to make it look like cum. She went into the bedroom and showed it to Teddy. "Now, you know I can't go outside with cum all over," she told him. "Let me go into your sister's room and borrow one of her outfits. I'll bring it back next time I come over to give you some of this good pussy," she lied.

Teddy didn't object because he was drifting off to sleep and couldn't be bothered worrying about his sister's clothes. Unique found Kim's room and changed into a black velour Fendi sweatsuit with the tags still on. Then she saw the sister had some brand new black hi-top Reeboks still in the box, which just happened to be her size. She cuffed those too. She didn't even bother to say goodbye to Teddy, who was snoring by now.

As she walked through the kitchen to let herself out, she noticed cases and cases of Heineken. She couldn't help herself. *Shoot, nigga, you gotta pay the piper because ain't NO dance free!* She grabbed a twenty-four pack of Heineken then left.

She laughed as she got into the car with Strolla.

"Girl, I love that outfit. It's cute as hell," Strolla complimented.

"Courtesy of Teddy's stuck-up ass sister. I know I need to go home and take this off because as good as this outfit fits me, it's a sure Slip outfit."

Strolla agreed.

"Girl, please! Tell me I couldn't work this and catch me plenty of victims on a Thursday night at the Slip," Unique bragged.

"Ghetto night at the Slip! Girl, that outfit is an investment." They both laughed.

Unique glanced in the back seat of the Beamer. "Got-damn, girl, you really hit him up," Unique said as she dug into her bulging backpack and pulled out the towels, washcloths and soap.

"Girl, he ain't gonna miss it. His deep freezer is running over. Girl, you ain't do too bad yourself," Strolla said, handing over two blank money orders she had found in the glove compartment of Teddy's car. They both laughed, amazed at what they had pulled off.

The next morning they went to pay the bill to get the phone reconnected. They headed to the laundromat to wash clothes and drop off some dry cleaning, hoping that by the time they returned home, the phone would be on.

Before they made it back to the house, they remembered they needed some weed. Neither one of them was about to pay for any weed, so Unique did what she did best. She called Fry, the Jamaican who sold the weed, and made a deal. She gave him a little poonanny in exchange for an ounce of weed.

Later that night, Unique sat on the couch and rolled a blunt while Strolla cooked filet mignon and lobster tails. They discussed their accomplishments. Both were proud of the fact that they had succeeded at everything they had set out to do. What a team they were.

For Unique, there was nothing that could make

the day more complete than a call from Took. Like
clockwork, Unique's phone rang at 10:01. She answered on the first ring.

"Halllllooo!"

"Hello," replied an automated operator. "This is
Bell Atlantic with a collect call from . . ."

"Took." Unique heard Took's voice as he spoke
his name. Boy, did he sound good. Now everything
she had been through the last two days was worth
it.

THE GOLDEN
ARCHES

For two months, Unique had been working the 5 A.M. to 1 P.M. shift at a McDonald's way out in the suburbs, about twenty-five minutes from where she lived. She had started looking for a job the same day she heard about the players' ball. As much as she hated the idea of working, she had to ensure that her paper was proper for the party. It made her sick that she came home every night smelling like greasy French fries, but she just kept reminding herself that she was making good money. It wasn't that the hourly wage was that good—after all, it was just a job at McDonald's—but since it was in the suburbs and not in the hood, this McDonald's didn't have surveillance cameras on its employees. Unique was able to tip herself at least $100 a day out of the drive-thru cash register. That fact alone was enough to motivate her to put on that ugly-ass uniform and go to work every weekday.

Unique spent her time during breaks daydreaming about the upcoming ball being hosted by Tall

Daddy, one of the richest dudes ever to set foot in Richmond. He grew up in North Carolina, but came to Richmond for a summer to visit his grandmother and never went back. Tall Daddy had his hand in some of everything, from drugs to guns and even some real estate. He felt like the world was his until the day he was shot during a drug raid that left him with six bullet holes. The gunshot wounds paralyzed him and he was confined to a wheelchair for the rest of his life. For a while the wheelchair slowed him down, but it wasn't too long before he got him a go-fast, chromed-out wheelchair and began driving the wheelchair like a racecar. Tall Daddy put himself back on top, and now he was hosting one of the biggest events Richmond had ever seen.

This was indeed a ghetto celebrity event, and only the elite ghetto superstars were even allowed. Since she was Took's girl and Took was a well respected player in the streets, Unique got a personal invitation from Tall Daddy. She knew the party would be full of retired ballers who hadn't shown their faces on the scene since around 1988, as well as all the established hustlers and up and coming multi-millionaires who would make an appearance. She was not about to miss this event, and she knew she would have to make sure her outfit, hair, nails and makeup were lined to the tee. Unique was out to make an impression on the heavy hitters, and if it meant working a bullshit job at McDonald's for a while, then oh well, she would just do what she had to do.

"Welcome to McDonald's. May I take your order?" she spoke into the drive-thru microphone.

"Ummm, let me have a double cheeseburger, and don't put no ketchup or pickles on it, two Big Macs, two milkshakes, one chocolate and one vanilla, two large fries, and two apple pies." The woman popped her gum constantly as she gave the order.

"Would you like to get the combo meal?"

"Did I ask for the gotdamn combo meal, bitch?"

Damn, who is this ghetto chick? Unique wondered, but stopped herself before she said anything stupid. All she had to do was remind herself of the money waiting for her in the cash register, and she could put up with just about anything to keep this job. She calmly repeated the order back to the customer. "Okay, that'll be $17.92. Please drive around to the second window."

Unique could hear the tires spinning as the car pulled off before she even finished what she was saying. She couldn't believe her eyes when big booty Brianna drove up to the window.

Of all the chicks, why she gotta come through here? My worst enemy in the whole world. This ho better not try no stupid mess. I will take this McDonald hat off and go right outside and pull her ass right out that raggedy Geo she driving.

"Make sho' my shit is fresh and hot too," Brianna demanded.

Unique took a deep breath and tried to keep herself under control. "No problem. Would you like any condiments to go with that?"

"Look, did I ask you for that?" Brianna sucked her teeth. "You just better make sure my shit is hot. That's all you need to worry about."

The drive-thru runner heard the hostility in Brianna's voice and hurried to bag the order. Unique handed the food and drinks to Brianna, who looked into the bag and took inventory of the order as she stuffed a handful of fries into her mouth.

"Fill these all the way up to the top," she yelled as she handed the container of fries back to Unique. "I asked for a large fry, not a small in a large box."

Unique turned her back before she rolled her eyes. She went to fill the container to the top for Brianna's big ass then returned to the window. She gritted her teeth and handed Brianna the fresh, hot fries with a smile as Brianna was stuffing the last of the Big Mac into her mouth.

"Sorry about the inconvenience," Unique said, as phony as could be. "Have a great day, and please come again."

Brianna was not happy. She had come to this McDonald's only to piss off Unique, and instead Unique was pissing her off by being so pleasant. It didn't look like there was anything to do that would ruffle Unique's feathers.

"Fuck you, you McDonald's-working bitch!" Before Unique even saw it coming, Brianna had tossed the chocolate shake right at her and sped off.

Unique was fuming now. *Oh, this bitch is taking it to another level. Now, she knows exactly where I live, but she wanna come all out of her way to try to make me lose my job. It's all good, though, because I'll see that ho again. Believe that!*

The feud between Brianna and Unique had been going on for quite a while, ever since an incident that happened a few months before Took got locked up. It all started the day Unique called Took's cell phone because she hadn't heard from him all day, which was rare. He usually called her every few hours. His guilt made him afraid that she might creep out on him the way he did to her, so he was constantly checking up on her.

Unique wasn't too concerned when Took didn't answer his cell phone. She figured he'd call back in a few minutes, so she started getting herself together so she and Strolla could go to the mall. As she stepped out of the shower, her cell phone rang. She looked on the caller ID and smiled when she saw Took's cell phone number.

"Hey baby," she said as she answered the call.

"Did someone just call Took from this number?" a woman demanded.

"Who is this?" Unique was shocked. For a minute she didn't know what else to say. She wondered how this girl could have Took's cell phone, which he usually guarded with his life. No one, including her, was ever allowed to answer his phone.

"This is his girlfriend, Brianna. Who this?"

Unique had to snap out of her daze and hop on her feet. "This is his wife." She said it with such pride that Brianna remained silent. Unique knew she had caught this chick off guard.

"His wife? His wife who?" Brianna finally asked.

"Unique."

"When did, um . . ." Brianna was tongue-tied. "Um, when did y'all get married?"

Unique was a quick thinker under pressure. "April twenty-sixth," she answered, naming the date she and Took had gone out of town to the Poconos. If this bitch really was messing with Took, then she would know he had been away that weekend.

"Well, I sure just got finished fucking his brains out a few minutes ago," Brianna responded.

"Oh, okay. I hope you sucked his dick too," Unique said without missing a beat. She was not about to let this ho get the best of her.

"Yup, I sure did, and he ate my pussy too."

"Thank you, boo. How much I owe you? Because I hate to swallow."

Brianna ignored the comment. Neither one of them was going to back down now. "Well, we surely worked up an appetite, and he's gone to get us something to eat. Ya know, he sure wasn't acting like a married man when he came to pick me up today and brought me over here to Motel 626."

Unique laughed out loud, but Brianna didn't get the joke. "What's so funny, bitch?"

"I know what Took thinks of you if he took you to some damn Motel 626. He would have never taken me there."

"Bitch, don't hate, congratulate. You just mad. We just came here 'cause we wanted to come somewhere where it was a pool."

"Well, what happened to the Marriott, the Hyatt, or the Radisson? Shit, all those have pools. He bypassed all those to get to that damn roach motel with your stank ass."

Unique heard a dial tone in her ear at the same time she heard Strolla ringing her doorbell. She let Strolla in the house and filled her in on the conversation she had just had. Strolla's first instinct was "Let's go up there and get to the bottom of this here shit."

The phone rang again, but this time the caller ID read MOTEL 626. Unique took note of the first three numbers, which let her know in which part of town the motel was located. Unique answered the phone while she continued getting dressed.

Now that she had her road dog, Strolla, with her, it was on and popping!

"You lying-ass bitch!" Brianna said. "He ain't married to you or nobody else."

Unique laughed. "Did you really expect him to come clean?"

"Oh, looka here," Brianna said. "He putting his key in the door right now. Guess that means I'm gonna have to keep him here and give him some more of this good shit."

"Put him on the phone," Unique said, not bothered at all by Brianna's threats. While she waited for Took to take the phone, she put on some shoes—tennis shoes, just in case she had to get into a brawl.

"Here, Took. Get on the phone. It's your *wife*," Unique heard Brianna say. Then she heard Took yelling, "Why da fuck—"

She heard fighting, tussling, and finally the phone went dead.

Unique and Strolla were out the door and in Strolla's car on their way to the motel, speeding, weaving in and out of traffic. Motel 626 was across town, but they got there in twenty minutes flat. As soon as they rolled up to the motel, they found Took's brand new Cadi, still with the thirty-day temporary tags on it, parked where it could have been seen by anyone passing by. This pissed Unique off. He didn't even have the decency to hide his shit.

"Take me to the store right quick," Unique demanded, her blood boiling. "This nigga got the nerve to be riding a bitch to the hotel in the shit that I had to go through hell to get financed for his sorry ass! Motherfucker, I don't give a gotdamn if this shit is in my name. This ma'fucka won't be riding around in this shit no more!"

Unique ran into the 7-Eleven and bought six chocolate candy bars. Strolla drove her back to the motel and parked behind the building. They walked over to the Cadi and Unique used her key to open the car so she could release the latch for the gas cap. She put the chocolate bars into the gas tank, one after another.

They tried to think of a way to get the room number from the motel clerk, but neither one of them knew Brianna's last name, and Took probably used an alias anyway. They thought they had done all the damage they could for now, until they were cruising through the parking lot and noticed Brianna and Took laid out, chilling in lounge chairs by the pool. Bingo! Today was Unique's lucky day.

Unique got out of the car and walked over to the fence surrounding the pool. She stood behind their chairs and eavesdropped for a while as they sipped on Mountain Dew, carrying on small talk as if the whole incident on the telephone had never happened.

"Oh, isn't this cute?" she said after she couldn't stand it anymore.

Took almost fell out of his chair when he heard Unique's voice. Brianna, on the other hand, just smiled as if she was happy she'd broken up their happy home.

Took tried to get over the shock as he wondered how Unique managed to find the hole in the wall motel. It only made matters worse when he noticed she had Strolla with her. Without a doubt, he was busted.

Unique took control of the situation while he

was still trying to get his heart out of his swimming trunks. "Took, let me holla at you real quick," she said in the calmest voice she could manage.

"Gotdamn," Took said under his breath as he headed over to her. *At least the fence is separating us, so she can't throw no blows at me.*

Unique looked Took up and down and then straight in his eyes. "Look, I ain't come up here to start no trouble. I just wanted you to know that I *know* where you at, so there really ain't no need in lying and denying, saying you wasn't with this chick."

"Look, baby, I love you," Took pleaded. He rarely told her this when things were going well between them, but now he would say anything to keep the peace.

Brianna approached them, amused at the whole circus. She said, "Oh, my name is Brianna. It's nice to meet you," in a sickeningly phony voice.

Unique was so mad and hurt that she couldn't even look at Brianna. Strolla, however, thoroughly checked her out, and if looks could kill, Brianna would have fallen to her death.

"Unique," Strolla announced, "this chick is pregnant."

Unique finally looked at Brianna.

"Oh, don't worry. He ain't one of the ones it could be," Brianna said with a smirk.

"One of the ones? Damn, you a straight up ho, ain't you?" Strolla said.

Took spoke up. "Fuck this shit, Unique. I love you, and I'm with you."

Unique shook her head in disgust. "You mean to tell me you up here creeping on me with some pregnant chick and the baby ain't even yours? You's a stupid asshole."

"But Unique, I love you, though. I swear I do." Took could see the smoke coming out of Unique's ears.

Unique didn't care what he had to say at this point. "Look, you got about an hour to get home and get yo' shit. If not, yo' shit gonna be in the dumpster," she said, though she didn't really mean it.

She heard Brianna's voice. "Look, Took, I've had enough of this interruption. Come on. You on my time!" Brianna turned to face Unique. "Oh yeah, if you didn't know, you better ask someone. Pregnant coochie is the best kind, boo!"

Up until now Unique didn't think she had any real beef with Brianna. Her problem was with Took, until Brianna decided to try to be funny.

"You nowhere ho, beggin' for a baby daddy for your li'l bastard. Bitch, please! You know you at the roach motel with *my* man," Unique said as calmly as she could. She was as hot as fish grease, but would never let on. "You dumb ass. I'm always gonna get the last laugh, bitch. You don't know who you fucking wit'. You should know I'm gonna always get the last laugh." She locked eyes with Brianna. "I promise you that!"

Unique turned to Took. "As a matter of fact, get yo' shit and come on now."

Without hesitation, Took gathered up his things. He knew Unique was mad and she meant business. He was on his way out of the pool area when Brianna ran up behind him.

"How am I supposed to be getting home?" she whined.

"Catch a cab," Took said, continuing his stride.

"But I don't have no money!"

"Well, that ain't my problem. You shouldn'ta been running your mouth, answering my phone and shit. Then you woulda been riding home in the Cadi." *Shit, that bitch is lucky the room is already paid for,* Took thought as he left the pool area and headed for his Cadi.

Unique and Strolla sat in the car, waiting for Took to try to start the Cadi. They expected it wouldn't start because of the chocolate bars in the tank. To their surprise, it started and drove fine, so they figured the chocolate bar thing was just an urban legend. What they didn't know was that in another two days the Cadi would start jerking, smoking, and ultimately the engine would die. In the meantime, Took drove that car back to the house, where he did everything he could to convince Unique to forgive him.

Brianna stayed at the motel after they left, hoping Took would come back to check on her, or at least send someone else to make sure she was all right. He didn't do either, so she lay awake all night, alternating between ringing his cell phone and blowing up his pager until he turned off his phone and took the battery out of his pager. Took was not about to be bothered with her. He felt Brianna had brought this on herself in the first place by touching his cell phone, so whatever happened from this point on, it was on her. She would have to fend for herself with no money at that damn roach motel.

The next morning, it was check out time and Brianna was stranded. The room phone had been cut off after she reached the $50 limit, calling

Took over and over. Now she didn't even have a quarter in her pocket to use the payphone to call for a ride. She went to the front desk and asked to use the phone, but the clerk informed her the phone was only for use by the guests. She knew she couldn't admit that she was a guest because then they would expect her to pay the phone bill from the room. Instead, she asked the clerk to have sympathy on her because she was pregnant. It worked, and he allowed her to use the phone. She tried to call a couple of rides, but no one was driving. With nothing else left to do, she called a cab, then stood outside and waited.

Once the cab arrived, she told them her destination, one block away from her house. When they arrived, she told the cab driver, "I gotta go get the money from my boyfriend."

Once she stepped out of the cab, Brianna took off running. The cabbie was pressed for his money, so he got out and ran behind her. At six months pregnant, Brianna was moving fast, but not fast enough. She looked over her shoulder to see the man hot on her trail, and ended up tripping on a concrete block. As she fell, she let out a scream before landing belly first on the ground. The cab driver stopped his pursuit and called 911 as he watched Brianna lying on the ground, moaning and bleeding.

As he waited with Brianna, the cabdriver realized where they were—in Blackwell, where dead bodies turned up and shoot-outs happened three, four, sometimes five times a day. He thought there would be a Red Cross station set up in the heart of one of the most deadly housing projects in Richmond, but there wasn't. Help would surely take too long to get there, so the cabdriver knew what he had to do. Without hesitation, he called a crack head over to help him get Brianna into the back seat of his cab. He rushed her to the hospital, running every red light and causing one accident.

He got Brianna to the hospital in time to stop the bleeding that was threatening her life, but they couldn't save the baby, who died from the trauma of Brianna's fall. As she lay on the table giving birth to her stillborn child, Brianna vowed to one day get revenge on the person responsible.

Like so many women around the world, it didn't matter to Brianna that it was a man who had done her wrong. In fact, Took hardly crossed her mind at all, and she definitely never considered the thought that she had something to do with her own fate when she chose to sleep with another woman's man. As far as she was concerned, it was Unique who was to blame for her being stranded at that motel, so it was Unique who was responsible for her falling and losing her baby. From that day on, every chance she got to torment Unique, she took it, knowing that one day the opportunity would come, and the ultimate revenge would be hers.

DA HO STROLL

The night that the whole town had been waiting for finally arrived—Tall Daddy's party. Everybody who was anybody in Richmond's street life wanted to bless the party with their appearance. Although there was a tight guest list, many stood around outside praying that they would somehow get into the exclusive party in the Arthur Ashe Center. The lines wrapped around the building, and cars were backed up all the way up to the CVS pharmacy on the boulevard. Tall Daddy had hired some off-duty police to direct traffic, but with so many folks coming out to party, traffic was still a mess. The police directing traffic called for more backup because the buses couldn't get in and out of the station across the street in a timely manner, putting them way behind schedule. When the additional police were called to the scene, so was the fire marshal, and the party was shut down.

Strolla and Unique had gone all out, intending to show up fashionably late to make a grand entrance to the event. When they rolled up in their rented limo, all they saw were blue lights flashing and officers directing traffic away from the Arthur Ashe Center.

"Damn, girl, this joint is packed than a ma'-fucka," Unique said to Strolla.

"Girl, I ain't seen this many people since Heavy Dee and the Boyz was here back in like '85."

"Guuurrrrlll, you ain't never lied." Unique laughed. "I remember that show. I can tell you what I wore."

"What? I know good and well you can't remember back that far."

"Girl, I wore a red-and-white Coca Cola suit with some white Delta Force Nikes." They were both laughing until they cried, reminiscing about the good old days.

It was clear that the party was over, but the crowd was too wound up to go home, and Strolla and Unique were not going anywhere. They had invested too much not to meet some type of heavy hitter to reimburse them for all the loot they had kicked out to make this night a success.

They instructed the driver to follow the traffic, which led them to a big block party at the intersection of the boulevard and Broad. For the next hour, it was lovely. Strolla and Unique instructed the limo driver to park, then they strolled up and down Broad Street looking like two of Richmond's finest, putting up a front like they weren't hearing some of the local mediocre hustlers calling their names, wanting to holla. On any other night, those same hustlers would have been ideal candidates, but not tonight. Unique and Strolla needed to meet a major playa to ensure that they recouped their expenses. Anything less wasn't going to cut it that night.

They zeroed in on a white 600 Benz sitting on twenties, with Cali tags. The ice around the driver's neck almost blinded them from across the street.

"Girl, if one of us—or maybe even both of us—could holla at that right there . . . our work here would be done," Unique said.

Without hesitation, they smiled at each other and crossed the street so they could walk past the car. They giggled at each other as they passed, never making eye contact with the guy, carrying on like they didn't even see the car or hear the music coming from inside. Just as they predicted, the guy couldn't resist the girls walking by.

He called Strolla over. "Hey there. Com'ere for a minute."

Strolla smiled and approached the guy. They began the basic conversation and exchanged numbers. Another dude walked up carrying a bag from 7-Eleven and started a conversation with Unique. He was fine, brown-skinned with curly hair, tall and slim. It didn't matter that his gear wasn't pimped out like the rest of the fellas. He was dressed in relaxed gear and still looked just as good, if not better than them. It was clear that he was holding paper.

"My name is Cali," he told her. For all she cared his name could have been Boo the Fool as long as his pockets were fat. His conversation was good and they exchanged numbers. Mission accomplished.

Now that they both had numbers, nothing else really mattered to Strolla and Unique, but they still continued on the "ho stroll." This was the place where all the ballers parked their cars along the side of the street and stood near their cars to examine each and every female who put herself on display. The chicks strolled by, showcasing what they were working with, waiting for the dudes to stop and talk to them.

While they were on the stroll they saw Train, a person Unique really didn't want to be seen by, but it too was late. The cat was out of the bag now. She was pretty sure that Train wouldn't say anything to Took about her being out because he was well aware how much Took loved her. He wasn't going to bring Took any unnecessary heartache while he was doing time. The man was already coping with the transitions from street life to prison life, so hearing that his girl was wearing next to nothing, showcasing his stuff all over Broad Street, was something no dude doing a bit needed to hear.

Aside from that, though, there was another reason Unique wished Train hadn't seen her out on the ho stroll. She had been so busy lollygaging, flossing and spending money that she hadn't paid the mortgage in three months. The money she had spent just to get ready for the Players' Ball was enough to make at least six months' worth of payments. She had intended to ask Train for the money, but now that he had seen her out partying, looking so fine, she had just messed up her whole plan. She couldn't ask Train for the money now, so she knew she had to really work Mr. Cali quick. It was only a matter of days before her house would be going into foreclosure.

Train called out to her. "Yo, Unique, let me holla at you right quick."

"Damn, I swear I don't need to hear this shit from Train right now, and I especially don't want

Cali to see me talking to him," Unique said to Strolla before she went over to talk to Train.

"Hey, Train, what's up?" Unique put on a fake smile, pretending she was so happy to see him.

"You look nice."

"Thanks." She was surprised at the compliment from him. He was usually so uptight when he dealt with her.

"Look, I ain't got a lot of time to shuck and jive, but you got 'bout five minutes to get the hell from up here because we 'bout to shut this shit down."

"Come on now, Train, don't be shooting up nothin' to get yo'self in no trouble," she pleaded, but the look on his face told her that he wasn't playing. Unique did what she had no other choice but to do—she got the hell up out of dodge.

"Come on," she said to Strolla and they started heading back to their limo as fast as they could. As soon as they shut the door and were safely inside the limo, they heard gunshots roaring.

Boom, boom, boom, boom! It was like the stroke of midnight on New Year's Eve in the hood. Unique and Strolla got away clean, but some folks were not as fortunate.

GOING BACK TO CALI

Strolla called Sam, the dude who was with Cali, from the limousine after they escaped the shootout. Sam and Cali had also gotten out of there injury-free. Strolla made plans for Sam to come scoop her up after he got his own car. Though she was a little disappointed that he wasn't the owner of the Benz she had seen him sitting in on Broad Street, Strolla wasn't surprised. It was often the case that the driver didn't turn out to be the owner. She could still tell that the clique Sam was rolling with was overflowing with money, so somehow she'd surely make herself entitled to some.

On the other hand, Unique wasn't going with any dude she had just met, especially one who she was trying to play "for keeps." She could just tell from the way he carried himself that Cali was doing major things, and in Richmond that meant one thing: he was getting coochie thrown at his feet every minute of the day. With the police's weed and seed program going on, so many of the major playas were catching cases left and right. There weren't enough of them left out on the streets to go around. With so many chicks looking for "the man" to take care of them, competition was fierce, and sistahs were coming off of whatever they needed to catch a man. Unique knew her best shot at Cali's pockets was to be different—well, at least pretend to be different than the rest of them.

Cali called and tried his hand with her, to see if she was just like her friend.

"My man just told me your friend was coming over. You coming with her?"

"No. I'll pass," Unique answered.

"Why? You don't want to see me?"

"I do, but it's too late for me to be leaving out the house."

"Oh, okay. Well, I can come over there."

Unique smiled. She was hooking him. "No, I don't take no guests this time of night unless it's a booty call, and we just met, so it's too soon for that," she said. What she really wanted to tell him was that he could stay as long as he wanted if he came over with a pocket full of money, but she controlled herself.

"I respect that," he said to her. She had passed his test, and was now worthy in his eyes. They continued with the small talk, then Cali brought the conversation to an end, promising to call her the next day.

Unique knew that the night didn't end for Cali after their conversation. She was willing to bet her last piece of ass that when Cali hung up the phone with her, he called the next girl, someone who was prepared to give him what he wanted that night. This didn't upset Unique in the least. Being a player of the game, she knew that this was how it was played. She just had to wait now, and hope that he really would call back, that he was interested in more than just a one-night stand. Eventually she would put out for him, and they could both get what they wanted.

The next morning at 10:01, Took called. Unique could set her clock to his calls, which always came in at the same time.

"Hey, baby," she said. "I'm glad you called. I wanted to tell you about somethin'."

She confessed that she had been out until the wee hours of the morning, because she didn't want to risk the possibility that Train might tell him. She wanted Took to hear her version instead. Of course, she had to stretch the truth a little bit to make Took understand. She explained that Strolla had convinced her at the last minute to go out.

What Unique didn't know was that word had already gotten back to Took that she had been hanging out the night before. That was one of the strangest things about the local jails. The people locked up often knew things faster than the folks living the life on the streets.

When he had first heard the news, Took was upset, but since Unique had come clean with him, like she had nothing to hide, he felt better. There was no reason for him to think there was any type of shadiness going on. It didn't even faze him when Unique's phone beeped with a call waiting.

Unique looked at the caller ID, saw the 323 area code, and knew it was Cali calling.

"Baby, this is these folks clicking in about this job," she lied to Took. "Call me back in about twenty minutes, okay?"

"No problem, baby. Good Luck."

Just like that, Unique was able to get Took off the phone with no argument. She checked the clock as she clicked over to receive Cali's call. It was still before 11:00, which surprised her. She hadn't expected to hear from him until after noon, which was checkout time at most hotels. She figured he'd wait until after he was done at the hotel with whatever skeezer he was digging up in the night before to call her.

"Hello."

"Hello to you." Cali sounded good.

"How did you sleep?"

"Okay, but I would have slept better had I been laying beside you. Can I come over and lay beside you in your bed?" he asked.

"Naw, this ain't the place for you. Only bill payers can lay up in here with me, and right now, I'm the only bill payer over here."

"Baby, you ain't said but a word. I can come over there and be a bill payer too. What bills need to be paid over there?"

"Every one of them," she said jokingly, though she was as serious as a heart attack.

"Oh, no problem as far as the bills are concerned. What you gonna do for me if I take care of all the bills?"

"What you want?" Now they were getting down to business, she thought.

"A brother needs a hot meal, a clean house to lay his head, no niggas running up through there, a place to hang my clothes, and a warm body to lay next to. Can you handle that?"

"I can handle mines," she said with confidence. "Just make sure you can handle yours."

"What's the address? I'm on my way."

She talked to him on his cell phone, giving him directions as he drove to her house. Just like that, he was in. There wasn't any kind of background check, no AIDS test, nothing. She didn't know his birthday, if he had kids, if he was married, nothing at all. She didn't have the foggiest idea if he was a mass murder, rapist or wanted for crimes committed out in Cali. She didn't know or care about his real name or social security number. The only thing she was sure of was that he had the potential to pay the bills and give her the finer things she had been missing. At that particular moment, that was enough for her.

On the other end of the phone, Cali didn't really care about the bills Unique had stacked practically to the ceiling. All he cared about was that he would have somewhere decent to lay his head when he was in Richmond. Unique's house would be more secure than the hotels he lived in, and shacking with her would almost be cheaper than how he had been living—eating out every day, spending $200 a night for his hotel room and another two bills if he wanted to entertain a chick.

For the next six months, Cali and Unique both benefited from their arrangement. Of course for

Unique, Cali's money made her feel secure. For Cali, it was other things about Unique that made him feel comfortable. He loved the fact that she was always available when he called, day or night. She cooked, and her house was clean. When he had to go out of town, he didn't have to pack all his stuff and carry it with him. It was safe at Unique's house. Although she lived above her means, it was worth it to Cali to have her on his team.

Cali actually only spent about fifteen days a month in Richmond, traveling back and forth to the West Coast. Even when he was in Richmond, he spent most of his time out in the streets, staying on top of his business. Unique learned his schedule and worked Took's calls in whenever she knew Cali would be in the street. She chalked the change up to her new job schedule at the pie shop, though she wasn't really working. Took still had no idea that Unique didn't have a job. The day before Tall Daddy's party had been her last day flipping burgers, since the only reason she had taken that job was to be able to do it up real big for the party. Now that she had managed to hook Cali, he was paying every bill in sight.

Train never knew that Cali lived with Unique because he rarely came across the water for leisure visits. He was always in some kind of beef with somebody from the streets. So, as far as Unique was concerned, she was juggling the balls of Took and Cali very well during those six months.

What she didn't know about Cali, though, was that even though he paid the bills, gave her good sex, and actually listened to her and acted as if he cared about what she was saying, it wasn't anything he wouldn't do for any other chick. His generous actions were motivated solely by business. He liked Unique a little—she was convenient—but if things started to get ugly for any reason at all, he had no problem leaving, and would never look back to Richmond, VA. That was exactly what happened when Big Tee and his boys from around the 643 robbed Cali one night when he was on his way into Unique's house.

They robbed him for $12,000 cash and an eighth of a kilo of heroin. He was almost certain Unique had nothing to do with it, but at the same time, Cali knew he had to move on. Any other time he would have brought the heat and dealt with Fat Tee in the most gangsta way, but he had too much at stake. He turned the other cheek this one time, shut down shop, and moved on to the next city. He never made contact with Unique again, and just like that, her money well dried up.

It didn't take long for the word to get back to Unique about who had robbed Cali.

"Gurrrl, I heard that Fat Tee and dem robbed Cali," Strolla informed Unique.

"Fo' real?"

"That's the word on the streets."

"Girl, I hate him so much. He fucked up everything for me. And don't you know all that money he getting, he ain't never paid Took what he owed him from before he got locked up."

"Girl, I know that nigga gonna get his."

Unique already had a nasty taste in her mouth toward Fat Tee. "The part that really pisses me off is the petty way that Fat Tee gave me the run around when I was tryin' to get the money he owed Took. I mean, if he ain't have no intention on giving it up, he shoulda just said so," Unique complained.

One day his fat ass is gonna get his for sure, she thought. *I just hope I be around to see him get his.*

WHEN THE GOING
GETS TOUGH

Once again hard times had taken over Unique's house. This time her mortgage was way behind. It had been eighteen months since Took had been locked up and almost three months since she had last seen Cali. She had met a couple other guys since then, but none of them were dishing out enough funds to make her life easy. Hell, they weren't coming anywhere close to half. It was almost like she was screwing and entertaining lame dudes for damn near free. Something had to give! She had to come up with some kind of hustle to catch up her mortgage payments.

In the projects, everyone had some type of hustle going on. Some were hustling and moving so hard that they wouldn't even notice their own momma. Unique's methods had always been to try to capitalize off the drug trade in whatever way she could. Her newest hustle came from a different angle. She started selling fish and chicken dinners, liquor, and sodas to all the neighborhood hustlers.

The hustlers would call and order dinners for themselves and family. Some would order seven or eight plates at a time.

Even though Unique was well known for her expertise on riding a dick, most dudes never knew of the skills she possessed in the kitchen. Once word got around about her fierce cooking talent and the bartending skills she had picked up while entertaining Took's friends, she was able to open up the Ghetto Kitchen. She was selling dinners for seven dollars, beer for three dollars, and any kind of mixed drinks the hustlers wanted. Her hustle filled a need in the hood; liquor stores around Richmond closed at 9:00 while she stayed open all night long. After a while, she added weed to her list of menu items. With this hustle, she made major paper on Fridays and Saturdays and didn't need to work anywhere during the week. Of course it meant she couldn't visit Took on the weekends, but she sent him a few dollars just to keep his mouth shut.

Unique had just finished taking a plate down the street to one of the fellas on the block when she noticed a black Denali with thirty-day tags parked on the corner. It was Baby Jon, a dude who always supported her and sent over a rack of dudes from the 321 to get dinners from her. All of Baby Jon's boys spent a lot of money with her—way more than the fellas around the street did. They all tipped real big, but Baby Jon was the biggest tipper of all.

She approached the new Denali, which she had never seen him in, and checked out what he wore. *Damn*, she thought, *Baby Jon look good as hell. He be doin' it real big—presidential Rolie, Prada sneakers, and lookin' good in that do-rag.*

She always thought he looked good, but now she was seeing dollar signs, and that was enough to make anyone look even better in Unique's eyes. *They say the blacker the berry, the sweeter the juice,* she thought. *Dat nigga cut up with a body like Vin Diesel. Mmm, mmm, mmmph. I wonder who he mess with. Shoot, do I even care who he mess with? I want Baby Jon's ass.*

"What up, Unique?" Baby Jon spoke to her.

"Nothing much. Just working hard; doing the same shit I do every weekend."

"Oh, y'all selling dinners down yo' house?"

"Yup," Unique answered as she thought, *As good as you look, I'll sell you anything you want.*

"I don't have no money on me now, so I'll be around there in a short, 'cause a nigga is hungry."

"I'm sayin', if you want to get a dinner, you know I ain't gonna let you starve. What you want, fish or chicken?"

He smiled. "Gimme chicken."

"A'ight."

In a matter of minutes she was back outside with a nice, healthy plate for Baby Jon. He thanked her and promised to be back later. When Unique crossed the street to head back to her house, one of Fat Tee's nickel and dime hustlers asked, "Unique, let me get a free plate. Look out for a brotha."

Unique broke western on him. "Look, when I used to buy weed from you, did I ever come to you with short money? No, 'cause I respected your hustle. Now respect mine. I sell seven-dollar plates, one-dollar sodas, ten-dollar weed bags, three-dollar beers, and it's anywhere up to fifty for the liquor. Feel free to do a li'l weekend shopping."

"Well, I don't have no seven dollars."

"Then you shouldn't be out here if you ain't got seven dollars," Unique said, then left him standing there hungry.

About an hour later, Strolla looked out the window and said, "Look, Unique, here come Fat Tee with his bald, egghead."

Fat Tee was the neighborhood kingpin who looked just like his name implied. He stood about five feet ten inches and weighed in at a burly two hundred ninety pounds. He was shaped funny because his stomach was big, but his butt was as flat as a pancake. He had every tooth in his mouth filled with silver caps, pretending they were platinum.

"Forget him." Unique rolled her eyes. "He always got something to say about everything and everybody. He don't never discuss how he need to go on that Subway diet, though."

Strolla laughed. "Girl, I remember I gave him some once. I couldn't even see his dick from his stomach covering it up."

"Girl, the chicks be chasing after him, though," Unique acknowledged.

"If he didn't have a bankroll I betcha he wouldn't have no chicks, 'cause that's the only thing that made me give him some. I just focused on how I was gonna be spending that money."

They heard the screen door open and Fat Tee entered the kitchen.

"Hey, Tee, I've been selling dinners all day. Had a whole bunch o' people stop through, but to what do I owe the pleasure of having the Ghetto Superstar himself stop by?"

"You know he hungry." Strolla joked to his face. "Came to buy a plate. Hell, to buy the whole chicken."

He ignored Strolla and focused his attention on the issue he had come to deal with. "Unique, I see you can give dem niggas from over the 321 a free plate, but you can't give my worker a free plate." Fat Tee was here to address what he saw as her disrespecting him.

"Look, Tee, the dudes from the 321, those cats tip me good. Your li'l workers don't even tip, and it ain't a time that your workers ever came with straight money. They always coming up with short money. Plus, this is my operation. I can do what I want to." She was not about to back down.

"Okay, yo' li'l red ass wanna get fly out the mouth? I'll shut this roach infested kitchen down."

"Do you, Fat Tee!" Unique looked dead into his eyes.

"Y'all's mouths is gonna keep y'all's pockets empty. I'm gonna see to that," he threatened as he turned to leave.

Strolla followed him to the door, running her mouth. "Matter of fact, Fat Tee, carry yo' ass back down the street where you can throw your weight around."

"Okay, you'll see," he said calmly. "I hope y'all said your prayers, 'cause you're gonna think I'm God after I finish with y'all."

"I hate his fat ass. One day he gon' get his," Unique said as she stood at the window and watched as he wobbled away from her house. She sounded confident, but she knew in her heart that he meant business.

"Girl, don't worry about Fat Tee. He just talking. I mean, how could he stop our little program?" Strolla tried to reassure her friend, but Unique knew Fat Tee was a dirty nigga and would get revenge. When he had it out for someone, he had it out for them.

Fat Tee couldn't accept that Strolla and Unique had stood up to him. It wasn't a secret; he went all out to make them pay. He took this beef to heart and went to work making them go broke. He purchased a pound of weed and had his workers selling dime bags at two for one, just to steal Unique's weed customers away. Then he had some crackheads selling dinners for four dollars a plate, three dollars cheaper than Unique's. The food wasn't as tasty, but it didn't matter to the hustlers when they were hungry. He did the same with the liquor, charging only enough to cover his costs. The kingpin hustler that he was, Big Tee didn't clear any profits at all, but it didn't matter. He didn't care that he had to go into his own pocket, as long as he felt they were getting his point. He was determined to teach them a lesson about going against his wishes.

There was nothing Unique or Strolla could do because Fat Tee had too much money. They couldn't compete. It was only a matter of time before Ghetto Kitchen was closed and Unique was back to being just as broke as before.

GOTTA PAY TO PLAY

After her food and liquor hustle came to a screeching halt, leaving her to struggle again, Unique got desperate. She began to go all across Richmond, messing with anyone who had a few dollars to put in her pocket. Then she started taking little pieces of coke out of their stash—not enough for them to miss, but just enough for her to sell for a few more dollars.

One of her victims was Lee, who had been an unfortunate kid growing up. His mother never bought him anything. All he ever got was hand-me-downs, but things had changed. Now the only hand-me-downs were the ones he gave away.

As a kid, Lee had worn thick glasses and clothes full of holes, so he never got any play from the girls. Although he'd been in the drug game at least a good six years now, he still was amazed sometimes at some of the women he pulled, and this made him vulnerable. When he saw Unique at the mall and she gave him a little play, he was willing to do anything to keep her attention, so he dumped out his pockets to her.

At first he was taking her shopping, giving her five hundred dollars every other day just to make her feel like he had it like that. This went on for about three weeks, then the five hundred turned into two-fifty every three days. Gradually, that turned into one hundred dollars a week. He made up excuses of how he'd been robbed or one of his workers hadn't paid him, but Unique showed no mercy. She still demanded money and accused him of giving it to another chick he messed with.

"Lee, you know I need two hundred dollars to get my layaway out because tomorrow is Friday, and I gotta go to First Fridays down at After Six."

"Look, I just took a hell of a loss. I'll be straight by Monday. I'll take you shopping then."

Unique didn't care anything about his plight. She did what she had become so good at doing. She waited until Lee went into the shower then searched through his pockets, helping herself to the two hundred dollars for her layaway and two more just because he should have given it to her from the beginning. *Lyin' ass nigga. I betcha he won't be tricking none of this money off to the stripper broads or none of those other lame chicks he mess with.*

Hiding the money in her shoes, she enjoyed the rest of the night with him as if everything was fine. The next day she spent hours shopping. When she arrived home, her arms were full of shopping bags as she struggled up the sidewalk. Suddenly, an unexpected guest greeted her.

"I thought you ain't have no money to get yo' layaway out. Where you get money from, huh?"

Lee screamed. His tirade was followed by a back-handed pimp smack and a powerful punch that sent her to her knees.

Before she could get up off the ground, Lee yelled, "Where the hell is my money, you thieving bitch?"

She never responded, but took her whipping like a champ. After Lee felt like she'd had enough, he left her lying on the ground. She got up, gathered her bags and went into the house to look at her wounds. Five minutes later she was out the door, headed to the mall to buy her some cute Fendi sunglasses to cover her swollen eye.

Not even four hours after she had gotten her butt tore out of the frame, she was spotted at First Fridays, sporting her new chic glasses, mingling with some of the "Who's Who" of Richmond. There was no shame at all in her game.

From talk at the club she learned that the reason Lee was so mad was that he was as broke as a broke-dick dog. He was just fronting to her like he was doing it real big and had it like that. In truth, he basically hustled and gave all his profits to her; trying to impress her. That's why the real cash flow had only lasted three weeks. It wasn't long before he had to cut out the charade. In the end, the money she had stolen from him was money he owed his supplier. Although it was only $400, those four bills really hurt his pockets.

Later that night at the after hours spot, Unique ran into Teddy. He was looking good; jewels sparkling and pockets bulging. He never mentioned that he had missed any of his towels, soap, and all the other things that she and Strolla had stolen from him. He grabbed her hand and whispered in her ear, "Can I get some of that tonight?" while he was rubbing on her ass.

"How much cash you got? 'Cause that li'l chump change you peeled off to me the last time was just that—change."

"I got whatever I need to get some of dat. Meet me outside in ten minutes. I'm 'bout to leave up outta here."

She nodded and went to tell Strolla that she was leaving the club. Strolla understood totally. When duty calls, a bitch gotta roll out.

Unique met Teddy outside.

"Look, I gotta drop my man off at home," Teddy told her. "He'll be out in a minute. He was waiting for some chick to give him her number."

They waited on the side of the club for Teddy's friend to come out.

"Come here and give me a big ol' hug."

She did as she was told and then some. No one on the packed sidewalk noticed that Teddy was finger-fucking Unique, because their coats concealed their action from prying eyes. Her coochie was so wet it was overflowing with juices, just like Teddy liked it. They were both talking dirty, whispering sweet nothings into each other's ears when out of nowhere came a shadow.

Klack! Klack! Klack!

Someone had dumped three shots into Teddy. Unique still had her arms around him and he had his hand in her thong as they fell to the ground. As bad as it sounds, Unique's opportunity had once again arrived and she took total advantage of it as she lay on top of Teddy's body. She robbed a dead man, not even caring that she too could have been killed. It was more important to Unique to get hers than to worry about her life and well-being. When she stood up screaming, she had all of his valuables in her pockets.

Those three shots set off a whole lot more. Unique, ducking and dodging bullets, was lucky to make it to her car, but she came across another guy who had been crouched behind a car and wasn't as lucky as she was. She didn't think twice, and again, she didn't feel bad about robbing the dead. *Shoot, a nigga—dead or alive—got to pay to play. I'm gonna get mines, by all means.*

It turned out the money she got out of their pockets wasn't even enough to cover the repairs from all the bullet holes in her car. Her car insurance had lapsed and been cancelled, so the car was a total loss. There was only one thing to do with the money she'd robbed—get a hoopty. She got a ten-year-old car, a 1992 Diamante that was priced right. She promised to give the Arab salesman $50 a week until the car was paid off, but once she put her champion's head job on him in the back of the shop, never caring that his balls were reeking a foul odor, she left there with the title. She promised to come back and give him more head whenever he called.

Next, she started messing with Baby Jon. She held the title when it came to giving a blowjob, and because of this, Baby Jon fell head over heels for her. Although he had a long laundry list of women, not to mention a waiting list, Unique was his number one pick. Still, Baby Jon was ashamed of their relationship. By now she was a burnt-out ho, and everyone including him, knew about it. She had even pulled the pregnant okie-doke on him just to get the abortion money. Baby Jon fell for it two times in a four month time frame, before he wised up. After a while, Baby Jon figured out that some of everyone had had her, so he couldn't possibly turn that ho into his housewife.

Though he gave her money and bought her gifts, he never took her anywhere public. The only rendezvous' they ever had were late night at his house. Baby Jon continued to deal with other women hoping to get Unique out of his system. What he didn't know was that he was adding heat to a fire that was already building, waiting to be ignited. When he didn't want to be bothered with the other chicks, he would turn off all his ringers and ignore their calls. Some of them would ride by and see Unique's car sitting in the parking space reserved for apartment 161. Unique's enemy list was growing longer by the day.

MEMORIAL DAY WEEKEND

Strolla was busy working a double shift at the Chick Pool, a ghetto car wash where females with hourglass figures washed cars in bikinis. Many of the girls worked there to pay their way through college, but Strolla was grinding up all the tips she could to make sure her bankroll was strong for Memorial Day weekend. She wasn't in the group using this place to further their education. She was with the girls who worked there as a stepping stone for their careers in stripping, prostitution, and porno. Those were the girls who dreamed about a "happily ever after" with one of the big hats who came through to get their cars washed. These girls knew that the tips were good, but what they were really looking for were the customers willing to pay by the hour. Dirty old men were Strolla's specialty.

Strolla watched the cars. She waited and searched for potential night customers to further fatten her weekend bankroll. Then she saw a customer pulling in who just had to be her next victim. Ironically, it was a woman. Plenty of women came in to get their cars washed, because they knew that while they were standing around waiting for their cars, they just might hook up with one of the fine men who rolled through there. When she saw this woman, though, Strolla's mind wasn't filled with potential dollars, but with sweet revenge.

They always say every bitch has her day, and today has to be the day, Strolla thought. *I ain't forgot about what this bitch did to my friend.*

On that note, Strolla called out to her boss, "Can I go on break in five minutes?"

"Sure."

Strolla waited until Brianna checked her car in, then told her co-worker, "I'll vacuum this one just to help you out. You don't have to split your tip with me because I need to kill time before I go on break anyway."

It was Strolla's pleasure to go through the glove compartment to find out where Ms. Big Booty Brianna lived. It was even more of a pleasure to slip two keys off the ring, leaving only the car key in the ignition. She ran to the nearby hardware store to make copies of the keys, knowing she had plenty of time. Brianna's car was so filthy it would take them twice as long as usual to wash. Once she had the keys copied, Strolla was able to get them back on the ring just in time. Brianna was so busy checking out the dudes in the vicinity, that she didn't even notice Strolla.

Strolla stayed out of sight and eavesdropped on Brianna's conversation with her home girl. She was talking loud, hoping to attract the attention of one of the ballers waiting for his car to be finished.

"Girl, when we leave here we gonna ride to D.C.

to get our outfits right for this weekend. Gucci, Fendi, Louis Vuitton, Nordstrom's, Saks, Neiman Marcus, here we come," Brianna announced, knowing full well they weren't hitting any major department stores, only the bootleg spots.

The girlfriend said, "mm-hmm," but then on the down low she told Brianna, "Girl, I hope ol' boy call us back so we can get that money too."

Brianna stopped talking loud enough for the world to hear. "Girl, you know I ain't heard from him in a few days. I believe he must have someone else riding his dick. I miss him so much. I am hoping and praying that I see him before I leave."

Strolla couldn't wait to tell Unique what had happened. She called her as soon as her shift was over.

When Unique heard the phone ring, she thought it would be Baby Jon. She was sitting in her filthy bathtub wishing she hadn't been too lazy to clean the ring out before she hopped into the tub. Not far from the tub was a Massengil douche bottle. She was trying to make her stuff tight after one dude had just left and before Baby Jon called her to meet him at his house. She didn't want to give Baby Jon any reason to believe that she had been with three other dudes before him. Like Strolla, she too had been working to ensure that she'd have her spending money right before she left to spend Memorial Day weekend down in Miami.

She had worked her magic on each dude, making it clear it would cost them $150, so by now her spending money was starting to add up. Still, Baby Jon was her biggest fish yet. She expected to get anywhere from $300 to $500 from him, especially after she did that trick she liked to do with a Popsicle, while she was giving head. While she added up her money in her head, she practiced contracting her coochie muscles until the phone interrupted her concentration.

She reached for the cordless phone that sat on the toilet. "Hello."

Skipping the hello, Strolla shouted, "All I wanna know is what the hell does Tupac say?"

"Girl, what you talking 'bout?"

"I'm talking about how revenge is the next best thing to getting the cat licked!"

"Girl, you so crazy. What's up? What got you all wound up?"

"Girl, I got that chick Brianna right where we need her. Come and pick me up from work right now."

Hearing Brianna's name was enough to make Unique forget totally about getting the cat tight. She hopped out of the tub and practically rollerskated around the house to get to the Chick Pool to see what exactly Strolla had in mind.

As Brianna saw the yellow, white, and red rose petals leading to her doorstep, she also saw the big silver envelope with a large gold bow taped to the door.

"Girl, he misses me after all." Brianna smiled at her girl, glad that someone was finally romancing her. "It's about time he comes around. And he used the key that I gave him weeks ago."

Her heart was racing rapidly as she ripped open the card. Written inside in big, bold letters was *Surprise, baby. The best is yet to come!*

Brianna fumbled with her keys, anxious to see

what waited for her on the other side of the door. Was it the man she longed for? Was it the man whose phone she'd been blowing up, leaving messages, begging him to come by to see her?

"Oh my God, he has finally come to his senses. I knew it wouldn't be long. I am so glad that while I was up in Georgetown I bought some cute lingerie." Her home girl didn't even bother to respond. She could see from Brianna's trembling hands that she was nervous and probably wouldn't care what she had to say.

Brianna turned to her girl. "How do my hair look? Is everything in place?"

Her home girl nodded and asked, "You want me to see you later?"

"Yeah, girl," Brianna said as she opened the door and saw the elegantly set table. The apartment smelled of vanilla and roses from the scented candles throughout. "I can't believe he went all out for me. You only see shit like this on TV. Wait 'til those hating-ass bitches hear this! Take notes so you can help me spread the word all over town tomorrow."

She spotted another envelope like the one on the door. The note inside read: *Ran out to Ruth's Chris to get our dinner. Have a glass of champagne while you wait for me. Look in the fridge. I poured it for you already. Get naked and wait for me in the bed, because you are going to be the main course tonight!*

"Call me from your cell so you can talk to me while I get ready and wait for him to get here," Brianna said as she pushed her home girl out the door.

Brianna couldn't have been happier than she was at that moment. She pranced around the house, sipping on her glass of champagne in the candlelit living room. In the bedroom she found more candles burning, and smiled as she pulled off her clothes and got under the covers. That was when she felt something against her leg, on the side of the bed she was supposed to be keeping warm for her man.

She turned on the light and pulled back the covers to find a silver platter with a cover. Confused, she lifted the cover and the odor hit her in the face. The platter was covered with shit!

"What da fuck?" She screamed as she jumped out of the bed, racing to the window as fast she could. She tossed the turds out the window then leaned out and vomited. When she finally calmed down and pulled herself back into the house, she glanced at the bed and realized the shit was smeared all over her sheets. It was too late. She had already laid on top of it when she got into the bed. She was outraged and upset, and smelling like shit. Brianna burst into tears, crying like a baby as she wondered why someone would want to do this to her. It seemed like every man she ever wanted always had some reason to hurt her, but this had to be the worst.

After she took a hot shower to get all the shit off her body, she changed her sheets then sat on the floor near the open window. She gulped down the rest of the champagne, trying to calm down, but she couldn't. As she was hyperventilating and feeling like she might have a nervous breakdown, she wondered who in the world could have been so cruel. She had decided her man could never or would never do such a thing.

Her phone rang. It was her home girl calling.

Brianna whimpered while she told her girl everything, but her girlfriend showed no sympathy. She laughed so hard at Brianna for playing herself. She told Brianna she had some nerve thinking those candles and everything were from this man who had never even taken the time to return a phone call.

"Bitch, it ain't funny!" Brianna yelled into the phone, directing her frustrations at her home girl.

"My bad, girl," her friend told her but continued to laugh.

Brianna hung up on her friend and threw the cordless phone against her nightstand. That was when her eye caught sight of the envelope on top. She tore it open and read with rage.

Dearest Enemy Number One,
EAT SHIT AND DIE, BITCH! By the way, that's not Cristal, it's PissTal. Kiss my ass.

Immediately Brianna knew who had masterminded this evil prank. Once again, Unique had won. First she took her baby from her, and now her sanity. With fury in her heart, Brianna vowed to get the last laugh.

SLEEPING ON THE ENEMY

Unique had a ball in Miami for Memorial Day weekend, but once she came back, things were up and down for her. Some days she coasted through life at some sucker's expense. Other days she struggled. Those were the days she blamed Fat Tee for her misfortunes. If he hadn't robbed Cali, she wouldn't be having so many problems. The icing on the cake was the day she and Strolla were walking past Fat Tee and his boys and they started cracking jokes on them as they passed by. One crackhead actually ran up and pulled Strolla's pants down. Everyone on the block just about fell to his knees in laughter. Strolla was so humiliated that when she got into Unique's house, she cried like a baby.

"I hate that ma'fucka!" she screamed. It took her a while to calm down enough to even listen to Unique.

"Don't worry. We'll get him back. I promise."

"How we gonna get him back?" Strolla asked while still crying. She didn't really believe there was any way possible to get revenge on Fat Tee.

"Look, baby, didn't we work it out to get Brianna back?"

Strolla nodded. Flashing back on the whole shit-on-a-platter episode made her chuckle a little, enough that they were able to come up with some ways they could get back at Fat Tee.

Two days later as they were walking to the Chinese restaurant, Unique noticed Fat Tee in there ordering some chicken wings. When they walked in, Fat Tee looked her up and down. He was surprised when she spoke to him.

"What's up, Fat Tee?"

"Nothing much, Unique."

Strolla rolled her eyes at Unique, threw some money on the counter for her stuff then stormed out of the restaurant.

Unique watched her leave, but didn't follow. "You know you ain't right," she said, smiling at Fat Tee. "That shit you did to Strolla weren't right. Why you get that crackhead to do that to her? She took that to heart. I told her y'all was just playin', though."

"Yeah, it was just playin'," Fat Tee said, surprised and relieved that Unique wasn't taking it personally. To show there were no hard feelings, he even paid for Unique and Strolla's food, then gave Unique a ride home. Unique sat in his car with him for a few minutes as they laughed and joked, carrying on like two old friends catching up on old times. It was almost like nothing had happened between them. Just like that, the beef between Unique and Fat Tee was squashed.

As Fat Tee drove away he gave himself a pat on the back. He was sure he had taught them a lesson. Just like the rest of the neighborhood, they would now bow down to him.

When Unique walked in the house, Strolla was sitting in the living room, furious. She felt like her best friend had betrayed her.

"Unique, that was real messed up. You up there kickin' it with that twelve-sandwich-eatin' nigga. You so damn phony."

"Bitch, you better pull yo'self together. What you saw was pure con."

"Look like it was from the heart to me," Strolla protested, but she still listened to Unique's story.

"How many times have I told you I was gonna get that ma'fucka? Girl, you know I gotta play the role to get that petty dude where I want him. He sleepin' on us. He don't know just how poisonous we are."

THE GETBACK

A few weeks went by and Unique came up with
the perfect plan for revenge. First she hunted
down Fat Tee like he was wild game.

"What's up, girl? What's so damn important?"

"Well, I got a li'l problem and I had to bring it to
you, since you the king of this empire around
here."

Fat Tee smiled, showing all the silver teeth in his
mouth.

"What's up? Whatever it is that's broke, you know
I can fix it."

"Look, man, thanks to you my house 'bout to go
into foreclosure, and my pockets are turned inside-
out broke, so I came to get your permission to have
a party so I can hustle up some money to pay everything that's 'bout to be turned off."

She described her plan to him. "I just want you
to let me have the liquor and the food. I'll need
you to run the Craps game for me and get one of
yo' boys to run the Poker table. You can have the

money. Just look out for me however you see fit from the profits from those."

"Oh yeah, that's what's up!" Fat Tee exclaimed.

She could tell he liked what he was hearing, so she kept it coming, putting on her best act. "I'll have one of my girls at the Tonk table since mostly only chicks play Tonk anyway."

"That's cool." Fat Tee listened attentively and stood in agreement.

"This is gonna be an all out money-getting party, and if they haven't been invited personally by me or you, niggas can't get in. So all that broke, riff-raff crowd won't be allowed to get in and just stand around. Ya feel me?"

"Yeah, I feel you. That shit gon' be like that."

"Oh yeah, my homeowners insurance just lapsed too, so I can't have none of that shoot 'em bang-bang going on in my house. I'm collecting all the guns at the door. Just like when niggas go to the club and they do a coat check—well, mines is a gun check."

"That's what's up," Fat Tee agreed. "And if niggas don't like it they can carry they ass somewhere else."

"I know that's right."

Fat Tee was counting his profits in his head. "I'm in, shawty. Let's get it on and popping."

Even before she went to him, Unique knew for sure that Fat Tee would take the bait because when it came to gambling, the house always walked away with the biggest profit. Folks never took into consideration that the odds of winning when shooting Craps are slim to none. If the dice isn't dropping numbers for you, it can be a nightmare, but if the dice is dropping numbers for you then it's a miracle. People are convinced that it's skill, but shooting Craps is pure luck. Some just happen to be luckier than others. Even if a few suckers get lucky, though, the houseman can't lose. He's the referee, the regulator, and the monitor of the money pit game. Fat Tee, without a doubt, knew all the ins and outs and jumped on this opportunity Unique was offering.

Everything was going as planned. Now Unique needed a silent partner with plenty of heart who wanted Fat Tee as much as she did and who would play fair with her. She brainstormed, and there was only one name that she came up with—Train. She blew up Train's cell phone until he finally answered. She told him it was an emergency and insisted that they meet right away.

The sight of Unique made Train sick, because by now her reputation was out of the bag. He knew exactly what she was, and didn't think she was worthy of his man, Took. Train hated the fact that he couldn't run her whole rap sheet down to Took, but he knew that Took still loved her. It would have been too hard on Took to learn the truth about his girl. As bad as he wanted to brush her off, Train didn't, out of respect for Took. He agreed to meet her by his place.

Unique went over to the south side to meet Train, and boy, did he look good with his permanent-tanned red complexion and bald head. It was something about that all-white SeanJohn sweatsuit and white Kangol cap that he wore. If he wasn't Took's boy, Unique might have tried to run some game on Train, but she knew he wouldn't have it. Since she couldn't have him that way, she stuck to her plan and asked for his help.

"Look, Train," she said with no shame in her game, "I really need you."

What's new, bitch? he wondered. *She always needin' something. I swear to God, if my man ain't love her no-good ass so much, I would enjoy every second of murking her ass. A bitch like her I wouldn't even shoot in the head. I'd straight stab her ass to fucking death so I could watch her nothingless ass suffer. Ummph, bitch! If only she knew.* Train gritted his teeth to keep from saying any of this out loud. Instead, he stayed silent and listened.

"I've got something for you sweeter than candy," Unique started, "and I'm gonna put everything in your hands. You gotta play fair with me, though. You'd be in complete control once I give it to you and set everything up."

"Unique, what in the hell you jaw-boning about? Calm down now, girl. You too excited. Give me what you have so I can make my play on it." Train was eager to hear what Unique had to say. He knew how scandalous she was, and for her to seek his help, it was surely something worth his while.

"It's like this, plain and simple. I found a way to get all these wack-jack hustlers into one place un-armed. All the niggas that's gonna be there is gonna have lots of money on them 'cause I'm gonna have a Craps table, Tonk, and a Poker table. I'm gonna have Fat Tee's pussy ass at the Craps table, one of his boys at the Poker table, and one of my girls at the Tonk table. I'll be at the door checking in the guns and helping out at the bar when I can, and Strolla gonna be making the drinks. They're gonna be a long way from watered down, so niggas can be nice and drunk. Ya feel me?"

"What do this have to do with me?" Train had to ask to be sure.

"After everyone is in and the party is at its peak, that's when you and your boys come and lay them down. Take everything—I mean everything, and just make sure you look out for me real decent." Unique was breathless with excitement.

Train was puzzled for a minute, wondering why she had come to him with this proposition, but then he decided he didn't care what her reason was. This plan was the perfect opportunity for him to get some payback. He gave her a list of clowns from across the water who he'd been wanting to get at for a while, but could never catch slipping. Some of them were Richmond's top of the class jokers, and a few were known city-wide as snitches who had somehow established a bankroll. Train felt they shouldn't be in the hustling game in any way. He knew he couldn't murk them, but robbing them would do for now. He stressed to her to make sure that they were all there, because there wasn't any doubt in his mind that they needed to be got.

The next few days Unique put her work in. She and Strolla went to all the clubs and onto every strip, set and corner, looking high and low, rounding up the fellas on the list to make sure the party was a big success. Some she knew and some she didn't, but nevertheless, by the day of the party they had tracked down all the fellas. The streets were talking loud about the party. Many renowned gamblers were promising to make their appearances, so everyone on the streets wanted to win a piece of the money they knew would be brewing in the jackpot.

A few of the guys who were invited saw Fat Tee at the club and one asked him, "What the bank worth?"

At the time, Fat Tee was damn near pissy drunk and taken off guard. The guy asking was the nerdy type wanting so bad to be a gangsta. Fat Tee looked at this dude and burst into laughter as he pulled out his fat bankroll. "Me and my money will be there," he said. "I'm tryin' to send you home broke, so make sure you be there."

Females were all around so Fat Tee had to showboat. He reached into his other pocket and pulled out another bankroll, holding them in both hands. "Bring your game, not your mouth, and that li'l bankroll you got is only one bet away from being in my pocket."

This one incident really hyped the party, raising the stakes even more. Word spread on the streets, and now everyone wanted a piece of Fat Tee's bank. Unique's party was sure to be a success. What people didn't know, was that if things went according to her plan, she would be the only one walking away smiling.

A HO FOR A HOUSEWIFE

Because she was putting so much energy into planning the party, Unique had not seen Baby Jon all week. To his surprise, he missed her more than he thought he would and actually started thinking that he wanted her to be a permanent fixture in his life. He called her Thursday night, demanding to see her, claiming he needed to talk to her. She agreed because she missed him too. Although she knew that after the party she would no longer need his money, she had started liking him for more than his loot. In the past she had dreamed of ways to clean him out, but now that she had the chance, she no longer wanted to do it. She had to try to convince him not to come to the party.

She drove to his house wondering what he wanted to talk to her about so urgently. She came up with all kinds of crazy scenarios for what it might be, but all of them turned out to be wrong. When she arrived, she saw that he actually had a candlelight dinner waiting for her. His need to see her was not about craziness, but about romance. After dinner was over, they didn't just screw. For the first time, they made passionate love, something Unique had not experienced since Took went to jail. After they were done, she lay in his arms and listened as Baby Jon poured out his heart to her.

"Can I confess something to you?"

She wanted to say no because she didn't want anything to mess up the moment. Instead, she let him get whatever he needed off his chest.

"For so long, I've made you meet me here because I was ashamed of you," he told her.

He paused for a moment, choosing his words carefully. "Look, baby, by no means do I wanna hurt your feelings, but I've got to be real with you so you can understand where I'm coming from."

"I feel you completely," she said with no hostility. Even if the truth hurt, she wanted to hear it.

He took a deep breath and kept going. "I was ashamed because you had slept with so many folks for a little money, and so many people in this town hate you. The females hate you 'cause you're good at what you do in the bed and you have your way with men. Men don't like you because you never try to have relationships. Instead, you scheme and steal whatever you want with no shame in your game."

Unique opened her mouth to try to present a defense, but he stopped her.

"You don't have to be that way."

Unique looked in his eyes and could tell his feelings were true. She was touched, especially when she heard what he had to say next.

"Look, I love you for who you are, the best and the worst. You've never brought that scandalous shit with you when you came to my door, so I respect you for that."

"Thank you, Baby Jon."

"I know we started out as a fuck for a few dollars," he continued, "but I've grown to care about you. Here's the thing, though . . . I don't know if you heard or not, but they issued a warrant for my arrest."

Unique was taken by surprise. She wondered how she hadn't heard this news out on the street. "A warrant? Damn!"

"I've been plastered all over Crime Stoppers and everything."

"Damn, boo! That's fucked up."

"Yup," he said as he explained the details. Then he dropped the surprise of her life right in her lap.

"Unique, the only way we can be together is if we could go away to North Carolina. Come with me, girl."

At that moment, life couldn't be any sweeter for Unique. His offer to take her out of Richmond fell right into place with her plan for the following night. Once she got her revenge on Fat Tee, she could get the hell out of there.

"Look, baby," Baby Jon said, "the only reason why no one has hurt you yet is because of the respect people have for Took. But word on the streets now is that Took's patience is growing very thin. It's only a matter of time before he writes you off." Baby Jon was trying to convince her to come with him. He didn't know she was already there in her head.

"I know, I know!" she said, pretending to be sad about Took. "What do you think I should do?"

"Just leave everything and we can start over with

a fresh beginning. No one will know anything about either one of our checkered pasts."

Unique lay in Baby Jon's strong arms and stayed quiet for a minute. He thought she was deliberating the pros and cons of his offer, but she had already figured out that this was the opportunity of a lifetime. What she was really thinking was that she knew her welcome would be worn out after tomorrow night at the party. Plus, her behavior was probably too far gone for things with Took to ever be like they were before he went to jail. She had done too much damage to try to mend anything with him. Her reputation on the streets was that of a petty ho. The streets were talking and screaming loud, and she had heard that the latest word was that people were referring to her behind her back as a hood rat. She had no reason at all to stay in Richmond.

As far as believing Baby Jon when he said he wanted to be with her for real, Unique didn't care if it was true. After the party, she would have enough dough. If he didn't play fair once they reached their destination, they could go their own separate ways and she'd still be okay. This offer that Baby Jon had on the table was the only way she was going to get a chance at a clean slate.

She looked into Baby Jon's eyes and promised that she'd go with him. "But I need a few days to get everything straight before we can leave," she explained. He agreed to keep a low profile until then, so they could make a clean getaway.

THE STICK UP

Party night rolled around and the high rollers rolled in. Feelings were hurt when dudes came to the door.

"I need yo' pistols," Unique announced.

One guy didn't understand. "Man, g'on ahead with that shit." The renowned corner hustler waved his hand at Unique like the rules didn't apply to him.

"I ain't playing." Unique looked at him without smiling. "I am dead serious."

"I am not 'bout to leave my brand new nine up here with you for you to give it to the next nigga by mistake. Shit, yo' ass crazy."

"Look, gimme the damn gun and take this ticket." She handed it to him as if he was checking in his coat at a club. "I promise I'll take good care of the nine," she said, batting her eyes at him. *A big gun for a little dick*, she thought.

He was mad. "Fuck it. I ain't going in if I can't be strapped."

"Carry yo' ass then. I don't give a got-damn. It's a line a niggas behind you that want to come in."

Other people got stopped at the door because their names weren't anywhere on the guest list, but the place was still packed. Everything went as planned with the gun check. The liquor was steadily flowing, and the fellas were drinking like sailors. All the tables were pulling in money, with plenty more people waiting to get their chance. Unique even added C-Lo, a game played with three dice instead of two. Odds were once again in favor of the house, and Unique was discreetly stashing away money in a special hiding spot all night. Not even Strolla noticed what she was doing.

When it was time to put her plan into action, Unique asked the nerdy-looking guy from the club to help her with all the trash that was running over. She bagged it up then held open the door so he could take it out back.

As he stepped out the door, four masked men jumped him. Unique had left the kitchen and was laughing and joking with Fat Tee, heading over to the C-Lo game when the door banged open. Unique turned around and saw a tall man dressed in black, holding a gun to the nerdy guy's face. The first masked man was followed by three more, also holding guns.

Tears were rolling down the nerd's cheeks as he begged his attacker not to shoot. "Please, please, please don't shoot me! I'll give you whatever you want."

The armed men came in and took complete control of the house in a matter of seconds, before anyone even had a chance to react. Everyone in there was wishing they had never checked their weapons at the door.

"Y'all know the routine! Get on the floor, kiss the ground." The first gunman raised his voice and threw the nerd on the floor.

A girl nearby dropped her glass and screamed, and another shouted, "What da fu—"

"Shut the fuck up!" the second guy pimp-smacked her.

Number one said, "Nobody moves, nobody gets hurt! Y'all know what time it is. We here for one thing and one thing only. This a stick up!"

They moved around the house swiftly and confidently, as if they had done this a million times before. One moved to the front door and put the doorman on the floor, then let two more masked men in. Now there were six of them in the house, and they were the only ones armed. It wasn't a problem for them to take care of business at that point.

Two of them took control of the Poker and Tonk tables, laying everyone down. Another pair took over the Craps room, emptying the bank and all the pockets that surrounded the table. Hundreds, fifties, twenties, and jewelry, filled the duffle bags of the stick-up kids. They retrieved over sixty Gs alone from the C-Lo game. One kid in there got out of order, so he was vigorously pistol-whipped to set an example for any other fool who got an idea. Blood spurted all over the floor and Unique covered her face and looked the other way.

The remaining two masked men were roaming throughout the house to make sure everything was running like clockwork. They planned to take everything worth taking. This heist was definitely a professional job.

"Damn, man, this shit is fucked up. Niggas can't have shit from niggas tryin' to take shit." Fat Tee was huffing and puffing, mumbling under his breath.

"Shut da fuck up!" The masked man shouted, but Fat Tee couldn't follow directions. He had to keep on mumbling.

"Niggas just like crabs in a bucket."

The masked man went over to Fat Tee and commenced to hit him with the stun gun. Unique saw Fat Tee's expression and how the tears couldn't stop rolling down his face. He was shaking a little, and she could see all the silvers in his mouth. For one minute she thought, *Damn, maybe I shouldn't have,* but then changed her mind. *Fuck dat nigga. Good for his ass! Cry, motherfucker, cry!* She had to bury her face in the carpet so no one would see her smiling.

After everybody was cleaned out, the stick-up kids backed out of the house with not only all the money, but the guns too. "The next time y'all decide to have a party and don't invite us, we'll invite ourselves. Y'all try to enjoy the rest of y'all's night, ya heard?" one of them announced before he closed the door. Just like that, the robbery went down, and without any altercations, the mission was accomplished.

After the gunmen left, a few dudes tried to jump on the nerd. "Nigga, we know you set that shit up."

"No I didn't," the nerd cried. "Shit, my money got taken too."

"How much money you had?"

"Shoot, it don't make a difference. I worked hard at UPS for mines."

"We work for ours too." One dude ran up and hit the nerd from the back and the rest of the dudes followed suit, putting some knots on his head and a few bruises on him before they were stopped.

The robbery had been masterminded so well that these dudes had no one else to blame. They were just taking their frustration out on the nerdy dude.

No one had any idea that Unique's larcenous butt was behind any of this, especially when they saw the big alligator tears rolling down her face. "One of you ma'fuckas got my shit hit!" she screamed at the crowd. "Now all you get the hell out my house, right now!"

One of the neighborhood girls was whining, popping trash. "Somebody gon' have to get my shit back. They took all my jewelry," she hissed. "It don't make no sense. I worked hard for all my rings."

"Girl, shut up. I am not trying to hear that shit, right now."

"I don't have no jewelry at home and I'm mad as I don't know what. What I'm suppose to do? I got some of that stuff on sale and bought it hot from junkies."

"Stop whining 'bout them bullshit-ass diamond chip cluster rings. Don't nobody even wear that shit stacked on every single finger no mo'."

"Whatever, bitch. You pawned all yours from when you went broke, depending on a nigga."

Before anyone saw it coming, Unique drew back

and hit her so hard she damn near knocked her into the next room.

Then one of the last people to leave, another chickenhead who had been at the Tonk game, asked, "Unique, you gonna call the police?" in a very sincere tone.

"Bitch, for what?" Unique screamed for everyone to hear. "So I can get locked the hell up? What I'm gonna tell them, that I was running an illegal gambling house? Get out 'fore I knock you out too. I already told y'all bitches to get the fuck out of my shit. Now get the fuck out!"

Strolla headed outside to talk with some of the fellas who were standing around their cars, trying to figure out what the hell had just happened. Unique went into her room, slammed the door, and turned the music up loud. She fell on her bed, laughing hysterically. Her plan was a success!

THE AFTERMATH

The next day Strolla spent all morning giving the house a thorough cleaning. She was worried about Unique, who was refusing to even get out of the bed. As she cleaned, Strolla brainstormed a few scams to help her friend out with the bills.

Fat Tee stopped by with his crew. He walked into the house and was directed straight to Unique's room, where she was lying in bed, looking a hot mess. Fat Tee could smell the liquor coming out of her pores as soon as he opened the bedroom door.

"Unique, get yo' drunken, hung-over ass up," he said, pulling the comforter off of her. "Look, it was nothing but a robbery. This shit happens. It's not the end of the world."

"I'm glad you see it that way," she said to him as she sat up to pull the covers back on her. "But I'm still in the same boat—broke! I don't have a safe with money caked up, a dope spot, and an out-of-town connect that can put me back on my feet when I've been stuck da fuck up, like you, so stop telling me shit is gonna be alight, 'cause it ain't! Tellin' me that ain't gonna get my shit back or keep me from having to sleep on the streets or keep my water on so I can wash my ass, is it?"

"Unique, when I find out who dem niggas is, I'm gonna clean house and paint the walls red. Trust me. Get your ass up and shake the madness." He raised his voice. "I said you'll be a'ight, and I meant what I said. Now get up and give Fat Tee a hug."

As Unique hugged him, she whispered in his ear, "Thank you."

Fat Tee gave her a knot of money and told her to take care of the bills. He promised there would be more where that came from.

"But I can't sleep in this house no more since it got robbed," she whined, knowing exactly what that little act would get her.

Fat Tee agreed to pay the deposit and first two months' rent on a new place, just like she knew he would. Later that night, he came back with the money for the new place.

Fat Tee was convinced that he was the king of the 643. He swore he knew everything that went on in his hood—every move made, who sold dope, coke, weed, sex, food stamps, who stole, who killed—but there was one thing that he hadn't the foggiest clue about. Unique had just sold him a solid gold dream!

It had been four days since the robbery and Unique was playing her position to the fullest. The whole "I'm depressed" role she had laid on Fat Tee had him nearly eating out of her hands. He felt so guilty that, he did everything possible to try to cheer her up. One morning, he stopped by early and gave her more money to get her hair, nails, and feet done, telling her to get out of the house to try to pull herself together. He only left after she promised him she would try.

As she got dressed, she got the phone call she had been waiting for from Train. He told her where they would meet—at the Radisson Hotel, Suite 229. She wasted no time getting there, her palms itching in anticipation of the loot she was about to collect.

Unique arrived sooner than Train expected. He had just stepped out of the shower, so he slipped on some Bill Blass pajama pants to open the door for her. Unique tried to focus on the pile of items on the table, but couldn't help noticing the print of his large dick, swinging from side to side.

Damn, Strolla would love to have some of that big, red horse dick right there, she thought. *Too bad I can't never hook them up.*

A while back, Train had asked Unique to give Strolla his number. Jealous, Unique lied and told Train that Strolla was gay and had a girlfriend who kept her totally satisfied. Now, even if she wanted to, she couldn't let them get together, because Train might tell Strolla about the lesbian story she had invented. Oh well, she would just have to hook Strolla up with another baller somewhere down the line.

"You spoke to Took?" Train asked as he went to the closet to retrieve a bag.

"I spoke to him last week, but he on lock for fighting," Unique answered. "He's on phone restriction, done caught a street charge. I swear I'm getting so sick of his ass. All he doin' is running up his time."

"In there, you gotta stand yo' ground."

"But damn! This is like the fourth penitentiary he done got moved to. Every time he bust a nigga upside the head he gets moved, and they move him further and further away. Who wanna drive six or seven hours to see a nigga locked up?"

Unique's last comment really infuriated Train, but he didn't respond. He got straight down to business. Unique stood mesmerized as Train dumped the neatly wrapped bundles of money onto the bed.

Unique rubbed her hand so the money could come directly to her, rubbed her ass so it could come fast, and rubbed her knee so it could come free.

"Look, I had to pay the shawties that helped me, and after I paid them, yo' cut is thirty-two grand. Now, if you don't go out of control like you've been known to do in the past, you can be a'ight for a good li'l while. I repeat, don't spend any money on no large items. But then again, you shouldn't really need nothing new, because you splurged and bought everything new when Took went to jail, right?" Believe it or not, Unique didn't even catch the frustration in his voice when he said that to her.

"I am gonna keep it on the low. Don't worry 'bout me." No matter what she was saying, Unique couldn't wait to get her hands on that money and go shopping.

"I'm keeping all the guns, but as far as the jewelry is concerned, you can take what you want. Whatever you take, just make sure you go to Georgetown alone, and trade that shit in right away. It ain't wise to wear no nigga's jewelry that got jacked from him during a stick up."

"I know, Train," she complained. "Come on, I ain't slow fo' real."

"So, you a'ight with yo' commission, shawty?"

"Yeah, I'm cool. Thanks so much. I honestly thought you were gonna just gimme a pat on the back," she said with a little chuckle. "Naw, I'm just playin'."

She looked at Train and realized that she was very impressed. He was the man who had come through for her, and he'd done it with total grace and professionalism. If only Took had played his cards right. He was so busy being Mr. Hothead in the joint, running up his time, that it was making Unique sick. Train, on the other hand, was looking good to her all of a sudden. He had money to spare, could roll in any car he wanted, and could pull off a heist and take over a house with over fifty people inside. *And to top it all off,* she thought, *he fine as hell and got a big dick too! Now, that right there is gangsta.*

With those kinds of thoughts running through her head, Unique did not hesitate to pull a bona-fide hoodrat move. Before Train even knew what was happening, she was slobbing all over his knob like there was no tomorrow. At first he was in total disarray. The blowjob was the best he'd ever had.

She had the mouth of a champion and could deliver blows to the head like Zab Judah. Her movement and jerk motions were unpredictable. She gave facial expression and body language with unbelievable stamina. Damn, she was the best lip boxer alive! She put so much effort into it that Train could understand why once Unique got hold of a nigga's dick, he would be gone.

Train was dizzy for a minute, enjoying Unique's skills, but not for long. He was quick on his feet, even with her deep-throating him. It didn't take him but a minute to remember who that was down there on her knees. This was Took's girl, and she had the gall to be giving head to him, the man who had bailed her out, over and over, only on the strength of his friendship with Took. How dare she disrespect Took in such a way? Train knew how to deal with a no-good, slutty guttersnipe like this, who had stooped as low as she could. *I got somethin' for this lowlife ho,* he thought as she continued to perform her state of the art blowjob on him.

Unique could tell that Train was really starting to enjoy himself and loosen up. He grabbed her hair and got aggressive with her. "Make sure you swallow. Don't stop 'til you swallow." And she didn't.

As soon as he came, he rolled her over on her stomach and began to lay pipe all up in her. It was rough, and he only did her anally, never vaginally. Unique thought he was just doing it that way because that's what he liked. She didn't understand that Train was doing it to her as a form of disrespect.

When he was done, he waited for her to get dressed then said, "Look, I'm not tryin' to be funny, but you gotta get yo' stank ass up out of here. Don't ever call me again and ask me fo' shit. Yo' scandalous ass is on your own, so take yo' li'l money and get the fuck up out my sight, you thievin', no good, low down, dirty bitch!" He spit on her and pushed her out of the room, throwing her shoes out behind her. "Bitch!"

As much as he didn't want to do it, Train made a special trip the next day to explain everything in detail to Took. He told Took what he had wished he could've reveal to him for a while. He learned the craziest thing, though. Took already knew the trifling, low-budget slut that Unique had turned into.

"Come on, man. You know niggas in the system know everything going on in the streets. When I first started hearing li'l bullshit I was fucked up— couldn't sleep, eat, nothin'. Shit, a nigga lost so much damn weight. Why you think I been busting the shit out of niggas left and right? My frustrations for that no-good bitch!"

"Man, I 'pologize on everything I love for not saying nothing earlier, but I know how it is to be locked down and in love with a broad who ain't playing fair," Train said.

"Man, I understand. You ain't gotta say nothing. Thanks for giving that dirty bitch what she deserved."

"Nigga, you know I was all twisted yesterday and the whole drive up here. I didn't know how you was gonna take it. You know I snapped and was straight out of character yesterday."

Took gave Train a brotherly hug. "Everything's cool."

Unique's name didn't come up anymore that day. They continued the rest of the visit, laughing and having a grand ol' time.

SWEET REVENGE

Baby Jon was blowing up Unique's phone. He was ready to get the hell out of dodge and was pressuring her to hurry up. Not only were they running the Crime Stopper commercial on the local news, but now both of the black radio stations, 106.5 The Beat and Power 92.1, were announcing his warrant.

With all the drama going on, Unique was ready to burn the road up. She went by her house, packed some clothes, gave Strolla a measly $500 and told her she'd be back in a week, though she had no intentions of ever seeing Richmond again. She drove cautiously to Baby Jon's house and parked in his reserved space.

Brianna was madly in love with Baby Jon, even though they'd only had a one-night stand. The morning after, she gave him a key to her house, thinking they were going to be a couple. He had

never used the key, and had never even bothered
to call her. Since then, Brianna had been doing
drive-bys and stake-outs, hoping to catch Baby Jon
so she could plead her case to him. Now that she
had seen the Crime Stopper ads, she was determined to aid him any way she could. She hoped
that by helping him in his time of need, he'd feel
eternally indebted to her and she would end up
becoming his woman.

Brianna was furious when she saw Unique pull
up in Baby Jon's parking space. She couldn't believe that out of all the women in the city of
Richmond, this was who he had chosen. Once
again, she had lost to Unique.

What does that bitch got that I don't? she wondered
then tried to convince herself he didn't really care
about Unique. *He probably just using her to help him
escape.* That thought was immediately confirmed
wrong when she observed how Baby Jon greeted
Unique at the door. The way he looked at her, his
body language said it all. Unique was his woman.

Brianna's feelings were so hurt that she began
to cry. Thoughts of suicide even popped into her
head as she drove around remembering everything Unique had ever done to hurt her. Then she
began to redirect her rage as she circled the block
and drove by the apartments again. This time she
noticed that Unique's car was gone. She wanted to
talk to Baby Jon now that he was in the house
alone, but she knew that if she knocked, he wouldn't
answer. There was only one thing left for her to do.
She made her way to the payphone, because her
cell phone battery was dead from repeatedly calling Baby Jon.

Brianna dropped her money in the coin slot,

called Crime Stoppers and gave them Baby Jon's exact location. She didn't call because she needed the reward money. She called because if he wasn't going to be with her, then she would make sure he wasn't with anyone, especially not Unique.

Brianna knew that Unique wasn't about to ride out a bid with anyone. She had proven that with Took, the man who practically kissed the ground she walked on. Once Baby Jon realized that Unique would leave him high and dry, Brianna could step up to the plate. Throughout the years he would see that she was worthy of his love.

While she waited for the police to come, Brianna parked her car where she could watch as they came to haul his black ass off to jail. Within minutes, the police surrounded the apartment and kicked in the door. She observed carefully as the police came out of the house with an evidence bag containing two guns, and another evidence bag that looked like it was full of drugs. She sat in astonishment then as she saw them escorting not Baby Jon, but Unique in handcuffs. All of a sudden, Brianna's tears dried up and happiness was spread across her face.

THE OUTCOME

Months Later

"Unique Bryant, you are sentenced to serve fifteen years in the federal correctional center for women. Lord have mercy on your soul," the judge said, glaring at Unique as he hit his gavel.

Unique didn't show any emotion. She took this too, just like a woman. She did her crime and she would pay her time. It didn't matter now that she wasn't even guilty of the gun and drug possession charges that were sent her away. Her list of real crimes was long: prostitution, extortion, robbery of a dead man, fraud, conspiracy, operating an illegal gambling house, accessory to robbery, grand larceny, claiming she loved Took when she didn't, and most of all, being a hoodrat. Unique had done many crimes and knew that some day she'd be punished. She just never expected it to be with hard prison time. Of course she could have snitched, but she didn't. She might have been a whole lot of things, but snitch bitch wasn't a title she wanted to acquire now, so she kept her mouth shut and went to do her time.

Unique wasn't too surprised that Baby Jon didn't come through to drop her a dime, even though he had her money. She left her money—not only the thirty-two Gs Train had given her, but the stash she had accumulated throughout the party, plus Fat Tee's gifts from afterward—in the trunk of the car, which Baby Jon had been driving when she got arrested. He had used it to meet someone before they left, and it turned out to be the thing that helped him escape.

The most shocking part of the whole ordeal was that Strolla was nowhere in sight. She hadn't been at Unique's trial to show any kind of moral support, but she had good reason. Strolla was too busy living in the lap of luxury with Train. They had finally hooked up and they were so happy. Well, at least they were happy once Strolla got over the pain of learning the truth from Train about her friend Unique.

Strolla always knew that Unique was scandalous, but had believed they were so much better than that when it came to dealing with each other. Strolla was shocked, however, when Train told her about the robbery. She couldn't believe that Unique didn't breathe a word to her about it. She was even more hurt when she found out that Unique had called her a lesbian when Train had wanted to hook up. It took a while, but gradually the love that Train showed Strolla wiped away all of her pain, and she never gave Unique another thought.

Brianna was the only familiar face in the front row of the courtroom when Unique was sentenced.

When the deputy came to put the cuffs back on Unique, she got a good look at Brianna, who was wearing a Kool-Aid smile, satisfied that she had gotten the last laugh.

Unique stopped in her tracks and spit on Brianna, wiping off that smile. "Now, beeaatch, I still get the last laugh."

Brianna had other plans, though. She had already decided that instead of trying to trap Baby Jon, she would redirect her attention to Took. She knew that with Unique in the slammer Took was very vulnerable. If she played her cards right, she could surely win his heart. It wouldn't even matter to her if his affection for her was real or he was just using her to pass the time. All she cared about was feeling like she was able to take something from Unique. She had taken her freedom, and now she would take her man.

Once the deputies took Unique to the back so she could begin to serve her jail time, Brianna was happy. She wiped the spit off her face and then she couldn't help herself. She practically ran to the ladies' bathroom, sat on the toilet, spread her legs open, pulled her vibrator out from her knock-off Prada bag, and went to work. She had finally gotten revenge on Unique, and she celebrated with an orgasm.

"Oh, oh, umph, umph," she moaned. "Sweet revenge. It's the next best thing to a good ol' nut."

For Unique, there was never a lesson learned. She never felt even one ounce of remorse, regret, guilt, humiliation or shame for any of her actions. Nothing at all. In fact, behind prison walls she continued to play her manipulative hoodrat games.

The only difference was that her victims were now female and her state of the art blowjob had to be modified to fit the needs of her new victims. Her game was, without a doubt, still state of art.

Acknowledgments

Roy Glenn

Thanks, Carl and Martha Weber

Nina

ONE

"So, it all comes down this?" I asked my lawyer, Wanda Moore.

Wanda looked over at me and slowly nodded her head. "All there is now is to wait, Nina."

Wait for a grand jury to decide if I was going to have to stand trial. I didn't wanna go to jail, but who does? And if I had to go, I couldn't blame anybody but myself. I chose to be where I was in life, and I chose to be doing what I was doing. Still, sometimes life leads you to make choices that you think you normally wouldn't. At every point where I should have turned right, I went left.

It was my first day back from Virginia. My girl, Teena, came and picked me up just like she did every time I came home. Only this time I was home for good. After five years I had finally graduated from Hampton with a degree in business administration. It took five years 'cause I lost my mind and went wild my freshman year. First time away from home, first time away from my parents' control—shit, I thought college was a social activity. You couldn't have a party and Nina not be there.

I got a little more serious about it my second year. I never was a great student, but I did enough to graduate. I figured I'd hang out for the summer, you know, have some fun—okay, have a lot of fun—then I'd get serious about getting a job in September. Maybe even October. After all, I had earned that break.

Teena had been my girl since I could remember. She was very pretty, and just the nicest, funniest person to be around. If there was trouble to get into, we got into it together. When I went away to college at Hampton, Teena, who always hated school, decided college wasn't for her and stayed in New York. For the last five years she'd been hanging out. Teena didn't work, and to my knowledge never had. She said her job was getting niggas to give her money. "The trick is doin' it without fuckin' everybody. That's what makes it an art form," Teena always told me. But it was working for her, 'cause everybody loved her.

Teena had taken some guy's Escalade to pick me up while he was sleeping. She said she met the guy a couple of days ago. "He likes to smoke weed, right, but he gets real sleepy when he does. So I told him when he picked me up that I wanted to borrow his truck, you know, so I could hang out with you or whatever."

"He probably thought you were crazy," I said.

"He laughed and says, 'We'll see.' So we had been ridin' around smokin' weed all day. Now, you know I can handle mine, but I know he's gettin' fucked up. So we get back to his house, right, and I say, you know, like, let's smoke another blunt. So we sittin' there smokin' the blunt, watchin' TV, and I ask him about the truck again, but he don't really answer me 'cause he's fallin' asleep. So I'm tellin' him, like, what a good driver I am and how I'm gonna take good care of his truck and shit, right. But by now he's breakin' his neck tryin' to stay 'wake. So I'm like, look, if you fall asleep on me, I'm takin' the truck," Teena said.

"What he say?"

"All he could do at that point was smile. He fell asleep, I got his keys and was gone. Then I called this other guy, told him that I needed some money to hang out with you, and said I'd come by later. Not!"

That's just how she carried it. So, now we were riding in some man's Escalade, spending another man's money. We hit the clubs.

We were hanging at this spot uptown when Teena says, "Hey, Nina, don't that guy look like Lorenzo?"

"What guy?" I got excited just hearing his name. I turned around quickly and saw him making his way though the crowd toward the bar. It was him, Lorenzo Copeland, my boyfriend from high school. My first lover, my only real boyfriend. I hadn't seen him in five years, and damn, he looked good. I told Teena I'd be back, went to the bar, and posted up where I knew he'd see me.

"Nina?" he yelled over the music as he got close enough to recognize me.

I turned around slowly like he was bothering me. I looked at him and made like I didn't know him. "Yes."

He stepped a little closer. "Don't you recognize

me?" He snatched off his sunglasses. "It's me, Lorenzo."

I took a step closer to him and slowly put on a little smile. "Lorenzo? Lorenzo Copeland." I held out my arms. "Come show me some love." He stepped up quickly and threw his arms around me. "How are you, Lorenzo?" I gave him a friendly hug and took a step back.

"I'm chillin', you know. But damn, Nina, it's good to see you."

"Really? I'm glad you feel that way 'cause I was just thinkin' about slappin' the shit outta you."

"Don't be like that."

"How come you never answered my letters?"

"Nina, I swear I never got your letters."

"Sure," I said and turned away.

"A lotta shit happened after you left. Gimme a chance to explain. Come on," he said and touched my hand. I pulled away. "Can we go someplace where we can talk?"

I stood there for a second and looked at him. I could tell by looking at him that he was a baller now. Standing there looking like money. I guess it was inevitable that he would grow up to be a baller; it ran in the family. Back then, two of his uncles went to jail for selling drugs, and the only reason his father stopped dealing was 'cause Lorenzo's mother had died when Lorenzo was young. Lorenzo was definitely bling-bling now, and his gear was all designer shit.

"Okay. Where can we go?" I asked.

"Come ride with me."

"I can't. Me and Teena are rollin' together. I can't leave her."

"Teena? From high school Teena?"

"Yup."

"Where she at?"

"Right there," I said and pointed to my girl.

"Wait a minute." He walked over to Chris, one of the guys he was with, whispered something to him then pointed at Teena.

Chris was fine too. He walked over and started talking to Teena. She was smiling and laughing, and the next thing I knew, him and Teena were coming toward us.

"What's up, Teena?"

Teena gave Lorenzo a big hug. "What's up, Lorenzo?"

"Y'all need to start callin' me Lo. Nobody calls me Lorenzo anymore."

"Whatever, Lo-ren-zo," Teena said, emphasizing each syllable. I had to agree with her. I had met him as Lorenzo, and to me, that would always be his name.

Teena turned to me. "So, where we goin', Nina?"

"I don't know. This is a Lorenzo production." I turned to him. "Where you talkin' about takin' us?" I asked, knowing that it didn't really matter where he wanted to go, and it really didn't matter what excuse he offered up for why he never wrote. I was going with him.

"Don't worry about that. We goin' to a little place I know. Come on."

Teena and I followed them to Lorenzo's rimmed-out Suburban. He threw the keys to Chris and we got in the back seat. Chris drove to a place called Jimmy's, a little hole in the wall bar where everybody seemed to know them. While Teena and Chris drank

shots of tequila and played pool, me and Lorenzo
sat in a booth in the back of the bar and talked.
While I sipped rum and Coke, he told me that
after I went away to Hampton, his father went to
jail for murder. Since he was only seventeen at the
time, Lorenzo had to go into a foster home until
he turned eighteen.

"I'm sorry to hear that about your father. For
real, I really am, but what does that have to do with
you writing me?"

" 'Cause he killed the man in our house, so they
never let me back in there. They just packed up
some of my stuff and shipped me off to this group
home. I tried to tell them that I had to get back
in the house to get some more of my stuff, but by
the time I got in there the landlord had thrown
out all of our stuff and moved someone else in
there."

I looked at Lorenzo, still playing the mad role.
"You probably wouldn't have wrote me even if you
had the address."

"That's not true, Nina. I loved you—still do. I'm
so glad to see you, you just don't know."

"Sure you do," I said, getting wrapped up in the
part. "All that is easy to say now, but all I know is
that you forgot about me."

A very sad look came over his face, but then all
of a sudden he stood up and started smiling. "You
gotta come with me, Nina," he said and started
walking away. When I didn't jump up and fall in
behind him, he stopped and came back to the
table. "Come on, Nina. You gotta come with me."

"Why?"

" 'Cause there's something I gotta show you."

"Show me what?"

"Come with me and see."

"Come with you where?"

"To da crib."

"Hell no! I see you after five years and you think I'm gonna go to your crib with you? I don't think so. What you wanna show me, your dick?" I asked. I wondered if he said yes, would I say okay. Truth be told, I love me some dick, and that had been my dick all through high school. On the morning that my parents drove me to Virginia to start college, I even snuck down to his house so I could fuck him one more time before I left.

Lorenzo smiled at me. "I could show you that right now if you wanted to see it, but what I got to show you, you gotta come with me to see."

"Why can't you just tell me what it is?"

" 'Cause I want you to hold it in your hands and know that it's for real."

"Sounds like we still talkin' about your dick."

"Yeah, you wanna see it, the way you keep on talkin' about it."

"You must be smokin' that rock you sellin'. I don't wanna see that dried-up little thing you got."

"Cool. Since we both know it ain't about no dick, you can come with me so I can show you what I gotta show you."

I went along with him. We told Teena and Chris that we would be back, and it wasn't long before we were in his apartment. I don't have to tell you that "Da Crib" was laid. The whole place had a black and white theme. The furniture was white leather and just about everything else was black. He had every kind of electronic device you could possibly imagine, plus a few things that I had no idea what they were.

"I hope I can find it. I ain't looked at them in years," he said as he went into the bedroom.

I followed him and sat on the bed while he searched in the closet. I picked up the remote and turned on the flat screen TV. While he searched the closet I flipped channels, wondering what I would say when he came out of the closet and sat down next to me, talking 'bout he can't find whatever it is that he's looking for. As far as I was concerned, this was nothing more than a clever way to get me here. I started to call him out on it, but I decided to just let it ride and see where Lorenzo was going with this.

"I know they're in here somewhere. I never throw anything out." The search continued for a minute or two more before he finally said, "Here they are." He came out of the closest and sat next to me on the bed. "This should prove to you that I didn't just forget about you."

"What are those?" I asked.

"Here," he said and handed me two envelopes. They were addressed to Nina Thomas at Hamilton University in Hamilton, Virginia. They were marked RETURN TO SENDER, NO SUCH ADDRESS. "I wrote those letters to you and mailed them, but they came back."

I couldn't help but laugh. "That's 'cause I went to *Hampton* University, in Hampton, Virginia, not Hamilton, silly." I suddenly felt myself getting all warm and sentimental. Not only did he try to write, but he saved the letters for five years.

"Oh shit. Really? Damn, I feel stupid."

"You should feel stupid. How many times did I tell you it was Hampton, not Hamilton?"

"A bunch of times, Nina," Lorenzo said, and that's when I saw it. I got up and walked over to his dresser to look at the picture stuck on the mirror. It was faded and the edges were all curled up, but there it was—my high school graduation picture.

"I can't believe you still have this."

"Never forgot you, Nina. I thought about you every day."

I felt a rush of warmth when he kissed me. It was like it was all happening in slow motion. Maybe it was him, maybe it was the rum and weed. I don't know, but it seemed as though his touch made my head spin. I felt myself losing control of the situation, so I pulled away.

"Slow down, handsome. We got plenty of time for all that."

"All right, all right, but I don't think you know how I'm feeling right now," Lorenzo said.

"Yeah, I do. But we left Teena and Chris at the bar."

"So? They'll be all right. They looked like they was gettin' along just fine."

"Maybe, but I would be mad as hell at her if she ran off with somebody and left me with a stranger."

"All right, all right," he said then kissed me. "We can go back for them, but you gotta promise me something right now."

"What's that?" I asked and he held me tighter.

"Promise you'll never leave me again," Lorenzo said and he kissed me.

"Never."

Lorenzo was right; Teena and Chris were getting along just fine without us. We got back to the bar in time to take Teena to the Escalade so she could follow Chris wherever he was going. After we dropped them off, I went back to Lorenzo's apartment with him. As soon as we got through the door, he was all over me. We were both naked before I knew it.

There we were, both of us standing in his living room, breathing hard, and surrounded by a pile of clothes. "What?" I said as we stood there staring at each other.

"You are so beautiful, Nina. Let's take a shower so I can bathe you," Lorenzo said.

When the water temperature was right, he led me by the hand into the shower and picked up a bar of soap. He began rubbing the soap between his hands until both were lathered heavily. I occupied myself by rubbing his rather large and very hard erection between my hands.

With the bar of soap in one hand, he began to lather my body, sliding his hands delicately over every inch of my body. My eyes fluttered shut and my head drifted back as I continued to massage his erection. Once he had soaped my whole body, Lorenzo pulled me to his chest and wrapped his arms around me. He slid his body up and down against mine, staring into my eyes the whole time. "You are so beautiful, Nina."

I tried to say something, but all I could do was moan. The feeling of his chest against my nipples made them swell. "Turn around," Lorenzo said, and I quickly complied, turning my body into the shower. He started again, sliding his body against mine. He massaged my breasts gently, squeezing my nipples as the water beat against my body, washing away the soap. Lorenzo ran his hand across my stomach, fingering my navel. His hand made the occasional pass across my pubic hair. He started kissing and licking my neck, sucking and gently biting my earlobes. Then his index finger found my clit. My eyes and mouth both opened wide. Again I tried to speak as his finger massaged my clit; again no words could escape. His touch was soft and gentle, yet firm all at once. It felt as if waves of electric current emanated from my clit and spread throughout my body. I reached for the wall to steady myself; my knees locked, my body shuddered from the inside out.

I forced myself to pull away from him. I quickly washed the remaining soap from his body and pulled him out of the shower. We slowly dried one another, each of us exploring the other's body with the towel, our hands, and our eyes.

"Lie down. I'm gonna give you a massage." He kneeled on the floor and poured a little baby oil on my legs, rubbing it in slowly. He began massaging my calves then did the same to my thighs, exploring with his tongue until I felt my body shake. Rising from his knees, he sat next to me on the bed and applied oil to my arms and chest.

I took the bottle from him. "Lay down on your back. Let me do you," I said.

Lorenzo smiled his reply and quickly complied with my wishes. Now it was my turn to kneel on the bed next to him. I poured the lotion into my hands and rubbed them together, then I began to massage his thighs gently. I straddled his torso as he looked on with great anticipation. I slid down on him and started to move up and down slowly, then in circles. I reached for the baby oil and poured it across his chest, rubbing it in with my fingertips. Once I had covered his chest, I leaned forward and kissed him. I moved from side to side, rubbing my chest across his in beat with the music. I started to move my hips faster while I tasted his tongue, then I sat up and went to work. After a while, I stopped and moved my legs so my feet were flat on the bed. In this position, I proceeded to fuck the shit out of him.

TWO

I guess you can tell that I'm just a little dick happy. You know, excited to the point of smiling from ear to ear at the sight of one and the feel of it in my hands—soft and silky to the touch yet hard and firm. So you know I was glad to be back with Lorenzo 'cause he had it going on down there. Besides, I still had mad love for him.

It's like we could feel each other sometimes, you know. One minute we'd be talking then we'd just look at each other. The next thing you know, we were into it, having mad sex. It didn't matter where we were or what was going on around us. We would do it anywhere.

I remember one Saturday night, we were on our way to the movies and I looked over at Lorenzo and said, "Turn down that street." Well, naturally he complied with my request; he knew what time it was. "Pull over behind that building there." As soon as he stopped the car, I got out. "You coming?" I asked and started walking toward the building. Lorenzo turned off the truck and followed me. Once I got to the building I walked down a short flight of steps leading to a door. I leaned against the door. "Come here." I kissed him, and he reached under my skirt. I stepped out of my panties and handed them to him. "Hold on to these for me." The kissing began again, until I stopped suddenly and pushed him away from me. "Sit down on the steps."

He did it. Quick.

"Take it out so I can ride you." I gathered my skirt around my waist and turned around. I grabbed hold of it and put it in me, then I started grinding my hips into his lap. Once we were done, we went on to the movies.

While I was at Hampton I never really had what you would call a boyfriend. There were guys I saw 'cause they were paid and liked to give me money, guys I saw just to go out and be seen with—but they had money too—and then there was Raymond. Me and him never went anywhere, we never did anything together, and he never had any money to spend on me, but damn, that nigga could fuck.

Just like I'd had other men, I wasn't stupid enough to believe that those last five years, Lorenzo had been saving all that dick for me. I knew that there had to be somebody he was fucking, more likely a whole bunch of women looking to fuck a baller—a baller with skills. Shit, I knew he probably had a gang of women. But it was cool; I wasn't worried. None of them had shit on me. And besides, I had history with him, and if that first night back together was any indicator, I could just relax and let it come to me.

And it did.

But you know there had to be some drama first. Like this one time we were at Sam Goody looking at CDs when one of his women walked up on him. I was on one aisle and he was listening to a CD on the headphones on the next aisle, so he didn't see her coming. I'd been watching her since she came in the store, wondering what possessed her to put that bad weave in her hair, and we are not even gonna talk about her outfit and that ridiculous shade of pink. She was looking around, but as soon as she saw Lorenzo she started straight for him. Well, Pinky walked her narrow ass up to him and threw her arms around his neck and kissed him on the lips. Lorenzo started looking around to see where I was. When he finally saw me, I was looking dead at him. I just stood there and waited to see how he handled it. Lorenzo eased her arms from around his neck, took off the headphones and put a polite distance between them. It wasn't long before he turned around and pointed me out to her. She looked over at me and waved. She said a few more words then she walked out of the store.

When I asked him who she was, he told me that she was one of his sister's friends and that he barely knew her. "Come on, now. I saw the way that woman kissed you. You gave her some of that dick. Only question is whether she still gettin' it."

Lorenzo put his arms around me and said, "The only woman I want is you. Believe that."

I always felt warm and safe in his arms, like, I don't know, like I could feel how much he loved me. Still, I couldn't let him off the hook that easily. "I hear you sayin' that, but what I see is something different."

That first chick went away quietly. The next one wasn't pretty.

We had gone to the club and just hit the VIP room when Lorenzo stopped dead in his tracks. He whispered something to Chris and they tried to walk me and Teena up outta there quick, but they weren't quick enough.

"Lo! Lo! You hear me callin' you, mothafucka. Don't try to walk away from me!" I heard a woman yelling over the music. Lorenzo stopped and faced her, but Chris was still trying to drag me and Teena out the club.

"Let me go, Chris," I said, struggling to get back to them.

"No, Nina. That ain't nothing for you to be concerned about," Chris said.

I kicked him in the ankle; not hard, but enough that he let go of my hand. As I got closer to them, I began to wonder when Lorenzo developed this thing for rail-thin women with bad weaves.

By the time I got back to them, she was all up in his face with, "Why you don't return my calls?"

"I been busy," Lorenzo said as I stood next to him.

I could see the fire light in her eyes when she saw me standing there. "Who the fuck is she? This who you been busy with, huh?"

Lorenzo looked over at me and smiled. "Yeah. This my baby, Nina. Nina, that's Karhonda."

"Well, bitch, you know I'm fuckin' him too," Karhonda said and took a step toward me.

"You mean you used to be the bitch he was

fuckin', 'cause I'm gonna make sure that your tri-flin' ass never see that again."

By that time, Slim was surrounded by two other women. Karhonda caught me off guard and slapped the shit out of me before Lorenzo stepped in between us. One of her girls stepped up and swung on me, but outta nowhere Teena clocked her with a shot to the jaw. "No you bitches didn't think y'all was just gonna group up on my girl and me just stand here!" She looked at the other women. "What, bitch? You want some too?"

Teena was my girl, and if it came to it, she was always ready throw down.

"Everything all right here, Lo?" a security guard asked. He was a big, huge mothafucka, backed up by two more just like him.

"Nah, them three there gotta go," Lorenzo said as he pointed them out. "And they don't need to come back up in here."

"I'll take care of it," the guard said and turned to the three women. "All right ladies, let's start making our way to the door," I heard him say as Lorenzo ushered me back into the VIP room.

There were a few others, but after a while I was the only woman Lorenzo was seeing, or that was the way he made me feel. I was his woman, and it felt great. At the clubs, I was the one on his arm, chilling in the VIP room, hanging out with the stars. It didn't matter where he was at night; Lorenzo would always come get me so I was the one he woke up next to every morning.

He bought me a white 2001 BMW. At first I was a little disappointed that it wasn't a new BMW, until he explained to me that he couldn't pay cash for a new car at any dealership without them reporting the transaction to the IRS. Even though he couldn't do it, I still felt good knowing he had cash like that. It wasn't shit for Lorenzo to hand me a thousand, sometimes two thousand dollars and say, "Why don't you go buy yourself something nice?" or "You haven't been to the spa lately. Why don't you spend the day pampering yourself?" At first I thought it was just his way of getting rid of me for the day, and that used to bother me, but I came to grips with it. One, that was a lot of money to throw away just to get some stray pussy, and two, even if he was trying to get rid of me, did it matter?

Lorenzo took me to Mexico for my birthday. When I got back I called Teena so I could tell her all about it. She said she was tired of smoking the weed that Chris had and was on her way to find some. I told her that I would ride with her. I sat patiently waiting for Teena to arrive, and two hours later when she finally did, she came with some fantastic story about what she and Chris were doing.

"So, how you doin', girl?" Teena asked as I got in the car. "I like that suit. Where'd you get it?"

"I'm doing fine, and I got the suit off the rack at Neiman Marcus."

"So, tell me. How was Cancun?" Teena asked.

"Girl, we had the best time, but I never wanna see another bottle of Jose Cuervo as long as I live. We stayed drunk the whole time we were there. We must have been on the alcoholics' tour, 'cause it seemed like we woke up drinking. Everyplace we went they had shots of tequila. And then we had the nerve to go on a tequila cruise. So picture this;

we're already drunk, right, staggering onto the boat. I almost fell in the water twice."

"No you didn't!" Teena laughed.

"Yes I did. We were dancing on deck when Lorenzo decides he wants to spin me around. I lost hold of his hand and went straight for the rail. Luckily he caught me before I went over. So we're standing there laughing about it, and me, like the drunk fool I am, spin around again. Bam! Right back to the rail. I sat my drunk ass down after that."

"I just bet you did," Teena commented.

The conversation, like any other conversation between me and Teena, was intense and all over the place. We jumped around from topic to topic while we rode around trying to find some weed. Finally the subject turned to men in general and Chris in particular. "And when we got back, there was Chris waiting at the airport to take us home. Which reminds me . . ." I turned to her with a questioning gaze.

"What?" she asked.

"Teena."

"What?"

"Teena," I repeated with more intensity.

"What!"

"What did you do to Chris?"

"What do you mean?"

"You know what I'm talking about, Teena. Don't sit there looking innocent like you don't know who Chris is."

"I ain't doin' nothing to that nigga. You know me, girl. Chris is just another nigga with money to me."

"You must have done something to him 'cause you were all he wanted to talk about on the way from the airport. I know at first he really wasn't feelin' you, but now all he talks about is Teena. 'Teena says this,' and 'Teena likes that.' I got so tired of hearing about you last night I had to throw Chris out."

"Tired of hearing about me, huh? I'll try not to take that personal."

I threw up my middle finger. "Anyway."

"What did he want to know about me?"

"Whether you were crazy."

"I know you told him I was."

"Well, you are out there, Teena."

"Out there? Bitch, please," Teena said as her cell rang. It was another friend of ours named Shay. The three of us had known each since junior high school. She got married and had two kids, which was the only reason she didn't hang with us all the time. "What's up, Shay?"

While Teena talked to Shay, I stared out the window and thought about how I was letting all the things I had planned for myself after college get further and further away from me. I had planned to work for a year and then go back for my masters. "Yeah, right," I said out loud and Teena looked at me like I was stupid. I had been out of school for almost a year by that time, and I hadn't looked for a job or filled out an application to grad school. I was getting so caught up in Lorenzo and what he was doing that I was losing myself to it. But I loved Lorenzo and was happy to be anywhere he was, doing anything he was doing.

When Teena got off the phone, she said that Shay was bored and wanted to know what we were doing. "I told her we were rollin' around trying to find something to smoke. She said she knows where the fire is, so come get her. I told her hell no, I ain't ridin' nowhere with her and them bad-ass kids."

"That's fucked up, but they are bad."

"I was being nice when I said that, 'cause them little fuckas is off the chain, but she said they're at her momma's house for the night. She said that her and Gary were supposed to be doin' something, but now he says he gotta work late tonight."

We rolled by and picked up Shay, and she told Teena where to go to find the weed. While Teena drove to the stop, the three of us were talking.

Shay busted out with, "You two are livin' the life and me, I got two little, bad-ass kids and a cheatin' husband."

"I tried to tell you before you married his ass. He was a ho when you met him. Did you really think he was gonna change?" Teena asked.

"Yes. We're married now."

"Hold up now, Shay. Let's be honest; that don't mean shit. You gonna tell me that you ain't never creeped on your man?" Teena asked.

"No, Teena. Never. I have more respect for myself than to do something like that."

"What does self-respect have to do with it?" Teena asked.

"If a woman respects herself, especially a married woman, she doesn't feel the need to sleep around."

"Well, let me ask you a question then," I said.

"Go ahead."

"Did you fuck Gary before y'all got married?" I asked.

"Yes, but that was different. We were in—"

"Y'all were in love. Yes, yes I know. Did you fuck any other men before you met Gary?"

"I . . . ah, ah . . ." Shay dropped her head.

"Ah, ah, ah, my big ass, girl. Did you or didn't you fuck any other men before you met Gary?"

"Yes," Shay answered reluctantly.

"I know that's right, 'cause you were one scandalous-ass ho," Teena said.

"I was not!" Shay protested.

"Bitch, please," Teena said and rolled her eyes. "She must be frontin' 'cause you here, Nina. You must have forgot about the time that you called me trippin' 'cause you had fucked five different niggas in three days. Where was your self-respect then?"

"That was different. I wasn't married then."

"So, as long as you ain't married it's all right to fuck around and have no respect for yourself, but when you get married is when it's different, 'cause you're in love."

"What you say to that, Shay?" I asked.

"Fuck you, bitch. That's what I gotta say to that." Shay smiled at me.

"Let me tell y'all about my aunt," Teena said. "She carries it like this respectable churchgoin' woman. She's been married for twelve years. Good job and shit, two kids in private school, and she's cheatin' her ass off."

"No," I said in mock horror.

"She's cheatin' with a guy that goes to church with her. Thursday is their night to creep, but Thursday is supposed to be her shopping night. So what this respectable, churchgoin' woman does, since her husband expects her to be out late anyway, is she does her shopping on Wednesday and takes all the food and stuff over her girlfriend's and leaves it there. Then after Mr. Churchgoin' Man fucks her on Thursday, she goes and picks up her stuff and goes home. Respectable woman. And get this—when she gets there, her husband helps her in with the groceries."

"Oh, no she don't," I said.

"I ain't lyin'," Teena said.

"Y'all saw Don at Chuck's party last week, right?" Shay asked.

"Yeah," I said. "I hadn't seen him in a long time. Where's he been?"

"In jail."

"What was he in jail for?" Teena asked, laughing.

"Indecent exposure and resisting arrest."

"Get outta here. What happened?" I asked, laughing at the charges, anticipating a colorful story.

"You know Vincent and Keisha, right?" Shay asked.

"Yeah, and?"

"Well, you know Don's still fuckin' Keisha, right?" Shay said.

"Yeah, yeah, we know. Even after she married Vincent," Teena said impatiently. "Everybody but Vincent knows that. Get to the story."

"Don told me that he went over to their house. You know, just kicking it with Keisha, right, when Vincent comes home. But that isn't any big deal, 'cause he's over there all the time anyway. So they sit around and talk for a while, Keisha cooks dinner and they eat. Then after dinner Vincent tells them about this party and tries to get Don to go with him."

"Vincent ain't stupid. He was trying to get Don out his house and away from his wife," Teena said.

"Yeah, but Don ain't trying to hear that. He tells him, now dig this, 'No, I'm just gonna stay here and kick it with Keisha for a while then jet'."

"Kid got nerve," I said.

"I'm sayin'," Teena agreed.

"So, Vincent breaks out to go to the party and leaves Don and Keisha. Don said that as soon as Vincent locked the door, Keisha was on him, grabbing on his shirt, pulling on his belt. Next thing you know, they're upstairs in the bedroom, butt naked, doin' it doggy style. So Don says him and Keisha are all into it when something tells him to look to his left. He sees Vincent sneaking up the stairs."

"Oh shit!" I shouted and Teena followed up with, "You bullshittin'."

"This is what Don told me. He was cold busted. So he pushes off Keisha just as Vincent dives at him. Vincent misses Don and falls on Keisha. Don starts grabbing for clothes while Vincent gets up and comes after him. Don said he was running around the room trying to put his drawers on, but Vincent jumps on him and they start fighting."

"I can see Don now, goin' for blows with Vincent while he's naked," Teena said, cracking up.

"What was Keisha doing while all this is going on?" I asked.

"Don said she was just kicked back on the bed, watching like she was gettin' off on it or something," Shay replied. "So Don says he knocked Vincent into the dresser long enough for him to get his drawers on, but instead of running out the house, he tries to explain. He said Vincent went wild, reached into the dresser and got out his gun, and just started shooting."

"I bet he got that ass outta there quick then," I said.

"No, he said since Vincent wasn't hitting nothing, he got the rest of his clothes. Keisha jumped on Vincent's back, Don ran downstairs and out the back door. He said he hopped the fence and was running down the street when the police rolled up on him and went spotlight. Don tries to run like a fool. They ran him down and locked him up."

"That's deep, Shay," Teena said, shaking her head. "That's the type of thing you just hear about, but you swear stuff like that don't happen."

"Hold up, hold up," Shay said. "Cops are putting Don in the car when Vincent comes running out with his gun, yelling that Don had raped his wife. Cops throw down on him, but Vincent keeps coming. Don said he got in the car quick. Finally Vincent drops the gun, but as soon as the cops relax, he rushes at Don again. Cops grab him, kick his ass, and they take both of them to jail."

"That's too wild," Teena said.

"Did they charge him with rape?" I asked.

"Yeah, but Keisha never would talk to the cops, so they dropped the charge," Shay went on to explain. "She told Vincent she didn't wanna go through all that drama. Pull over there, Teena, where those guys are standin'," Shay said. Teena dimmed her lights and pulled over. One tall, skinny guy who looked like JJ from *Good Times* came to the car. I rolled down my window.

"What's up, ladies? Can I go with y'all?"

"Hell no," Shay said quietly and we all giggled.

"What y'all lookin' for?"

"What you got?" I asked.

"Got these fat dub sacks," JJ said.

Teena leaned toward me. "Let me see them," she said and held out her hand. While JJ got out a couple of sacks, Teena dropped the car in drive. It had been a long time, but I knew what was coming next. When he reached in with two sacks for her to look at, I slapped them out of his hand and Teena hit the gas. We drove away laughing our asses off.

"We haven't done that in years!" I yelled over the laughter.

"You two are crazy," Shay said, almost to the point of tears.

"Just livin' the life!" Teena screamed.

My slide into the life continued, and after awhile, there was no more talk about finding a job. For what? I didn't need a job. I always had money, I had a car, and I shopped practically every day. I didn't want for shit. "Who needs a job?" I told my parents.

"You do, that's who, Nina." My parents kept pushing the job thing down my throat. It was starting to get old. I started talking to Lorenzo about me getting my own place.

"What you wanna do that for?"

"I need to get out of my parents' house," I told him.

"Why don't you come live with me? You're there just about every night anyway."

And that settled that. I moved in with Lorenzo. I didn't take anything with me, I just bought all new stuff. To me, it was like leaving my old life behind and starting a brand new life, a life where Lorenzo was a king and I was the queen. Expensive cars, big money, new clothes, and anything else I wanted. It seemed like the money never stopped coming. Everything was great in my corner of the world. I was living the life, but what I didn't know was that fate was getting ready to get it all twisted.

THREE

"**L**orenzo Copeland, this is your last warning! Come out with your pants on!" Chris yelled while he rang the bell and banged on the door. We heard him out there making all that noise, but we didn't care. Lorenzo and I continued to make love in spite of the noise, at least until it got so loud that it broke my concentration.

"Damn!" I said as I rolled off Lorenzo, folded my arms, and pouted like a child who had her toy taken away.

"All right, all right! I'll be out in a minute!" Lorenzo yelled.

"It ain't nobody but Chris. Just ignore him and he'll go away."

"You know if I don't answer it he's just gonna keep banging."

"You're right," I said and wrapped up in the sheets.

"I'll get rid of him."

"Lorenzo, you know I like your friends, right? And Chris is my boy and whatever, but he always seems to show up at the worst times."

"You're right. Chris does have a nasty habit of dropping by while we're doin' it," Lorenzo said.

"But you gotta admit I'm cool about it, though. It's become sort of a running joke."

"It ain't like I'm glad to see him either. You were tryin' to fuck the shit outta me."

"I sure was, so make it quick. I'm not finished with you yet."

"Keep it wet for me," Lorenzo said as he got out of the bed and put on his pants. He went to the door to let Chris in then came back to the room. "What are you gonna do today?"

"I saw the cutest outfit yesterday. I'm gonna go back and get it."

"Why didn't you get it then?"

"I'm ashamed to admit it, but my hands were already full." I laughed and rolled out of bed.

"Maybe that oughta say something to you about the amount of shopping you do. I mean, you got shit in that closet that you ain't looked at since you bought it. Still got tags on them and shit. It's like shoppin' is your drug of choice."

"You want me to look good for you, don't you?" I asked, walking around half in a daze, half looking for something to put on.

"No doubt, but you don't need to shop to look good for me. You look good to me just the way you are now."

I looked at Lorenzo and smiled. He smiled and stared me down.

"What you smiling 'bout?" I asked.

"Lookin' at you."

"Oh, really?"

"I don't mean to be crude, Nina, but those are the prettiest titties I've ever seen."

"Even if you didn't mean to, yeah, that shit was crude. But thank you anyway," I said and got back in the bed. "If I look so good, maybe you could get back in this bed and finish what you started."

"I am thinkin' about gettin' back in that bed, but I know I got someplace I gotta be, so I been tryin' to talk myself out of it," Lorenzo said as he finished getting dressed. When he was ready to leave, he came to the bed and kissed me good-bye.

Trying to be a good girl and prove that I wasn't a shopaholic, I didn't buy anything that day. We didn't even go to the mall. We just hung out around the way until I was ready to go home. I sat in the back seat listening, but not really hearing what Teena and Shay were arguing about. My mind was in a completely different place. I was thinking about putting the BMW down and getting a Lexus. The BMW had served me well these last two years, but I just felt like driving something different. And I wanted a black one this time. I hate white cars 'cause no matter what you do, you can never keep them clean.

Teena turned down my street and into a sea of police and other emergency vehicles. A cold chill came over me; I instantly knew this was not good. We got out of the car and tried to make our way though the crowd. As I got closer, it became obvious that whatever was going on, Lorenzo was in the middle of it.

"What you think is happening?" Teena asked.

"I don't know, but it can't be good," I said as I got near the building. I shivered as I watched the coroner come out of the building with a body bag. I was just about to cross the police barricade when somebody grabbed me by the arm.

"You don't wanna do that." I turned around and saw Jay, one of Lorenzo's people.

"Jay, please tell me that's not Lorenzo they bringing out in that bag."

"It's not. They brought Lorenzo and Chris out already. They're both in jail," Jay said.

"What happened, Jay? Who's in the body bag?"

"I don't know. I went to the store and all this was here when I got back."

"You didn't try to find out?" I asked, mad as hell at him.

"No. I ain't goin' anywhere near them cops right now."

Shay stepped up. "I'll find out what's happenin', Nina," she said and walked up to one of the police controlling the crowd. They talked for a long time, which drove me crazy, then the cop handed Shay a card and she made her way back to us.

"Well?" I demanded.

"Both Lorenzo and Chris are in jail. He said that one of them killed a cop, but he don't know which one."

"Killed a cop? In our apartment? What were the cops doin' there?"

"They came to arrest Lorenzo on a warrant for conspiracy to distribute," Shay explained.

"Oh my God," I said as I began to cry.

"I don't think that you should try to go in there anytime soon, Nina," Teena said. "You know how they like to arrest the girlfriend and shit. They figure that you know everything about how Lorenzo does business and then try to make you testify against him."

"Shit, that ain't gonna happen," I said. I took out my cell phone and called the lawyer. "Let's get out of here."

The worst thing about waiting for information is that you have plenty of time to speculate, and the three of us were off the chain with it. We had been sitting at Shay's house for an hour, coming up with all kinds of stuff. When the lawyer did finally call, he didn't do much to end all the drama. He confirmed what we already knew: both of them were charged with murder and conspiracy. He said that Chris was in jail and Lorenzo was in the hospital, and that he was on his way to see Chris. He couldn't tell us anything else, and said that he would call back with more information as soon as he could.

"What's Lorenzo doin' in the hospital?" Shay asked when I told them what the lawyer had said.

"He didn't know. Or if he did, he didn't tell me." I looked at Teena. She had been uncharacteristically quiet since we got to Shay's. I mean, she was talking or whatever, but she wasn't her usual self. She wasn't talking any shit, and that's what was uncharacteristic. I wondered if Chris was becoming more than just another nigga with money to her.

The next day the lawyer called me back to say

that Lorenzo was the one who killed the cop. I went numb, only hearing half of what the lawyer said after that. I knew then that nothing about my life would ever be the same. At the time, I couldn't even imagine how true that was.

FOUR

I wasn't allowed to see Lorenzo while he was in the hospital. They told me some bullshit about his condition. When I tried to get information they told me that I needed to talk to the police, but the police weren't telling me shit. After two days, he was released from the hospital and went straight to court. I was late getting there, so I had to see him when he got to jail. When he came into the visiting room, all I could say was, "Damn! What the hell happened to you?" Lorenzo's right eye was bruised and swollen, and his lip had stitches.

"Cops."

"The cops did that?" I asked him, thinking it was more of a statement than a question. This wasn't the first time I had seen the type of brutality that the cops could deal out. I just never in my wildest dreams thought it would happen to anybody I knew, and definitely not Lorenzo. He was much too smart to put himself in a position for the cops to bust him up like that, but there he was, all busted up.

"Yup. It looks a lot better now. Yesterday this whole side of my face was swollen."

"They say you killed a cop."

Lorenzo just nodded.

"What happened?"

"Me and Chris were at the crib chillin' when the cops come to the house with a warrant to search the place. I looked at Chris, he looked at me. I knew I had shit there, so I knew we were goin' to jail. But we talked about this, you know what I'm sayin'? Keep your mouth shut and do what they say. Don't give them no excuses. So we sittin' there on the bar stools, like we always do, waitin' for them to find the stash. While we sittin' there, one of the cops is talkin' big shit to us, but you know we ain't payin' that shit no attention. So when they find it and they're about to arrest us, this cop steps in front of me and points his finger in my face and says, 'I guess you *boys* are goin' to jail.' Now, you know I hate that shit, so I stood up and said, 'That's all right. I'll be back on the block playin' stickball before dinner time.' Then he hits me in the face, and I don't know, maybe it was reflex, but I swung back. Another cop pulls out his club and hits me in the shins and I drop to my knees. I tried to get up, then both of them start hittin' me with their clubs and kickin' me. All I could think about then was dyin'. I knew they were gonna kill me, Nina. I couldn't just let them kill me, so I grabbed one cop's gun and I shot him."

"Damn, Lorenzo. You killed a cop."

"It was self defense. He was gonna kill me, Nina.

I know it. After I shot the cop, the other cop pulls his gun and shoots me in the arm."

"You're lucky it was just your arm. He coulda aimed for your chest."

"He did, but I moved. Just not quick enough. The bullet caught me in the arm and I dropped the gun. Then it seemed like all the cops started kickin' me and hittin' me with them clubs. I heard somebody yell, 'That's enough,' and I blacked out. The next thing I remember is waking up in the hospital."

"Where was Chris while all this was goin' on?"

"I don't know."

Over the next few months the government took everything. Yes, everything. I never did get back in the apartment. I was told that it had all been purchased with the proceeds of a criminal enterprise or some shit like that, so now I had nothing—no home, no car, no clothes. It was a good thing that I did leave my old stuff at my parents' house, 'cause I needed it then. Since my parents wouldn't let me move back in the house, I had to get a small apartment. It was a dump, but it was all I could afford. I had given just about all the money to the lawyer.

At the trial, the prosecution presented their case and rested. This was when it became apparent what part Chris had played in all this. He became one of the star witnesses for the prosecution. Lorenzo's lawyer told him that Chris began telling everything he knew as soon as Lorenzo blacked out. Chris didn't want any part of the murder charge, so he rolled on Lorenzo and did it quick. He wasn't the only one. Lorenzo had another partner named

Bryce who had seemed to disappear about four months earlier. As it turned out, Bryce had been busted on a possession charge, and he was the one who gave them Lorenzo.

Lorenzo's lawyer didn't have much of a defense to mount. He tried to discredit Chris and Bryce on their drug-related testimony based on their admitted involvement in a criminal enterprise, but the bomb was already dropped when they put Chris on the stand to talk about the murder. He testified that he heard Lorenzo talking shit to the cops then the next thing he saw was Lorenzo grabbing the cop's gun and killing him. Not a word about the cops beating Lorenzo. That bitch didn't say shit about that. I wanted to shoot that nigga myself. How you sell out your boy like that? Lorenzo said he understood, but I could see in his eyes that shit hurt him. Both of your boys rolling on you—you can't tell me that shit is easy to swallow.

It took the jury less than an hour to find Lorenzo guilty on all charges. I can't ever remember crying harder over something than I did for Lorenzo that day. Inside, I felt like my life was over too. In those two years I had built my whole life around Lorenzo Copeland. What would my life be without him? Did I even have a life without him?

His lawyer arranged for Lorenzo to see me for a minute before they took him away. I began to cry again as soon as I saw him.

"Don't cry, baby. We knew this day was coming," Lorenzo said.

"I know." I continued to cry and Lorenzo held my hands.

"There's something that I gotta say to you," he said.

"What's that?"

"I want you to know that I love you. I have always loved you, Nina."

"I love you too."

"If you ever need anything, you gotta call my cousin Leon in Jacksonville."

"I will," I said, still not able to stop myself from crying.

"I been thinkin' about this for a long time, and I know it's gonna be better for you this way."

"What are you talkin' about?"

"I don't want you to come see me anymore."

"What do you mean? Why don't you want me to come see you?"

"I know that I'm never gonna get out of here, and if I do, it won't be for a long time."

"What are you sayin'? Lorenzo, I love you. I don't care how long it takes, I'll wait for you."

"Nina, you gotta listen to me. It's not fair to you. I can't do that to you, make you live your life alone, or worse, lying to me."

"No, Lorenzo, don't do this. I promise to be faithful to you. I love you. I promise to come see you, and I'll write to you all the time."

"I don't want you to come see me. I don't want you to write to me. You are a young, beautiful woman. You have the rest of your life in front of you."

I broke down crying hard. I couldn't believe what I was hearing. "I don't have a life without you. I need you. You're my whole life." I couldn't breathe. How could he be saying this to me?

"I can't be a part of your life anymore. That life is over for me."

"No," I cried. "Your life is not over. Don't say that."

"My life is inside now with my father and my uncles. It's like this is where I always been goin' all my life," Lorenzo said as the deputy opened the door. "I'm dead to you now."

"That's it," the deputy said as he uncuffed Lorenzo from the table. "Sorry, ma'am, but it's time to go."

Lorenzo stood and put his hands behind his back. "Good-bye, Nina," Lorenzo said as the deputy put him in chains.

"What am I supposed to do now?"

Lorenzo smiled at me and mouthed the words *sell drugs.*

FIVE

When Lorenzo was sentenced to life without parole, the reality of my situation finally began to sink in. I was alone, I was about to be broke, and I was depressed about it. I stayed in bed for a few days. When I did get out of bed I wouldn't come out of the apartment. Everybody came by to holla, make sure I was all right. I told them all the same thing: I was fine and just needed some time to get myself together.

One afternoon a friend named Amel came by to see me. She worked as a masseuse at the spa that I used to go to. She had been my masseuse for the last couple of years. I knew she did a little private dancing on the side, but there was a whole other side to her that I never would have even suspected. When an attendant walked in on her while she was having sex with one of her customers, she got fired. And yeah, that customer was a woman.

It took me a minute to come to grips with the fact that the woman who had her hands all over my body was, as she called it, a woman who believed in choices. She said she hated the term bisexual. By the time that happened, we had come to be friends. Our relationship had gone beyond her providing me with a service, so I accepted her. We could be cool as long as she never came at me like that, and she never did.

In spite of that, Lorenzo would have freaked if he knew. Although he'd never admit it to me, gay and bisexual women intimidated him for some reason. "Maybe it's because we come at a woman on a level that he could never understand, much less compete with," Amel told me once, but that shit was too deep for me to even wrap my mind around.

Naturally, I couldn't afford to pay her for her services now, so she dropped in to gossip and smoke a blunt. "What are you gonna do now, Nina?"

"I don't know. I'm not ready to sell drugs, and I'm definitely not ready to get a job," I said, but that was exactly what I should have been ready to do. I had a degree in business administration. I could hear Lorenzo telling me that I was a young, beautiful woman, and that I had the rest of my life in front of me. Still, I wasn't ready to make that choice.

"Why don't you dance?" Amel asked me.

"I never even pointed my mind in that direction, but I could damn sure use the money."

"And it's good money. You're a very pretty woman. You're young, your breasts are big and firm, and your stomach is flat."

"And I have the kind of ass that makes men follow me around."

"You'll get nothin' but paid. Believe that."

"Okay, you talked me into it. Who do I need to talk to?"

"Don't worry, Nina. I'll take care of everything." Amel went on to explain that she worked for an agency that provided dancers for private parties.

"Y'all just dancin', right?"

"Some of the girls sell pussy, some don't, if that's what you're asking me," was Amel's answer, never saying one way or the other which side she came down on. "I can tell you the money is out there if you want it. I can also tell you that it's something you'd have to decide on your own."

Anyway, two days later Amel called me and told me she was on her way to dance for a private party. She asked me to come along. "You don't have to dance if you don't want to. Just come with me and see if it's something you can do."

I said cool, so she came to pick me up to go to the Hyatt. When I got in the car, Amel wasn't alone; some guy was driving. "What's up, Nina?" Amel said as the guy drove off. "This is Ricky. He's my security. Ricky drives me to all of my jobs, stays with me during the show just to make sure that everybody behaves themselves, and drops me off at home when I'm finished."

"What up, Nina?" Ricky said. He was a large man with a thick West Indian accent.

"Hi," was all the greeting that my nervous ass could get out.

"If you decide to get in this business, you better find somebody like Ricky that you can trust," Amel advised.

When we arrived at the suite, the party had already started. It was a small set, just four men who

all looked like business types. Once Amel got her
outfits ready she began her show. I stood in the
doorway and watched her as she danced in the
middle of the floor, then to each man. While Amel
danced, she allowed the men to touch her, but
when one got a little too happy with his hands, she
would move away or remove his hand. As I watched,
I thought *I can do this*. I was definitely a better
dancer than she was. I could shake my ass like a
salt shaker.

When she came back to the room to change
clothes she asked me, "Well, what you think?"

"I wanna try."

"I was hoping you would say that. Take off your
clothes."

"What?"

"No time to get shy on me now. I got an outfit
that would be perfect for you. My breasts aren't
big enough to fit it right."

It was at that moment that I had to decide what
I was going to do. If I felt uncomfortable getting
undressed in front of a woman who had seen me
naked plenty of times, how was I gonna do it in
front of a room full of horny-ass men?

I began to undress, then I tried on the outfit she
had chosen for me. It was black and lacy and fit me
perfectly.

"Perfect. Now pick a name for yourself," she instructed.

"Simone, no doubt."

"I'll never be far away from you. Ready?"

"As I'll ever be."

The radio was playing "Slow Motion" by Juvenile,
and the only thing that was keeping me from throwing up was the dollar signs I saw when I closed my

eyes. I opened my eyes, moving my body seductively to the music as all four men stared at me. Once I made my way to the center of the room I began my show. I moved my hips in wide circles as I made eye contact with each man in the room. They were hypnotized. I let my ass drop practically to the floor a few times; their eyes and mouths opened wide. They all started throwing money on the floor around me—mostly ones, a few fives, a ten, but no twenties. I guess I had to do more than just bounce my ass a few times to earn a twenty.

I started to pick up the money. "I'll get it," Amel said. "You keep dancing."

While Amel gathered up the money, I began to move around the room. I danced around to each man, just as I had seen Amel do. One of the men grabbed me and tried to pull my bottom off, but Ricky took care of that. "Take it easy, mon. You get the whole show soon enough," he said, proving his value immediately.

As I danced, I looked around for Amel. She had changed into a different outfit and was dancing around the room. Once she made her way to me, she said, "Pick out another outfit and get back out here as quick as you can."

I made my way to the bedroom and closed the door. While I looked for another outfit to put on, I heard the men beginning to get loud as Amel worked her show. Once I had changed, I cracked the door a little to see what was going on. By this time, Amel was butt naked. She was standing on the coffee table; one of the men was lying on the table with his face in perfect position so that every time Amel dropped her body, she had her pussy in his face. I closed the door and went straight to the mini-bar. I grabbed the first bottle I got my hands on, Jack Daniel's, and downed it. "Whoo! That's some rough stuff."

When Too Short's "Shake That Monkey" came on, I burst though the door and got back to it. The men started yelling, "Take it off! Take it off!" I turned my back to them and came out of my top. With one arm covering my breasts I turned around, swung the top over my head and threw it to one of the men. He put it on his head as I lowered my arm and moved around the room quickly, shaking my tits in everybody's faces. Once I reclaimed my spot in the middle of the floor, the music changed. One of my favorite old school slow jams came on: the live version of "Reason" by Earth, Wind & Fire.

At that point, I closed my eyes and tried to forget the fact that I was in a room dancing naked for a bunch of strangers who, before that day, I would never have let near me much less touch me. I thought about Lorenzo. I missed him so much and wanted desperately to feel him. In my mind I was dancing just for him. With my eyes still closed, I slowly and very seductively wiggled my way out of the bottom of the outfit. When I opened my eyes, every eye in the room, including Ricky's and Amel's, were on me. Once again, I swung my outfit over my head and threw it. It landed on the floor and two of them dove for it. One grabbed it, immediately smelled it, put it in his mouth, and let it hang from his teeth.

I moved closer to one man and turned my back to him. I slowly bent over and allowed him to slip a twenty dollar bill into my garter. He got so close and was looking at my ass so hard, I thought he was going to try to crawl inside me. As a thank you,

I softly clapped my butt cheeks together and moved onto the next one.

One down, three to go, I thought as I slithered to my next stunned victim. He was hard, rock hard. I could tell by the print that was lying parallel to his thigh.

"Damn, baby," he whispered.

"You want to talk to me?" I purred. I couldn't believe I said that, but I might as well have some fun with this. "That's right. I can be your ho tonight if the price is right," I started to say, but thought better.

"Yes," he answered. Then started slinging curse words at me. "You're getting me hard as a rock. Bring it a little closer."

I obeyed his command and moved closer to him. They were all drunk, but he had passed drunk and moved to fucked up. He unzipped his pants and began to masturbate. *No he didn't take that little dick out of his pants.* On the inside, I was laughing all over myself until he said, "That's it, you nasty black bitch of a whore."

Oh, no he didn't, I thought, *but I guess that's what I am today.* I quickly dismissed the thought of cursing him out.

I creeped onto the floor and onto my back. I spread my legs and allowed him to talk dirty to me as he slipped another twenty into my garter. I thanked him by pulsating my pussy before rolling over to the next man. He was already there, shirt unbuttoned, tie loosened, pants down to his ankles, choking his limp dick. "Go, go, go!" he shouted as he finally reached his climax.

Gross.

One move from me sent him over the top, and

he threw his wallet at me. Amel grabbed it, emptied all the bills that were in it, and handed it to me. I took it between my breasts. I let him slide his wallet from between them then gently pushed him, at arms length, until his back was against the wall. I was shaking the twins at him along the way as I prepared to make my exit.

The last man was sitting in a chair, so I danced my way behind him. I leaned over and pushed him out of the chair. "Turn around and look at me," I demanded as I took his seat. I was really getting into the spirit of this now. He stumbled to his feet and turned around. He loosened his tie as I pulled my legs back practically behind my head. He stood there mesmerized as the others looked on. He started rubbing his head, and before I knew it what was happening, he was on the floor. I guess he was so drunk that he passed out.

We were there for an hour. After we left, Amel handed me two hundred dollars, and I had made another two hundred in tips. I became a private dancer, and the money got nothing but better. Amel took me along on all of her jobs, and every time she called me I got no less than two-fifty plus tips. Most nights I came away with five hundred dollars. I had quite a few customers who tried to proposition me, but I would tell them I was just there to dance, get my money, and leave.

Then I got lucky.

Amel called me and said she had an easy gig that night. "It's just one guy and he said he would pay big time for two, so come on and get paid. We'll pick you up in an hour." When we got there, though, the guy said he would only pay if he got to watch us take a shower together. "I wanna watch the two of you do each other, and then I wanna join in. How much would that cost me?" the guy asked.

"Fifteen hundred. Each," Amel said quickly.

I said, "Oh, hell no!" got my shit, and got out of there. It was a good thing that I did, too, 'cause that guy was a cop and he arrested Amel. That was the end of my career as a private dancer.

SIX

Now I was addicted to having that cash again, so once again I had to decide what I was going to do. What I decided to do was something that I swore I would never do. I walked up in a strip club and asked the manager for a job.

My thinking was that I would be all right on stage dancing, 'cause I would just dance and the customers would bring me money. That's what I was used to from working with Amel. I would dance around the room teasing men then they'd pay me.

Unfortunately, I learned that in the club the way to make money is to walk around all night saying, "You want a table dance? You want a table dance?" Then when you get a guy who's paying, you gotta sit there and listen to him try to mack. I told one guy, "Look, I'm just here to get paid. I don't wanna hear that shit."

As you could imagine, he told me to get the fuck on, which I gladly did. I lasted two weeks before I quit. I was making money, but I was never really built for all that anyway. Still, whether I was meant to be a dancer or not, the fact remained; I still needed to make some money. And I don't care how good they make it sound on TV, I was not getting a job at Wal-Mart. I decided that if I was gonna have to hustle, I might as well get paid.

But was I really ready? I thought about Lorenzo. Damn, I missed him. What was more important to remember, though, was why I missed him. I missed him 'cause he was in jail, and I certainly had no desire to do any time. So, if I was going to do this, I had to be smart about it.

Me, Shay, and Teena sat in my living room and talked about getting into the game, and most importantly, avoiding Lorenzo's fate.

"One thing you won't have is a woman like you," Shay said. "You were the flashy one. Drivin' that BMW, spending all that money shoppin'. And Teena, you weren't too much better. Both of y'all caught up in that lifestyle."

"Don't hate, Shay," I said.

"I'm not hatin'. Come on, Nina. You know me better than that. I'm just being real. Y'all two heifers was caught up in that baller's girl lifestyle, spending money like it was water. Now what you got to show for it? Government took everything but the clothes you had on your back."

"You're right, Shay. I don't have shit. But what's that got to do with avoiding Lorenzo's fate?"

"I'm just sayin', you should have opened an account in your name," Shay went on without answering my question. All me and Teena could do was sit there and look at one another 'cause we knew she was right. I had some money, but without any coming in, it was going fast. "If y'all are gonna do this, then you gotta tone it down a whole lot, ladies. Cut out all the flash and understand that this is a business, not a lifestyle," Shay continued, "When you start livin' that lifestyle, you get desperate to make that money."

"That's when you get careless," I added when I understood Shay's point. "You gotta have money to fuel that lifestyle, and you start takin' risks to make that money." I paused and thought, *Was I the cause of Lorenzo being locked up? Did my flashy lifestyle draw the attention of the police? Or maybe it was my shopping addiction that forced him to take greater and greater risk, like doing business with that bitch-ass Bryce.* Lorenzo always said that even though he had known him for years, he never trusted Bryce, but he brought in so much money that he had to keep fucking with him. I was glad Bryce was bringing in so much money. "More for me to spend," I remember saying at the time. Now I wished I hadn't.

While I was lost in my thoughts, Shay continued her sermon. "That's right, so let's try not to make careless or flashy mistakes," she said, looking dead at me.

"That's what we're talkin' about, Shay. Tryin' to roll and keep from goin' to jail for it."

"But Lo is in jail for murder," Teena said, "not selling drugs. So as long as we don't blast nobody," she said, pointing her fingers like a gun at Shay, "we won't get locked down for life." Then she blasted her, "Boom!" and we all laughed.

"True," Shay had to agree, "but drugs are the reason the cop was there for him to murder. So, when you break it down a little further, he's in jail because Bryce and Chris rolled over on him."

"True that, true that," I said, feeling the guilt once again that Bryce was on my card and it was a weight I had to carry. "So, how do we avoid the same thing happening to us?"

"You start with people around you that you can trust," Teena said.

"Yeah, but Lorenzo trusted Bryce, and I know he loved Chris like a brother," Shay pointed out.

"No," I said. "Lorenzo never trusted Bryce."

"Okay, let's be real. We all know that Bryce was a snake," Shay commented.

"Since we being real, Nina, Chris was always real envious of Lorenzo. He was always talkin about how he was smarter than Lorenzo and how it should be him runnin' the show," Teena admitted.

"Why didn't you say something before now?"

"I didn't take it as anything more than pillow talk. Something to get his dick hard again. I never thought it would come to this."

"The only people I trust is the two of you," I said quietly.

"You can trust me, Nina," Shay said as she sat down next to me.

We both looked at Teena.

"What the fuck are you two bitches starin' at me for? Y'all know you can trust me," Teena said and sat by my other side. "We're down together to the bloody end."

"Let's hope it ain't that deep, Teena," Shay said, and I had to agree.

"So, we gonna do this or not?" I asked, smiling.

"What we just say, Nina?" Teena asked.

"You won't be alone, Nina," Shay said. "We're down with you. So, what do we do now?"

"How much money y'all got?" I asked.

SEVEN

Now that the decision had been made it was time to put it into action. I had twenty-four hundred dollars. That was enough money to cover expenses, get a couple of ounces, maybe two and a half. That would be enough to get us started.

My partners didn't have much money to invest in our new business venture. Shay had no money, which I understood; she got kids to take care of. Teena came up with four hundred, but I was cool with that for the time being. I figured that I should start with a couple of people who did business with Lorenzo and build up from there. My thinking was that if everything went the way it should, I would recoup my investment in no time.

Before the deputies took Lorenzo away, he told me that if I ever need anything I should call his cousin Leon in Jacksonville. Lorenzo would go down there all the time, and I went with him on a few of his trips. Lorenzo never said and I never asked him, but I always thought that Leon was his supplier.

I was a little nervous about talking to Leon. We got along okay and he treated me with respect, but I always felt that he really didn't like me. It was nothing he said; it was just the way he looked at me sometimes like I wasn't good enough for his baby cousin.

"Hello."

"Hello, can I speak to Leon?"

"This is Leon. Who is this?"

"This is Nina. I'm Lorenzo's girlfriend."

"What's up, Nina? How you holdin' up?"

"I'm okay."

"How come it took you so long to call me? We're family now, girl. Remember that."

"I will. And thank you, that means a lot to me."

"So, what's up?"

"I need to talk to you about something, but I don't wanna talk over the phone."

"Come down here. Spend some time with me. Call me when you get here."

"I'll call the airport now and call you back with my flight info."

"No, I think you should drive. It ain't safe to fly. Terrorists and shit, you know. Much safer if you drive."

"I understand. I'll call you when I'm in Jacksonville," I said and hung up the phone. I looked at Teena and Shay.

"Well?" Shay asked. "You in there or what?"

"He said I was family now and should drive down there and spend some time with him."

"Either you in there or he wants some pussy," Teena said.

"Yeah maybe, but I don't think that's it."

"What's he like?" Teena asked.

"He's in his thirties. Tall, good lookin' and dark-skinned like Lorenzo, but he's a big guy. Not fat, but a big guy. Anytime we went there he always had a different woman with him. Big house, always got mad cash to spend, you know what I mean."

"Sounds like somebody I should know," Teena said.

"Maybe next trip, Teena. Besides, he wants me to drive to Jacksonville, and you hate long trips. Only problem with that is a car, and I don't have one."

"You could rent one," Teena suggested.

"No credit card."

"You can use mine," Shay volunteered. "It's not fancy, but Gary keeps it in good condition."

"He should. He's a mechanic," Teena said.

"Are you sure, Shay? I'm just sayin', what you gonna drive?"

"I'll be all right for a few days without it. If I need to go somewhere, Gary will take me," Shay said.

I was set. The next morning I hit the road for Jacksonville in Shay's old Escort station wagon. She left the baby seat in the back along with all of her kids' junk. Shay said it was too much trouble to take out the car seat, and she was just too lazy to clean the car. I didn't care; I just got in, said good-bye to my girls, and headed south. Shay was right about one thing: the car, junky or not, ran like a champ. All it had, though, was a radio—no CD, not even a tape player. "This is gonna be a long ride."

I rode down I-95 south, changing stations on the radio. I found that listening to music that you don't like keeps you awake. A lot of the time I spent with the radio off, just letting my mind flow. Naturally, I spent a lot of time thinking about what I was driving to Jacksonville for. The same question kept rolling around in my mind: Was I ready to sell drugs? And at this point, did it matter? I was going to do it. In my mind, there was no turning around now.

I thought about Lorenzo a lot too. I wanted so badly to talk to him, to tell him just how much I loved him, how much I missed him. I wanted to tell him about all the things I had been through since he'd been gone.

I thought about my parents and how much the choices I'd made had disappointed them. I could almost hear my father's voice telling me that he didn't raise me to take the easy way. It was hard work and making the hard choices that was going to carry me in the long run. But there I was, living and making short term choices. My thoughts were fuckin' with me, so I turned the radio back on to drown them out.

When I got to Jacksonville I called Leon and he came to meet me. After he laughed at the car, I followed him back to his house where there were two women lounging by the pool. They were both pretty, in their late twenties, I guessed. One had no top on, and both of them had big, fake-ass titties. I could tell 'cause they were too round at the top.

He introduced one as Diamond and the other as Pearl. I practically had to bite my lip to keep from laughing in their faces. He introduced me as Lorenzo's woman. Both of them acted like they knew exactly who Lorenzo was, which led me to believe that Lorenzo had fucked one, if not both of them when he came here without me. I started to cop an attitude with them, but then I caught myself. Lorenzo was in jail for life; no point in getting all twisted about it now.

"Are you hungry, Nina?" Leon asked.

"Starvin'," was my one word answer.

Leon turned to his other two guests. "Y'all get us something to eat," he said to them then turned around and went back in the house. I stood there looking at them until Leon said, "You coming, Nina?"

"It was nice meeting y'all," I said to them.

"I hope you like seafood," one of the women said to me as I walked away, " 'cause I'm goin' to Red Lobster."

I followed Leon back in the house and he took my bag upstairs to one of the bedrooms. He opened the door and held it for me as I walked in. Once I was in the room, he closed the door and locked it. *I guess Teena was right. This man really does want some pussy.*

I guess he could tell by the look on my face that I was apprehensive about him locking us in. "Don't worry, Nina. I only locked the door so we won't be disturbed. We don't need nobody walkin' in on us while we're talkin'."

"Oh."

"Now, make yourself comfortable. You consider this your home, you hear me? Like I said, you're family. You need anything while you're here, you just have to say so. Understand?"

"I understand, and thank you."

"Now, talk to me, Nina," Leon said as he sat down in the chair across from the bed. "Tell me what's been goin' on with you."

I sat on the edge of the bed and told Leon everything I had gone through since Lorenzo went to jail, eventually working up to my decision to get into the game. I even told him that I had been dancing and how I felt about the whole experience.

"You don't have to feel ashamed about that, Nina. A lot of women go down that road and find that it's not what they thought it was."

"Don't get it twisted. I'm not ashamed of what I did. I was just doin' what I had to do."

"It's called survival, baby girl," Leon said and stood up. He walked over to the window.

"But sometimes, Leon, I feel like I'm just out here spiraling out of control." I was surprising myself with how open I was being with Leon. He was just so easy to talk to. He was a good listener. Talking to him now, I no longer felt like I wasn't "good enough" for his baby cousin. That's when I realized that he was the same person, treating me with the same respect that he had each time I was a guest in his house. It was my attitude that had changed.

"I have an idea, but I hate misunderstandings. So, what was it that you wanted to talk to me about, Nina?" Leon asked and returned to his chair.

"Lorenzo said if I ever needed anything to call you. Well. I saved up some money and I'm ready for whatever."

Leon sat quietly and listened while I talked. I explained that I had some money and I wanted to get as much product as I could for what I had. He laughed a little when I said I had two thousand dollars, but he tried to play it off as a cough.

"How did you know to come see me about that?"

"I didn't."

"Well, I can help you, but first I gotta ask; are you sure this is what you wanna do?"

"I'm sure."

"I can help you with that. In fact, I've been expecting you, but I was expecting you three months ago. Lorenzo said that you'd be coming," Leon said and stood up. "You get settled in and relax. I'll call you when they get back with the food."

"They said they were goin' to Red Lobster."

"I know they had to go somewhere. Neither of them can boil water." Leon laughed and closed the door behind him.

Over the next four days me and Leon became inseparable. We didn't sleep together or anything like that; Leon was always a perfect gentleman. At the end of the day, Leon would say goodnight and go to his room, where the tittie twins were waiting for him.

We would talk all day about the game—what to do, what not to do; who to fuck with and who to leave alone; how to deal with the cops. We talked about seeing the bigger picture and not getting caught up on bullshit, and we talked a lot about trust. It was like going to school. "Damn, you mean there's more to this than just collecting money?" I joked early on, but Leon was not amused.

"This shit ain't no joke, Nina. You get to fuckin' around in them streets, thinkin' this shit is funny, and you'll get yourself killed or locked up like your man," Leon advised.

Some things I knew from being with Lorenzo, some things were just common sense, but most of what he was telling me I had no clue about.

"Do you like football, Nina?"

"I love football."

"Really?"

"Really."

"Then you understand the game?" he questioned. "You're not one of these woman who *love football* because it's men in tight pants?"

"No, Leon, I really understand the game."

"Good. I would have been disappointed in you if it was just the pants."

"Why would that disappoint you?"

" 'Cause it's so much deeper than that."

"How so?"

"Football is like life, Nina. Each time you step on the field, your objective is to score a touchdown, right?"

"Right."

"So the natural temptation is to go for the big play every time. The fans go wild, and it's great for your ego. However," Leon said, taking a timely pause and raising his finger to emphasize his point, "the defense is there to prevent this from happening. But the objective remains."

"To score a touchdown," I added.

"Exactly. This poses a problem, so you got to study the defense. You have to understand its strengths and learn how to exploit its weaknesses. Now you can take advantage of what the defense gives you. You run the draw up the middle, you run the short passing routes, but you're moving the ball down field and moving closer to your objective. You've got to play your hardest on every play until you've put yourself in a position to complete your objective."

"To score a touchdown."

"Just like life," Leon said.

"That was kind of deep, Leon," I said as I stretched and yawned. Leon stood up. "Hey, Leon, how come I never met you before? I mean back when me and Lorenzo were in high school. I thought I met his whole family."

"You met his Uncle Wayne, right?"

"Yeah, we used to go and visit him in jail sometimes."

"Wayne is my daddy."

"I didn't know that. I guess drug dealing does run in y'all's family."

"It's the family business," Leon said.

"So, you used to live in the Bronx?"

Leon nodded his head in response.

"Why'd you leave? What's the matter, you don't love New York?"

"Let's just say that I left New York for business reasons, and leave it at that, Nina," Leon said, and as he did every night, went off to slay the tittie twins.

The following day I came downstairs and found Leon sitting at the kitchen table while the twins tried to cook breakfast. "Good morning. I'm ready for another day of drug dealer 101."

The twins started laughing until Leon cut his

eyes at them. They stopped laughing quickly and resumed their discussion on the best way to fry an egg.

"Good morning, Nina," Leon said. "Sit down and pay them no mind."

"I thought you said they couldn't cook," I whispered.

"They can't," he whispered back, "and I damn sure ain't eatin' anything they cook. It's my fault. I said a home-cooked meal sure would be nice once in a while. What I wanna say that for? Look at them. Between the two of them you'd think they could fry an egg. Anyway, they mean well."

"I'm sure they have other talents."

"You just don't know, Nina. You couldn't imagine the talents those two have," Leon said as he looked over at the twins. Diamond glanced over at Leon while he was looking at her. She ran her tongue over her lips and went back to doing what she was doing. Leon smiled more of a smile than I'd ever seen on him. It still wasn't much, but I could see what the twins saw in him; Leon was sexy.

Leon always had this serious look on his face. It was like he was always thinking; thinking about what was next, thinking about that bigger picture that he was always talking about. Sure, Leon was teaching me how to play the game, but what was more important to me was when he told me, "Nina, what you have to do is stay focused on the objective instead of the game. How to work from a position of strength, making allies out of enemies to accomplish your objectives. And one other thing; always be right, and when you're wrong, make sure you have a backup plan. It's a poor rat that only has one hole," Leon told me. I nodded my head like I understood exactly what he was talking about, even though I was clueless.

"Now, you go and get dressed and we'll go to the Waffle House," he told me. "By the time you're dressed I'll have put a stop to this."

The more I thought about what he was trying to get me to see, the more it made perfect sense. To put it simply, don't get caught up on bullshit, 'cause it will only take time and energy away from what you're doing.

"I could cook breakfast," I volunteered.

"I know. I was talkin' about the last time you were here with Lorenzo and you cooked us that big-ass breakfast, but I don't want you to show them up. Let them go on believin' that all women are just as useless in the kitchen as they are."

That day, Leon and I sat out by the pool and talked. He was still on trust. "I know what you're thinkin', Nina, but don't do it. I'm tellin' you. Don't fuck with anybody that Lorenzo used to do business with."

"Why not?"

" 'Cause you don't know if you can trust them. You don't know which ones the cops got their hooks in. Cops had Lorenzo under surveillance; they know who he was doing business with. You see some of them went to jail behind his shit. The ones that are still on the street are the ones who gave the cops something to stay out."

"I never thought about that."

"Build your own team," Leon said and pointed at me. "People who'll be loyal to you."

"I understand. I need a loyal team to achieve my objectives."

"You have been listening."

"More than that, I've been paying attention. So, I'll stay away from the guys he used to do business with."

"Good. They won't respect you anyway."

"Why not?"

" 'Cause they will always see you as Lorenzo's ho." I didn't particularly like being called a ho, but that's probably how they all saw me. "Gimme the keys to your car." Once I handed him the keys he said that he would be back in a couple of hours. "You'll be ready to leave in the morning, so relax for the rest of the day." He got up. "Diamond, come follow me," he yelled to one of the tittie twins and she left with him.

Once Leon was gone, Pearl came and sat with me by the pool. "You smoke weed?"

"Yes."

"Good," Pearl said and pulled out a blunt from her cleavage. "It's a little damp, but we'll fix that," she said and took a lighter to it. "You wanna drink too?"

"Sure. Why not?"

"Don't worry, Nina, I make drinks better than I cook. Come inside with me," she said and I followed her. "I used to be a bartender until I found out I could make more money dancin' than pouring drinks. Now I'm gettin' too old for that shit too. Anyway, I'll make us a couple of Blue Muthafuckas," Pearl said.

"What's a Blue Muthafucka?"

"It's a Long Island Iced Tea with this blue stuff

mixed with it," she said, holding up a bottle of Blue Curaçao. "Now, how does that sound?"

"Great." I smiled at Pearl. Even though I had been there for a few days, this was the first time I had been alone with either of the twins. There was something I'd been dying to ask. "You mind if I ask you a question, Pearl?"

She stopped making our drinks. "Go ahead." She gave me this *What you wanna know, bitch?* look.

"Is your name really Pearl?"

She started laughing, so I laughed a little with her, but I still wanted to know. "Yes, Nina, my mother and father named me Pearl. You know, people been callin' us that for years, and nobody's ever asked me that," she said, still falling all over herself with laughter. "But you asked the right one. Diamond's my girl, but she is a little sensitive about her name."

"So, what's her name?"

Pearl stopped laughing, got this real serious look on her face and waited until I stopped laughing. "Alice Fae." She busted up laughing again.

By the time Leon got back with Diamond, me and Pearl were fucked up—I mean giggling all over ourselves fucked up. Leon just shook his head and made himself a drink. Diamond, on the other hand, seemed just a bit jealous, but Pearl didn't seem to care.

The next morning when I got ready to leave, I got my money together and tried to give it to Leon. "What's that for?"

"For the product I'm gettin' from you."

"Yeah well, put your money away. Go buy yourself a better looking cheap car than the one you're drivin' now," Leon said and laughed. "I'm just fuckin' with you, Nina. But when you do get a car, make sure it's nothing fancy, just something to get you around."

"You told me that a hundred times, Leon."

"And you ain't gettin' no two ounces. I'm givin' you a kilo." My mouth dropped open. "That one is on me. Make your money, and when you come back to see me, we'll talk about a price for the next one."

"Thank you, Leon."

"You don't have to thank me. You're family now. I ain't ever gonna see Lo again unless we run up on each other in jail, and you know I'm never going to jail. You're my cousin now. Whatever you need to make it, all you gotta do is ask me."

"I will," I said and gave him a hug.

"Don't you worry about a thing. You're gonna be fine. Lo always said you were the brains of the outfit."

"What?" I asked, looking at Leon like he was stupid.

"He said that you gave him the best advice whenever he asked you what to do and how he should handle situations."

"You're kidding." *Damn.* I never thought he paid any attention to what I was saying. All I ever told him was what I thought would bring in the most money. Who knew the shit was working for him?

"That's what he told me." Leon turned around and started walking toward the house.

"Leon," I called to him. "I don't mean to ask stupid questions, but where is it?"

Leon stopped and looked at me. "Strapped under the driver's seat. You'll need to take the seat out to get to it. If you get stopped, it won't be easy to find without dogs. And be careful in South Carolina; the state patrol is hot there."

"Good-bye, Leon."

"See ya, cuz."

So, I was on my way home with a kilo under my ass, feeling like I had the world by the tail. Although I was nervous about what I was carrying, I was bubbling over with excitement and anticipation about the future. Having a free kilo to go into business with was a whole lot sweeter than a couple of ounces. My mind began to open up to the possibilities that I was sitting on. There was no longer any thought in my mind of me, Teena, and Shay hustling to flip a couple of ounces so we could re-up. Now we would be able to sit back and wait on the money to come to us.

Now, all the things that Leon had said we could do on price would come into play. He said since I was entering a very competitive market, it would always be to my advantage to have a high quality product and to be very competitive on price. That was how I would get new customers. They would be loyal as long as I treated them right. He told me to remember that anybody I dealt with was liable to snitch me out the first time I fucked them over, but if I gave them a good price, they would come back to buy more. The more they bought, the more I could buy. My costs would go down, but my selling price would remain the same, so my profits would go up. It was damn good advice.

I got on I-95 and headed north, staying with the flow of traffic for the most part. I got into South

Carolina and remembering Leon's warning, I made sure to do the speed limit. That was cool until I got behind this old woman coming out of Florence who was driving really slow. I took it as long as I could, then pulled out to get in front of her. I passed her without a problem and was cruising along nicely when I realized I was doing eighty. I took my foot off the gas to let it slow down and blew right by a state trooper. I kept going, watching the rearview mirror, hoping that he wouldn't come after me.

"Shit. Here he comes."

As soon as I saw the blue lights come on I pulled over. As quickly as I could, I put on some lipstick, unbuttoned the top two buttons on my blouse and emptied my purse out on the seat next to me. He pulled over behind me and got out of the car. *Thank God he's black,* I thought. When he knocked on my window I went into my act. I looked up at him, rolled down the window, and started crying. Not no big boo-hog cry, but I forced a few tears down my cheeks.

"Can I see your license, ma'am?"

"Here it is," I said tearfully.

"You're a long way from home, Ms. Thomas," the trooper said as he leaned on top of the car to get a better view of the cleavage I had put on display for him. "What's your hurry?"

"I'm visiting my family in Florence. I didn't mean to be speedin', but I was diggin' around in this junky purse for my cigarettes, but I don't see them, so I guess I must've left them at Aunt Steph's house, and I guess I got a little heavy-footed," I lied. I don't even smoke, but the plan was working. The cleavage had his ass frozen. I knew then that he wasn't gonna search the car. Now it was time to get out of getting a ticket.

"Well, Ms. Thomas, I clocked you doing seventy-eight in a sixty-five mile per hour zone," the trooper said.

You're losin' him, Nina. I knew then it was time to close the show. I began to cry a little harder and made my breasts bounce. I looked at his face; eyes bucked wide, mouth open. He shook his head. "Don't cry, Ms. Thomas. I'm gonna let you go with a warning this time," he said and handed me back my license, "but just try to keep it at the speed limit. And maybe you should quit smoking. A pretty lady like you doesn't need to smoke anyway."

"I know. It's a nasty habit."

He reached in his shirt pocket, pulled out a card, and handed it to me. "If you wanna get together some time, give me a call," the trooper said. He was kinda cute for a cop, so I thought I just might. As he walked back to his car, I buttoned up my blouse and put my stuff back in the purse. I pulled out slowly into traffic and drove on, knowing that I had dodged a bullet big time. But the fact remained that I had dodged it, and was on my way to do this thing.

EIGHT

Now that I had it, it was time to make it work. Me and Teena posted up at a table in the back of Jimmy's, the same hole in the wall bar where Lorenzo and Chris first took us. I remembered what Leon had told me. "The ones that are still on the streets are the ones who gave the cops something to stay out." And here they all were.

I'd been low-profile since Lorenzo went to jail. First I was depressed, then I tried to be a dancer, so this was the first time I'd seen a lot of these people in a while. One by one each one of them came up to me to show their respect. Their women asked me where I'd been and filled me in on all the latest gossip. Some wanted to see if I was doing okay on my own. Some of the fellas who hadn't seen me in a good while told me how sorry they were that things went down the way they did. Some of that was sincere, some was bullshit, some of these muthafuckas were glad Lorenzo was locked up.

Some offered their help, others offered themselves. Imagine what I must have represented to them, what a prize I would be. One of them had taken my man's position, now they wanted me.

"Look at these muthafuckas, Nina. All of them tryin' to get with you," Teena said.

"All of them sold out Lorenzo to stay on the street."

"You sure you don't wanna recruit none of these muthafuckas?"

"Yup."

"Not even the cute ones?"

"Especially not them. I thought about it, believe me. This is where I thought I was gonna start, with these mugs. But now, looking at them, seeing how they trying to play me, we don't need none of these sell-out muthafuckas to do this work for us. No, Teena, we gotta build our own team."

"We?"

"Yeah, we. Or were you just talkin' that 'together to the bloody end' shit?"

"No, I wasn't just talkin'. You know that. But I was just thinking that since things had changed, you know, with you getting a whole lot more than you thought, and with you handin' me back five hundred on the four hundred dollars I gave you. I thought maybe shit had changed."

I looked at Teena; it hurt me a little to hear her say that. It was like she was questioning the strength of our friendship. "No, Teena, we're in this together. We gotta build this team."

"Well, maybe you should tell me exactly what *we* means."

"It means we're partners. Me, you and Shay are partners in this. I'm distribution, you're recruitment, and you know Shay."

"Yeah, she'll get done anything that needs to be done."

"So, the first person we gonna go see is Kenyatta," I said to Teena and motioned for the waitress.

"You just said you wasn't fuckin' with none of Lo's people."

"I know what I said, but Kenyatta is different. That's my girl. I was the one who brought Kenyatta to Lorenzo." I laughed. "She's been tellin' me since the day Lorenzo got locked down that I needed to do this."

When I went to see Kenyatta the following day, it was like she was waiting for me. She swung open the door to her apartment before I could knock. "I hope your grand appearance at Jimmy's last night means you're ready to take this thing to a new level."

"Hello, Kenyatta," I said and walked by her. "How are you today?"

"Just answer my question, ho. What were you doin' at Jimmy's last night?"

"That's what I came to see you about."

"Talk to me."

"You ready to take this thing to a new level?"

"Yes! Nina, I been ready. I just been waitin' on you."

"Good. You still hold down that same stop?"

"Of course."

"What's gonna happen if you change suppli-ers?"

"Since we're talkin' business, let's say you give me a reason to change suppliers."

"I'm in a position to give you a much better price than what you're paying now."

"Then in that case, I'd be doin' business with

you. They'll come around, make some noise, but my set is deep enough to make them think twice about takin' it any further."

So, now we had a place to sell and it all began from there. The way Kenyatta ran her program was tight; no hand-to-hand exchanges and little or no conversation. You say what you want, drop your money on the ground and go up the steps. On the ground at the top of the steps you'd find what you paid for.

Kenyatta immediately bought into the concept of making money on volume. She didn't put a lot of cut on it. Once the word got around that we were rolling with a quantity and very high quality, I couldn't get the product to them fast enough. That would become my foundation, and I would build up from there. It wasn't long before I was back in Jacksonville.

I made a point to stay in Florence on the trip down. I called that trooper and went out with him. Not that I was feeling him all that much, but I was going to be driving though there on a regular basis. Any information I could get from him would be useful.

In less than a year, we were able to move four kilos a month. In that time we had put together a team of nine players, male and female, who were buying weight on a regular basis. As a recruiter, Teena had found her special place in the world, hanging around with people—mostly men, mostly with money—feeling them out, seeing where their heads were at, and taking the ones that fit into our program. "Same shit I've been doing for years," Teena boasted. "Sizing men up is what I do."

On one of my trips to Jacksonville, I was with

Leon, having one of our usual conversations, when the subject turned to sex. "To be honest with you, Leon, I haven't been with anybody since Lorenzo."

"Why? If you were with Lo, I know you like sex."

I looked at Leon, unsure how I felt about him knowing that about me. "Yes, I do like sex, but I love Lorenzo."

"Lo is never getting out."

"I know that. And I know he told me to move on with my life."

"So, what's up?"

"What do you mean, what's up?"

"I mean are you planning on being celibate for the rest of your life or you gonna let somebody play with that vicious campaign you call a body?" Leon asked and showed me that look he had reserved for the tittie twins. "You're a young, beautiful woman. You have your whole life ahead of you. You shouldn't deny yourself that pleasure, especially if you enjoy it." I thought that Leon was about to try and talk up on some, but he got up and said goodnight. I watched Leon walk out of my bedroom and wondered if I would have said no if he had asked for some.

When I got back from Jacksonville, Teena introduced me to a guy who went by the name of Smoke. She had been sizing him up for a little over a month because of the weight he was talking about. Smoke came though the door talking a kilo a week. That doubled my business right away.

Smoke became my best customer, but he was one freaky dude. One night, I was hanging out with Smoke and this white chick I knew named

Gina. She was mad cool. Not mad cool for a white girl; Gina was just mad cool. Anyway, Smoke started telling us about all the freaky shit he's done and would like to do. Then he tells us that he always wanted to have sex with two white women at same time. Two blondes to be exact. "So, what about it, Gina?" Smoke asked.

"What about what, Smoke?" Gina asked.

"What about you callin' up one of your freaky, blonde girlfriends and y'all two come over to my place and let's do the damn thing."

"Oh, please. I wouldn't open my legs for you if you were the last swinging dick on the planet and I had to fuck you to stay alive."

So, you could imagine my surprise when three months later, Smoke told me that him and Gina were getting married.

Which brings me to Cedric.

I had gone to the wedding with this guy I'd met named Omar. There was nothing going on between us, a fact that Omar hated, but he was such a lame that I couldn't even point my mind in the direction of seeing him naked. However, since my talk with Leon, I'd been slowly coming around to the idea that I had moved on with every other part of my life, maybe I could move on with that part too. But not with Omar; we were just friends. Besides, he was good company sometimes, so I asked him to come to the wedding with me.

Anyway, I was watching Cedric watching me and thought about how long it had been since I felt a man inside of me. Cedric was fine in a rugged sort of way, and I found myself fantasizing about having sex with him. Finally, he found somebody to walk him over to introduce me. Not wanting to disrespect Omar when they got to the table, Smoke introduced him to everybody sitting there. With eyes focused on me, Cedric politely spoke to everyone, taking his eyes off me only briefly. Finally Smoke got to me. "Omar, Nina, this is my former roommate, Cedric. Cedric, this is Omar Parker."

"Nice to meet you," Cedric said to Omar and held out his hand, but his eyes were still focused on me. Omar accepted the gesture without speaking. "Cedric, this is Nina Thomas," Smoke said.

Our eyes locked. "It's good to meet you, Ms. Thomas."

"Please, call me Nina. And it's good to met you too, Cedric."

"Maybe you'll dance with me, Nina."

The deejay started playing "Diary" by Alicia Keys, and I was really feeling him, so I said, "Sure."

While we were dancing Cedric asked, "So, what's up with you and busta there?"

"Who, Omar? Nothing. We've been out a few times. He nice, but he's . . . I don't know."

"Well, who would know? Should I ask him?"

"No, he's probably already jealous of you."

"Why?"

"Maybe you should ask him," I said and Cedric started to pull away from me. "Come back here. I'm not through with you yet," I said. "You were going to ask him, weren't you?"

"Yeah. I need to know these things."

"Why?"

"I'm just an informational kind of guy. I make a livin' on information." The song ended and I started to pull away from him. "Come back here. I'm not through with you yet."

"Stay In My Corner" came on, and he drew me back to his chest. I liked the way it felt there in his arms. Cedric was tall, six-three, maybe four. I looked into his eyes. He held me tighter. "I hate to be the one to break this on you, but that thing with you and that busta . . ." Cedric frowned and shook his head. "It ain't gonna last."

"Oh, really? What makes you say that, Cedric?"

"I don't mean to sound overconfident, but I intend to take you from him, and I am prepared to spend all my time, all my energy, and all my resources to do it. Let's get out of here now. We can find a nice, quiet place where we can talk. Get to know each other."

"No, Cedric."

"Tell me what you want to do and that's what we'll do. I just wanna talk to you, Nina. I wanna know everything you want me to know," Cedric said with a confident smirk. "I wanna know what makes you cry, and what I can do to make you smile."

"I don't smile much these days," I said, leaning back.

"Tell me why you don't smile," Cedric said and drew me back to his chest.

"Maybe I don't have anything to smile about," I flirted.

Cedric laughed out loud. "That's why you need to be with me. Come on, let's go."

"No, Cedric."

"Then meet me in an hour at the Shark Club."

"No, Cedric," I said and wondered if he could tell that I wanted to go with him. I could feel how hard he was from dancing with me. "You don't waste any time, do you?"

"When you don't have a lotta time, you can't waste it. So, what about tomorrow?"

"No, Cedric." I looked at Omar. "Not tomorrow. Thursday, seven o'clock."

I hooked up with Cedric a few times, and the more I talked to him, the more I began to realize what an asshole he was. How could somebody that fine be such an asshole? In spite of that, he was kind of cool to hang out with. But even more, I was horny. It had been almost two years since Lorenzo went to jail and I was ready, but not in a rush. You know what I'm saying.

Cedric told me that he made his money robbing. You know, anyplace he could find cash on hand—hotels, restaurants. He said he even robbed a couple of post offices.

One night Cedric called and woke me up around 3 o'clock in the morning. "First of all, do you know what time it is?" I said, still half asleep but mad as hell.

"Yeah, I know what time it is. It's 2:58. You ain't got no other nigga over there, do you? 'Cause I'll kill that mothafucka."

I rolled my eyes. "What do you want, Cedric?"

"I wanna see you."

"Have you lost your mind? Hell no, you ain't comin' over here at 3 o'clock in the morning."

"I ain't talkin' about now. I mean when I get back."

"Back? Back from where?"

"Ohio. I'm on my way back from Ohio."

"What you doin' in Ohio?" I don't know why I

asked. I really didn't care; I just really wanted to go back to sleep.

"Me and my boy Tilly took a little road trip there to handle some business. I'm still in Ohio, just outside of Cleveland. But when I get back, I'ma come by there. I got something to show you."

"Cedric, don't come over here at the crack of dawn."

"Relax. We got a long way to go. Pennsylvania's a long state to ride through."

"Try callin' before you come this time. You seem to have this bad habit of just showing up places, unannounced and uninvited," I said and hung up the phone.

That next afternoon, Cedric was ringing my bell. No call; he just showed up. "I remember asking you to call before you came over here."

"Yeah, whatever," Cedric said and pushed his way past me. He walked into the dining room and poured twenty grand on the table.

"What's that?"

"What does it look like, Nina? It's money."

"I know that. I was askin' how much money and where did it come from."

"It's twenty grand, and it's my share of the job I just did."

I guess he was thinking that I was supposed to be impressed at the sight of twenty grand on the table. I'd seen Lorenzo with a lot more money than twenty grand. Shit, I was making damn near that much profit. But I knew a lot of women would be impressed. Impressed to the point of fucking him. In fact, I was sure when he left and did this same thing, some woman's clothes would fall off.

But I know how fragile the male ego is, so I tried my best to act like that was more money than I had ever seen in my life. "That's a lotta money, Cedric. What'd you have to do for it?"

"Let's just say he's no longer breathing."

"Are you sayin' y'all killed somebody for money?"

Cedric looked me dead in my face and said, "Nina, I will neither confirm nor deny anything like that," with a slick half grin on this face.

I didn't say anything; it didn't matter anyway. Cedric was on his way to being dropped into the friend zone. But what a shame to let a package like that go to waste.

"Yo, Nina, check this out. I'm going back out of town."

"Where you going this time?"

"Shippensburg, Pennsylvania."

"For what? Another hit?" I laughed to myself.

"My boy been there surveying a group of dope boyz who sellin' out of there. It's just some little college town. Anyway, after a week of careful spying and surveillance, he runs up on the house, and now we goin' to rob them."

"You going down there to rob some dope boyz? It was nice knowing you." I laughed out loud this time.

"No, Nina, you got it all wrong. These ain't nothin' but some college kids that's sellin' drugs. From what Earl say, they're unorganized, but they're clockin' big dollars."

"Well, like I said, good luck."

"I need a favor from you, baby girl."

"What you need? And stop callin' me that."

"Whatever, baby girl."

Asshole.

"I need you to drive me, Earl, and Tilly out there."

So, now I was looking at him thinking that he was crazy. I was not gonna be the wheel man for any robbery. But then I thought about it. I sat in that apartment all the time watching Jerry Springer and those dumb judge shows. The only time I really went out was to make money, and then I was right back here. Maybe I did need to add a little excitement to my life. After Cedric assured me that nobody would be at the house when they hit it, I agreed to drive them.

When we got there, the three of them agreed that if anything went down, it was every man for himself. They went in the house, no loyalty to one another, and probably no trust between them either. While I was sitting there thinking how that was a prescription for failure, a car rolled into the driveway. I honked the horn as three men got out of the car and went inside. When I heard shooting followed by the sound of glass breaking, I looked up and saw two men jumping out of the second floor window. Remembering that it was every man for himself, I started the car and was about to leave when I saw Cedric get up off the ground and start running toward the car. He got in and I floored it.

"What happened in there?" I asked as I drove.

"Shit got wild after you honked the horn. Me and Earl were upstairs searching the house and Tilly was alone downstairs. We heard them yell something and then we heard the gun shots. I guess they shot Tilly and were coming up the stairs after us, so me and Earl jumped out the window."

"What happened to Earl?"

"I don't know. He didn't get up. All I know is he didn't get up!"

"Okay, you don't have to yell at me. Are you all right?"

"Yeah, I'm all right," Cedric said.

I looked at Cedric; he didn't have a scratch on him. The whole thing excited me, I mean made-me-wet excited me, so when he asked me to have a drink with him when we got back to the city, I told him how the whole thing had me feeling. "But not tonight. I'll meet you someplace tomorrow."

We settled on a spot, and the next night I pulled into the parking lot looking around for Cedric's car. I was early and wasn't all that surprised when I didn't see it. I went inside and headed straight for the bar. To my surprise, not only was Cedric sitting at the bar, but he was halfway through with his drink. I walked up behind him. "Hello, Cedric."

It must have caught him off guard, because he almost spilled his drink.

"Did I scare you?"

"No, of course not. I meant to do that," he said and smiled.

"Mind if I join you?"

"Sure, beautiful. Have a seat. I got here a little early, so I started without you. I knew you wouldn't mind."

I did think it was a little rude, but whatever. "No, as long as you give me an opportunity to catch up." I sat down and motioned for the bartender. "Blue Muthafucka." I turned to Cedric. "Would you like another?"

"Yeah, bring me another double gin and grape-fruit juice. And can we see a menu, please?" The bartender handed us a menu and proceeded to his task.

"I didn't see your car outside, so I didn't think you were here yet."

"I had a friend drop me off," he said as he leaned toward me. "Hope you won't mind taking me home."

I smiled. "No, not at all," I said, but I wasn't feeling that either.

By the time I finished my third Blue Muthafucka, my judgment was impaired and I was feeling no pain. In simpler terms, I was drunk and so was Cedric. He was knocking down doubles like it was water. We weren't sloppy, stumbling-over- our-words drunk, but we were both pretty far out there. Our conversation was getting more and more sexual in nature. We had talked about what we liked and disliked in the opposite sex, and naturally that led to what we liked sexually.

"What you thinking so hard about over there?" I asked.

"Thinking hard about you. Thinking if you only knew just how hard I was thinking about you and how hard those thoughts were getting me. Thinking about getting out of here while I can still walk."

"You ain't drunk, are you?"

"No, not drunk, but I definitely got my buzz on."

"Good, 'cause I was thinking the same thing."

"Oh, really?" He smiled and leaned close to me—close enough to smell the gin on his breath.

"That's not what I'm thinking about," I said.

"How do you know what I'm thinking about?" Cedric asked and sat back in his chair.

"Hello! It's that *I wanna fuck you so bad it hurts* look. It's written all over your face. I may have my buzz on too, but I'm not blind."

"Am I that obvious?"

"No more than any other man. Pay the check. I'm ready to go."

Cedric signaled for the bartender and paid the check. We walked out to the car together and got in. I knew what was going to happen next, but I started lying to myself at that point.

During the ride to his apartment, the lying continued. Those lies allowed me to live in the delusion that somehow, being this high and horny, some bizarre scenario existed where I would drop Cedric off in front his building, say goodnight and go home. I kept telling myself that I wasn't gonna fuck him; I was just gonna drop him off and go home.

I pulled up in front of his building and looked over at him. "You wanna come in for a drink?" Cedric asked me.

I sat there and thought for a second. "Okay, but just one. Then I gotta go," I said and got out of the car. I followed Cedric to the door. I knew once I crossed the threshold it was over.

He locked the door behind me and offered me a seat on the couch. At that point it was over for me. As far as I was concerned, Cedric was getting fucked that night.

I watched Cedric shaking a canister of whatever we were going to drink and I thought about the consequences of what I was about to do. I would have to justify this with myself. Or could I just take a shower and shrug it off?

He gave me a glass and sat next to me on the couch. I took a sip of my drink. "Gin and tonic?"

"Shaken, not stirred," he said, trying to sound like Bond.

I took another sip and looked at Cedric. He was looking at me. Staring, really. "What you looking at?" he asked and continued to stare.

"I could ask you the same question."

"You could, but I asked you first."

"Thinkin' about the same thing you're thinkin' about." I leaned forward.

"Really? Then what am I thinkin'?"

"You were wondering if you should kiss me."

Cedric put down his glass. "You're right."

I could feel him getting harder as I tasted his tongue. I undressed him slowly and Cedric removed my blouse and bra and made slow circles around my nipples as they began to harden. I stroked his hardening dick with long, even strokes from tip to shaft. His body shook and he squeezed my nipples. My stroking became more intense, more focused.

I spread my legs. Cedric slid his hand along my thighs and gently fingered my clit. I felt it getting harder under his touch. I lay down on my stomach, Cedric sat beside me and ran his hands along my back, my ass, and then to my thighs. He entered me from behind. My pussy was so wet, he was so hard, and it felt so good inside me. I could barely control my passion. I began bucking my ass while he pounded against me. I yelled, "Fuck me harder!"

He did as I asked.

I felt the muscles inside me tighten around him and I came hard. Only problem was, so did he. Just that damn quick. I waited all this time to give somebody some, and this was all I got.

Damn!

After that night, I couldn't get rid of him.

NINE

I was right; Cedric was an asshole. And possessive. He was always calling me, wanting to know where I was, what I was doing, who I was with. Damn, the sex wasn't that good. In fact, it wasn't good at all. He'd tried on several occasions to explain to me that it was the excitement of the moment and me making him wait so long that made him a preemie, but I wasn't buying that. The excitement of the moment? Nigga, please. If you're a premature ejaculator, you're a premature ejaculator. And that's cool, it's just not cool with me.

I'd tried to tell him, get this, that it was the excitement of the moment that made me wanna have sex with him. Unfortunately, he wasn't buying it. He swore that I was in love with him and that day I was showing my real feelings for him. He said that if I just gave him another chance, he'd prove that he had real staying power.

He started worrying the shit of me about it and it was getting on my last fuckin' nerve. I finally said, "Okay, Cedric, but if the sex ain't good this time, you don't need to ever call me again," I told him. My thinking was that if the shit was good, I'd have me a new fuck buddy. You know, like Raymond back in college. If not, he would be so embarrassed that he would never bother me again.

I don't have to tell you what happened the second time.

Preemie!

So, now his excuse was that I put him under so much pressure that he lost his concentration and, you know, lost it. It only made him more obsessed with me. He started sending me flowers every day, and a singing telegram. I didn't think they still did that stuff. Cedric was following me around, calling me all the time. One night he called me twenty-seven times, but I didn't answer the phone. He knew I was home 'cause come to find out, he was sitting outside my building in his car the whole time. " 'Bout time you answered your phone, Nina."

"What do you want, Cedric?"

"I wanna see you."

"Yeah, well, I'm busy."

"Probably with some other nigga, ain't you, Nina?"

"As a matter of fact, I am," I lied.

"Why, Nina? I thought we had an understanding. You asked me to give you some time and I did that. Now you with some other nigga."

"First off, I didn't ask you to give me some time. And if I gave you that impression, I'm sorry. What I remember sayin' is there was no need for you to call me anymore."

"You don't mean that, Nina. You know you love me."

"Nigga, please. I am not in love with you."

"That's 'cause you won't give us a chance."

"Us? There is no us. There is nothing between us and there never will be."

"Don't say that, Nina."

"We went out a few times and that's it."

"There was more to it and you know it."

"What you talkin' 'bout? I was stupid enough, or let the truth be told, horny enough to give you some, and it wasn't good either time. Not good for me at all."

"I told you what the deal was with that. It won't happen no more."

"What, you go out and get you a fresh supply of Viagra?"

"Don't talk to me like this, Nina. I love you."

"I don't love you. I don't even like you. The more I get to know you, the more I realize what an asshole you are."

"You don't talk to me like that!"

"Why not? You're an asshole. An asshole that can't fuck long enough to satisfy me. So, if you'll excuse me, I'll talk to you later!" I yelled and hung up the phone. I changed my phone number and got a new cell the next day. After that, I didn't hear from him for about a month, so I just figured that he had gotten the hint and went on to terrorize some other woman. I was so wrong. Wrong to the point that he is the reason I'm sitting here now, waiting for the grand jury to decide my fate. And it all started one night when this guy named Victor called me.

It was a rainy Friday night, so I decided to relax and read *She's Got Issues* by Stephanie Johnson, the book I'd been putting off for weeks. It turned out to be one of the best books I ever read. Now, once I start reading a book, especially a good book, it takes me in and I can't stop myself. I have to suck it all in until it's dry. I made myself a drink and settled in for a good read.

I had gotten though about a quarter of the book when the phone rang. I looked over at the display. "Bell, VR?" I didn't recognize the name or the number. I usually didn't answer if I didn't know who was calling. Caller ID sure makes you anti-social. But my eyes were tired from reading in bad light, another bad habit. Besides, how long would it take to say wrong number and get back to the book? So, I answered the phone.

"Hello."

"Can I speak to Ronda?" said a voice so deep it sent chills though me. *Damn, he has a nice voice,* I said to myself. I could feel the vibration in between my thighs.

"There's no Ronda here. You have the wrong number," I said.

"Oh, I'm sorry to have bothered you."

"You're not bothering me," I said quickly. "I was just sittin' here reading a book."

"I'm sorry," he said. "I didn't mean to interrupt your reading. I'll let you get back to it."

"Has anyone ever told you that you have a nice voice?"

He laughed. "Maybe once or twice. My voice has taken me places and got me into and out of more things than I can count."

"You should be on the radio, 'cause your voice is so sexy I could just listen to you talk all night."

"Thank you. You have a very pleasing tone to your voice too."

"Well, thank you," I said and squirmed around in my chair. "No one has ever told me that before, Mr. Bell."

"How did you know my name was Bell?"

"Caller ID never lies," I said and giggled like a teenager.

"I forgot about that. But why don't you call me Victor?"

"Okay, Victor. My name is Simone," I lied, using my old dancing name and sounding as polite and professional as I could.

"Well, Simone, it's a pleasure to meet you."

"It's a pleasure meet you too," I said. "So, how does it happen that you're home on a Saturday night?"

"The rain. I was planning on doing some writing, but I just didn't feel motivated enough to sit down."

"You're a writer?"

"Yes."

"What do you write?"

"Fiction."

"You ever been published?"

"Not yet, but I'm submitting my manuscript to publishing companies."

"What's the name of your book?"

"*Crime of Passion*," Victor said proudly.

"What's it about?"

"It's a mystery about a guy who beats his wife and her lover to death with a golf club."

"Okay. Well, good luck with that. I'm not much of a reader," I lied as I looked down at the book on my lap. I am such a reading snob. Besides, I didn't want to give up too much personal information about myself. I already had one strung out pest on my hands; the last thing I needed was another.

"Oh," he said, sounding just a little hurt that I didn't show any interest in what he was writing. "What about you? How does it happen that you're home on a Saturday night?"

"I'm tired. Your body lets you know when you need to rest yourself, so I just took some time to myself. This afternoon my grandmother had a birthday party, so I went over there and I had the best time. It's fun hangin' out with old people."

"A lotta wisdom goin' on in there. You can learn a lot from old people."

"You sure can. So, I hung out over there, stuffed myself like a pig on finger food and cake and pies. It was nice, especially since I really hadn't been out in a while."

"Why is that?"

"I was goin' through some shit—excuse my language."

"It's okay. I've been known to say a curse or two myself."

"I know we should be able to express ourselves without cursing, but it does have its place in our vocabulary. Let's face it; people curse. Some just take it to unnecessary levels. But yeah, I was goin' through some really foul shit and I just needed a change."

"That bad, huh?"

"You just don't know the half of it." I really didn't feel like going into my problems with Cedric. The fact was that I was trying to forget about Preemie Cedric altogether, and the sound of Victor's voice was quickly helping me do just that. The way Victor sounded over the phone made me curious, and I began to wonder what the man behind this voice looked like. "Mind if I ask you a question?"

"Ask me anything you want, Simone."

"Anything?" I asked flirtatiously.

"Anything you wanna know."

"You are black, aren't you?"

"Last time I checked."

"Good. Would you mind describing yourself to me?"

"I'm six-two and my skin is dark. I have no hair by choice."

"I'm glad you said by choice."

"No, male pattern baldness hasn't set in yet. I have a beard."

"How old are you?"

"Thirty-four."

"I knew it. For some reason, I kept thinking you were thirty-four," I said.

"Why? Do I sound thirty-four?"

"No, silly." I laughed. "How does thirty-four sound, anyway?"

"I don't know. Like me, I guess." He laughed too.

"Are you fine?" I asked, bringing an abrupt end to our laughter.

"I've been told that a time or two, but I've never thought so. I consider the people who said it to be biased."

"Why's that?"

" 'Cause I was involved with them at the time."

"I'll accept that," I said, then I got a call on my other line. I said, "Victor, would you mind holding on a minute?"

When I clicked back over Victor said, "I didn't

mind you excusing yourself, but it allowed my mind to wander. Since we were on the subject, I began to give some thought to what you looked like, wondering what kind of person you are. Back in the day, what type of person you were wouldn't have even been a concern, but those were simpler times."

"Oh, really? Why don't you tell me what it was like back then?"

"You see a girl, you dig her. She digs you. Only concern at that point was where and when. But things are different now."

"Just a little." I laughed. "You're kind of funny."

"Thank you. I'm glad that I amuse you."

"So, I take it that back in the day you were livin' on the wild side?"

"I guess you could say that."

"Well, what would you say?"

"I would say that I've had my share of women. My share and somebody else's share, if I really wanted to be honest with you."

"Do you?"

"Can I?"

"Of course you can. You can be as honest with me as you like."

"Good. I've always thought that there was entirely too much pretense in conversation between men and women."

"You're right. There is." I had to agree since I had dropped a couple of lies in this conversation already.

"Each one is so busy trying not to say the wrong thing, not really saying what they mean, talking all around what you really want to say."

"Not being yourself," I threw in because I was guilty of it.

"Let me ask you something," Victor said and cleared his throat. "How many times have you said damn, if I'd known he was like that, I woulda never got involved with him?"

"One time too many," I said and thought about Cedric.

"See, that's pretense. So, I'll just be myself and hope that you do the same. Picture that, an honest relationship."

"Interesting concept."

"I have to try that one of these days," he said and I laughed.

"I don't know if it's possible for a man and a woman to have a completely honest relationship."

"Why is that?"

" 'Cause men lie."

"So do women."

"Yeah, but y'all take it to a whole other level," I said excitedly.

"Please. Give me a break."

"What's that supposed to mean?"

"It means while we're down here scheming and lyin' on level one, a woman is on level five, running a program of lies and manipulation that is so sophisticated that our dumb asses could never even imagine, much less know what's goin' on."

I had to laugh.

"You're laughing, but I bet that you've run some sophisticated games on men, haven't you, Simone?"

"Yeah. Well, first of all my name is Nina. Simone is the name I used when I danced," I confessed.

"The pleasure is all mine, Nina. And thank you for proving my point."

"Anyway," I said, hating to be caught in my own shit.

"Nina Simone, huh?"

"That's what my father used to call me," I said and thought about my daddy. It had been a while since I had seen my parents and I missed them. I would have to try to heal the wound that had grown in our relationship.

"Do you like Nina Simone?"

"To be honest with you, Victor, I know that she was a jazz singer, but I've never heard her sing."

"Really?"

"Really," I replied, feeling just a little stupid. I mean, here I was going around using the name and don't know anything about her.

"You should check out some of her music. She really does have a beautiful voice."

"You seem to know quite a bit about her."

"A bit. Like that's not her real name."

"Get outta here."

"What, you think you're the only one who can make up a name?"

"Okay, okay, you got me." I hate getting called out like that, but he had me. "So, what's her name?"

"Eunice Waymon."

"Eunice Waymon?"

"Yup," Victor said and I giggled a little.

"Where did Nina Simone come from then?"

"To support her family, she started working as an accompanist in an Irish bar in Atlantic City. The bar owner told her she had to sing too. So she changed her name into Nina, which means little one, and Simone, which she took from the French actress Simone Signoret."

"I never heard of her."

"Neither have I."

"Good," I said. "Now I don't feel so bad."

"So you dance, huh?"

"I used to. I used to dance at private parties, and then I danced at a club for a minute."

"Oh, really?"

"Really."

"Which did you like better?"

"Private parties. I hated working in a club."

"Why?"

"Too many people. All those men grabbing at me, trying to rub on me. I just didn't like that. And women hittin' on me got a little old too. See, at private parties, there's maybe four, five men. I could handle that a lot better. When I dance for a man, I feel the music inside me, and I move to the flow. I can look into a man's eyes, while he's watching me and make him feel me without ever having to touch him. It's more personal."

"Personal, huh?"

"Yeah, I know what you're thinkin', and no, I don't sell no pussy. I know some girls do. Do it all the time. I knew one got locked up trying to sell some pussy. You can get hooked on that money. I wasn't tryin' to do all that."

"Guess you made good money dancin', huh?"

"I got a flat fee plus tips. Depending on the crowd, I did all right."

"Sometimes the whole dancer/customer relationship amazes me. I mean think about it; we sit there for hours, giving sometimes large sums of money to a woman whose job is to get your money and make you feel good about giving it to her."

"Right. And she can accomplish this most times by making you think that there's a light at the end of the tunnel, and that tunnel leads to sex."

"Most times this isn't the case. I had a relationship like that. I used to go to this place to be entertained by a woman who called herself Starr."

"Starr, huh? At least my stage name showed some imagination, even if I didn't know it." I laughed. I couldn't remember the last time I laughed that much in a conversation with a man, especially a man I'd never met. Of course, that was an issue that I planned to remedy at the first opportunity.

"It started out like every dancer/customer relationship does. I tipped her while she was on stage, and when she came to thank me, I had her dance for me."

"That's how the club scene works. Hustlin' for every dollar you get. But you really liked her? I mean beyond just dancing for you."

"Yeah, I did," Victor continued. "She was cool, quite intelligent and pretty good company. Good enough that I became her regular customer. When she'd notice that I was in the club, she'd leave whoever she was sitting with and sit with me."

"You must have been a good customer for her to do that."

"I guess. But that went on whether I had money or not. Naturally, on nights when I had no money to spend, she'd leave me when she'd see a mark, but she'd always come back."

"Bet she'd have some stories to tell."

"She'd always have stories about the things men would say to her. Weak, lame lines. Starr gave me the run-down on all the other dancers: who was trickin', who got high, which ones stole money, the whole nine. Some nights she wouldn't feel like being bothered and would dance only when it was her turn on stage, or she'd dance for me when a song came on that she liked."

"I guess she really liked you too."

"I guess," Victor said quietly.

I could tell by the way he talked about her that she really meant a lot to him. "You wanted to have sex with her?"

"Bad. But for as long as the relationship lasted, there was no sex. Each night some guy in a gold Lincoln would show up to get her. She'd say goodnight and they'd drive away, leaving me broke and feeling foolish."

"She was just doin' her job."

"So what about you, Nina? What do you do now?"

"Excuse me?"

"What do you do? Where do you work?"

"Oh . . ." I laughed. I knew what he meant. I was just trying to decide how I should answer. "I'm in business for myself," I said quickly.

"What type of business do you do?"

"Wholesale/retail business," I said. "You know, I buy things wholesale and resell them for a profit."

"Really? What product, or maybe it's products, do you carry?"

"That depends on the customer," I answered. trying not to trip over my own words.

"So, you run a customer-driven business?"

"Right," I said. "Victor, would you mind holding on a minute? I got a call on my other line." I put the phone on mute and left him there for a while.

When I got back on the phone, Victor was more interested in my life as a stripper than knowing what products I carried.

Ah, men.

"Nina, you begin to interest me, and not just 'cause you were a dancer. Although that is a major factor, I am really enjoying this whole conversation."

"Well, I'm glad I'm able to amuse you."

"You never did say what you looked like. Describe yourself to me."

"I'm twenty-five, just turned, in fact."

"Happy belated birthday," Victor said.

"Thank you," I said. "I'm brown-skinned with long, shoulder-length hair. A lot of people think I'm Puerto Rican 'cause my hair is wavy. I'm about five-seven, taller in pumps, and I won't tell you how much I weigh."

"A woman thing, I guess."

"You know that. But I assure you that you won't be disappointed when you see me."

"I consider this a good thing. I've been on blind dates before. Most turned out to be nights I'd soon forget."

After a bit more small talk, I told Victor I was tired and I would call him the next day, and maybe we could get together. Victor, on the other hand, didn't seem too excited about meeting me in person. He kept saying that he had some business to handle the next day. If I'm nothing else, I am persistent, and I wouldn't give up until I got my way.

The next day, I was on the phone with Victor, and I was talking about him coming to get me for dinner, drinks, or whatever. I was going to meet the man behind the voice.

TEN

"Victor?"

"Nina?"

"Come on in."

"Thank you."

"Well?" I said, standing with my hands on my hips.

"Yeah, I could see where you could pass for Puerto Rican. You're very pretty. No, that's an understatement too. You're beautiful."

"Thank you, Victor. You're a very handsome man yourself. Have a seat. I'll be ready in a minute," I said and went into the bedroom. *Very handsome* was an understatement, too. This man was sexy as hell. His voice was just the tip of the iceberg.

We rode around for a while and talked. Once we settled on a place, we went inside and took a seat at the bar. I ordered my signature rum and Coke; I had to cut loose them Blue Muthafuckas. Victor ordered Remy Martin neat. That means straight, if y'all didn't know. I didn't.

We had the usual amount of uncomfortable, getting-to-know-you conversation over the first drink. The conversation turned back to the night before and his lack of enthusiasm about meeting me. "That's because I've had blind dates before and they never turn out to be about anything. But I'm flattered just to be here. Women that look like you don't usually do this. Getting a man definitely ain't your problem in life."

"I tried to tell you," I said with attitude. "I knew you wouldn't be disappointed." But the truth was, I didn't have a man and I was lonely.

"I don't think that *disappointed* is a word that applies to anything about you, Nina."

The way he looked at me when he talked, the sound of his voice, and the way he ran his tongue over his lips was moving me in ways that only Lorenzo had. We ordered a second round of drinks and a very interesting, not to mention tasty, spinach dip. "I'm glad I decided to call you today. I needed this. I'm enjoying myself."

"I'm glad you called too," Victor said and reached for my hand. "And I'm glad I came to meet you, Nina."

The whole time we were there, Cedric was blowing up my phone. He'd started calling again when he got a hold of my new number. He told me that he broke into my mailbox every day waiting for my cell phone bill to come so he could get the number. I didn't know if that was true or not, but he had it. Each time I felt the phone vibrate I'd look at it, put it on my hip and keep talking. Except once. "Excuse me, Victor. This may be some money calling." I walked out to the lobby and answered the phone. It was Cedric calling from another number.

" 'Bout time you answered your phone, Nina."

"What do you want, Cedric?"

"I wanna see you."

"I don't hear from you for a month and now you start blowin' up my phone, talkin' 'bout you wanna see me?" I cursed him out quick and went back inside and re-joined Victor at the bar. My phone rang again. I snatched it off my hip, looked at the number, and rolled my eyes before returning it to its resting place. I looked up and caught Victor staring at me.

I smiled. "What?"

"What you doin' to that man, Nina?"

"Nothing."

"Yeah, right. You're not doing anything to him, but he can't go twenty minutes without calling you."

"I talked to him," I fired back with an attitude. "I told him I was busy and I'd talk to him later."

"Well, you know later means different things to different people. I guess to him later means in twenty minutes." I rolled my eyes and took another sip of my drink. "No, Nina, you turned that man out, and now he can't stand the thought of anybody being anywhere near you. So, I will ask you once again; what did you do to that man?"

I still didn't offer an explanation, but I did smile a confident *Yeah, I got the nigga pussy whipped* smile. Quietly, though, I wished I didn't.

"You should be careful who you throw that monster on. He might start stalking you," Victor commented casually.

"I been stalked before. Not by him," I quickly lied again, "but I've been stalked before." It was becoming a pattern, but if I wanted to be honest, I would have to say that Cedric was a stalker. For some reason, I felt compelled to lie to Victor.

"Somehow, I'm not surprised," Victor said, sounding disappointed.

"I know what you're thinking, and it wasn't like that." I smiled and shook my head. Suddenly it was important that he understood and not be disappointed in me. I really liked Victor, and not just because he was so damn fine. When I was in college, Victor was the kind of man that I said I was going to marry and spend the rest of my life with. "For real, I never even kissed him. I was just fourteen. He was just obsessed with me. Callin' me all the time and shit."

"So, what you're telling me is you never even kissed the guy but he was stalking you? That's strong, Nina."

"All we did was talk on the phone a few times. He was one of my cousin's friends. That's how I met him. He used to come by with my cousin all the time, but he used to sit outside. So, one day I told my cousin to invite him in, you know, 'cause it wasn't polite to have him waiting outside. After that he just started callin' me. I talked to him a few times, more not to be rude than anything else, and from that he thought we were going together. Finally, I had to tell him that it wasn't like that, and that's when it started. He would come by the house and my moms would tell him that I wasn't home, so he would sit outside for hours before he'd get tired and leave. At first it was funny, you know, but then I started getting worried. I told my cousin that he needed to talk to his friend, but that didn't do any good. My father threatened him, but he wouldn't stop."

"How did you get him to stop? Or is he still at it?"

"No, silly. I finally had to call the cops. They told him he was goin' to jail if he had to come out there again. You ever been stalked?"

"No, not like that. I've had some people that didn't take the fact that it was over too well. I've had to call the cops a couple of times. Had a broken window or two, but not a sustained stalker."

"Big as you are, you had to call the cops on some woman?"

"Damn right. If I did anything, I mean looked at her hard, and she called the police, she could say anything and they'd lock my dumb ass up. Black man ain't got no win in court. Especially a big black man. No, Nina, I'll call the cops at the drop of a dime."

By the third drink we were both pretty comfortable with one another and were enjoying each other's company. I was really feeling Victor—or maybe it was my anger with Cedric. I don't know. We ordered another round of drinks and I said, "Let me run something by you."

"What's that?"

"I wanna spend the night with you. I know you said you got stuff you need to do, so if you can't, I'll understand."

"But you're not used to men telling you no."

I smiled. "No, I'm not."

"I see this."

"You know, you could write a story about this. I mean, it would make a good story. The first chapter would be last night on the phone."

"Tonight would be the second chapter."

"Right. And we both know what the third chapter is gonna be."

ELEVEN

"I just need to stop by my house to pick up a few things. I won't be but a minute," I said. "You got anything to drink at your house?"

"Sure. I always keep a little something around the house."

"You smoke weed?"

"Yes."

"Got any?" I asked with a smile.

"No, but that's no problem. I always know where to find something to smoke."

"I get my drink on and smoke a blunt, and it's on. I may even dance for you."

We drove back to my apartment then we swung by this spot, picked up a couple of dimes, a few blunts, and continued on to his house. I rolled a fat blunt and we smoked most of it along the way. By the time we got there, I was pretty fucked up. He told me to make myself comfortable and that he wouldn't be gone long.

When he got back to the house, *The Best of Sade*

was playing. I had his living room lit with candles and had changed into a sheer black robe with a black teddy underneath. I had rolled another blunt, had two glasses and the bottle waiting. I was asleep on the couch and didn't hear him when he came in.

Like Prince Charming, he kissed me softly on the cheek and I woke up. We talked for while and then "No Ordinary Love" started to play. I smiled and said, "Let me show you something." I stood up and began to dance for him. My movements were slow and seductive, and I could tell he was loving every minute of it. I ran my fingers though my hair and down my body. I pulled down my teddy just enough to reveal a hint of nipple. I danced my way close to him, close enough for him to touch. As he reached for me, I turned around and bent over.

He stood and started to move in unison with me. I stopped and turned to face him. "No, baby. You sit down and relax. This is my show."

He gladly obeyed my instructions and sat quietly, watching each movement of my body in anticipation of what was to come. I smiled and eased the robe off my shoulders then began to tease him with it. I leaned forward and gently ran it along the back of his neck and between his legs. One of the straps on my teddy fell off my shoulder. He quickly ran his tongue over my nipple. Just as quickly, I moved out of reach. I continued to dance, each movement more seductive than the last, and I knew I was making him want me even more.

When the song ended, I took a sip of my drink and lit the blunt. When "Kiss Of Life" came on, I started to move again in perfect time with the music. I danced, a drink and a blunt in either hand.

"You've done this before, haven't you?" he said and poured himself another drink.

"Maybe once or twice," I answered as I slowly allowed my teddy to drop to the floor. I moved toward him again, and this time I allowed him to touch me. He ran his hands along my skin while I moved. My arms, my legs, and my stomach were fair game, but like any good seductress, I always moved slightly out of reach each time his touches approached the more sensitive areas.

"Please Send Me Someone to Love" caused me to glide like wind toward him again. I stood before him and eased his back against the couch. My head began to spin, and I felt myself getting caught up in the erotic excitement of it all. Or maybe it was just the cognac and weed; I didn't seem to care. I eased myself down on him and my eyes opened wide. I had never felt anything so hard, so long, and so fat. It felt like he was contoured to fill me up. I ground my hips into his. I pinned his shoulders against the couch and stared in his eyes. I felt paralyzed; eyes wide open in disbelief at the sensations he was creating with each subtle movement of his body.

I got up, finished my drink, and poured us both another glass. When I went into the kitchen to get some ice, he took his shirt off and followed me. I got up on the counter and he came to me. I tasted his tongue. It glided slowly and smoothly over mine. I broke our embrace and he spread my legs. He kissed my inner thighs then tasted the wetness between them. I held his head in place while his tongue slithered along my lips and made circles around my clit. My grip grew tighter, my thighs twitched, my stomach muscles locked, and my head drifted back in quiet ecstasy.

After a while he said his knees got weak and we headed for the bedroom. We got as far as the hallway before we were doing it on the floor. Once we finally made it to the bed, he smiled and touched my face. I smiled at him and rolled over. He ran his hand over my shoulder and down my arm. He moved closer and his hands continued to glide along my body. He kissed my back. I began to move in response. I rolled into his arms and he kissed my lips. It wasn't just the quick exchange of tongues we had experienced earlier. He kissed me delicately and methodically, pressing his lips against mine. His lips were soft. I drew him closer to feel his skin against mine. I opened my eyes and he kissed my cheeks, down to my neck then up to my earlobes. I closed my eyes and he guided his tongue along my eyebrows, then kissed my eyelids. When he flicked my lashes, I opened my eyes. I put my hand on his chest and gently pushed him on his back.

He lay spread eagle across the bed and I crawled across to him. I looked at his manhood again, gawked at it actually, and contemplated going down on him. *I had broken all the rest of the rules, so why not that one too?* I asked myself as I straddled his torso. I grabbed hold and guided him inside me. He smiled and placed his hands on my ass. My hands dropped to his chest. He spread my cheeks and slowly moved me up and down, inching deeper and deeper inside me. The deeper he got, the wetter I got. Soon, I was sliding up and down on him effortlessly. He didn't move at first; he seemed very content to allow me to work at my own pace. My pace was slow and steady; there was a true rhythm to my movement, almost musical.

I closed my eyes, enjoying the feeling of his stiffness inside me. The thickness of him filled me, the warmth of him inside me, long and stiff, excited me. My hips shook. I began to quiver from the inside. I stopped moving, tried to slow my roll, but I couldn't. My entire body was quivering uncontrollably. For a second, maybe two or three, I felt like I was outside of myself. My excitement only proved to intensify the motion of my hips. He held me tighter, began to move with me. When I felt him throbbing inside me, I was no longer able to control myself. "Yes, oh yes!" I screamed as we thrust our bodies against one another. I could hear him moaning quietly, his face twisted and contoured. He throbbed and I felt him expand. My fingers dug into his chest. His body became rigid; I pumped harder. His mouth was open, his eyes were locked on mine now. I knew I had him.

TWELVE

We were both pretty exhausted after that, and our drinks were pretty watered down. He went back to the living room to get the bottle and the remainder of the blunt. On the way, he stopped to put the CD player on random then returned to the room. As he handed me a drink and the blunt, I glanced at the clock on the VCR. It was a little after midnight. "Thank you," I said and lit the blunt with one of the candles I had set out earlier.

I wondered, what do you say to a naked man you met on the phone the night before? Up until now, we hadn't had any problem talking to one another. Now, there was an uncomfortable apprehension that slid in between us. We smoked our blunt and drank our drinks in silence. That is until my cell phone rang.

Thinking that it was Cedric çalling again, I answered it with fury. "Hello!"

"What the fuck is your problem?" Teena asked.

"Nothing. I thought you were Cedric."

"Cedric? Now there's a name I ain't heard in a minute. How did he work his way back in the picture?"

"He didn't, but for some reason he's been callin' and bothering me all night, that's all. What's up?"

"You busy?"

I looked at Victor. "Yes, very busy."

"Then you shouldn't have answered the phone, bitch." Teena laughed. "Come make this money."

"What money?"

"This five thousand I got sittin' in front of me. And before you ask, no, I don't have enough product to handle it, and no, it can't wait until tomorrow. So, get your greedy ass up and come make this money."

I looked at Victor again. Normally, I wouldn't have had to think twice. Five grand? Shit, I would jump and run for a grand. This was five grand sitting and waiting for me to come get it. I was greedy, but what I was more was satisfied and looking forward to getting some more. Still, I had to be practical. "Where you at? I'm on my way."

After Teena told me where to meet her, I apologized to Victor about having to run out on him in the middle of the night, not to mention in the middle of great sex. I got dressed to meet Teena. Victor looked at me strangely while I got dressed. He had never asked me again what product I sold, and I never volunteered the fact that I was a drug dealer, so he was probably wondering what somebody could say to make me jump up and run out after having such great sex. I walked up to him in bed, kissed him, and apologized again. "Victor, I'm real sorry about havin' to leave you like this."

"It's okay. Really, Nina. I understand that you gotta go do . . ." Victor said and paused, "whatever it is that you gotta go do."

"Do you?"

"Yes, Nina. I understand."

"Good," I said and started to leave the room. I grabbed my purse. "Get up and walk me to the door, Victor," I said, smiling when he got out of bed. "Damn," I said with my eyes focused. "You make a sistah wanna strip down and get back in the bed."

"If that's the case, then why don't you come back after you do . . . whatever it is that you gotta go do?"

I smiled. "Can I?"

"Of course. Just call when you're on your way."

I started out of the bedroom and Victor followed behind me. "Ain't you gonna put nothin' on?"

"No. This is my house."

"You always walk around here naked?" I asked.

"Yeah, this is my house."

I caught a cab to my apartment to pick up some product and then to Jimmy's to meet Teena. On the way, I gave some thought to why Teena wanted to meet me there. I hoped that she wasn't doing business with none of those guys who hung out down there. We had talked about this time and time again. Leon's words kept ringing in my mind. *You don't know which ones the cops got their hooks in . . . . The ones that are still on the street are the ones who gave the cops something to stay out.*

But at this point, it didn't matter. I just wanted

to handle my business with Teena as quickly as possible and get back to Victor.

When I walked into Jimmy's bar I started to make my way through the crowd. I passed by these two women who seemed to be staring at me. *Probably just a couple of lesbians that wanna get with me*, I thought and continued to where Teena was waiting for me. Even though it had been a minute since I'd been there, the faces were still the same, and even though it had been a minute, I still looked at them the same way. These were the people who sold out Lorenzo, or at best gave up something or somebody to stay on the street. I still commanded some respect in there, so just about everybody spoke. Only difference was now it wasn't just 'cause I was the bitch Lorenzo used to fuck. I had become a respectable player in my own right, and it felt good.

"What took you so long?" Teena asked, staring at me as I sat down.

"What are you staring at?" I asked.

"You," Teena said with this look on her face.

"What about me?"

"Well, you got your hair pulled back in that fucked-up-ass ponytail, and you ain't got on no lipstick. You been fuckin'."

I just looked at her without answering.

"I'm sorry I pulled you off some dick to come here."

"That's all right. Let's just do this quickly so I can get back to him."

"I was gonna say that I hope he can keep it up longer than Cedric, but I can tell that he did."

"Yeah, yeah, I'll tell you all about it in the morning," I said and noticed that the same two women had moved and were staring at me again. "Teena, you know those two bitches?"

"Never seen them before in my life. But you know you have that type of effect on women.

"Yeah, whatever. The product is under the front passenger seat," I said and pushed the keys to my car in front of her. "I hope that you're not doin' business in here."

"Oh, hell no," Teena said and pushed her keys to me. "I was just in here hangin' out when Jay rolled up on me all frantic and shit. Black Thunderbird," she said and got up. "Call me tomorrow. I wanna hear all about this nigga you in such a rush to get back to."

"Money in it?"

"No doubt. It's in a bag in the trunk."

"Go on, get out of here," I said and watched her walk out the door. Then I saw Jay. He waved and smiled at me as he followed Teena out the door.

I sat there for a minute and looked around for the two women who were watching me. Not seeing them, I got up and made my way out of the bar. I wandered around the parking lot looking for the black Thunderbird that I now had the keys to. As I walked, I gave some thought to whose car it was that I was gonna be driving. I saw it parked two rows over. I weaved through the cars and was about to unlock the car when I heard a familiar voice. "I'm surprised to see you here, Nina."

"What are you doin' here, Cedric?"

"I come here all the time. I hear that you think you're too good to hang out in a place like this."

"I'm here to handle my business and get outta here, Cedric. And I don't care what people think."

"So, you finished your date?"

"Cedric, that's none of your business."

"Yes, it is my business, Nina. I wanna know where you were at tonight and who you were with."

"You're crazy, you know that? How many times I gotta tell you it ain't like that between us? Why can't you understand that? You are not my man. I don't love you. I can't even stand to be around you!" I yelled, and that was when he hit me so hard that I saw bright lights flash then I hit the ground hard.

"Who were you with?" Cedric yelled.

I saw a bottle on the ground near me. I picked it up and threw it at him. It hit him in the face and he grabbed it. I got up off the ground and ran back in Jimmy's as fast as I could. Once I told everyone what happened, half the bar ran outside to look for Cedric, but he was gone.

THIRTEEN

No man had ever hit me. Not even my father. He always left that task to my mother, who turned it into an art form. Now I wondered what was gonna happen next. I mean, I never imagined that anything like this would ever happen to me, not even with Cedric. But *maybe* I should have seen it coming.

After about an hour, I left Jimmy's. I started to go straight back to Victor's house but decided to go home first. I didn't want to go there with this money. It would only take a minute, and Victor didn't live that far away. I parked the car, got the money out of the trunk and put it in my purse. I walked in my building thinking about the way I'd been living lately. You know, how my recent sexual decisions had contributed to my current situation.

I took out my keys and had just unlocked my door when, out of the corner of my eye, I saw the two of them coming. Before I reacted, they had their guns to my head. One took my purse and the keys from me then the other one pushed me inside. They quickly gagged me, ripped the phone cord from the wall, and hog tied my hands and feet with it.

Although neither one of them ever said anything, it didn't take long for me to realize that they were women. These were the same two women who had been watching me at Jimmy's.

I was sure of it.

I watched them while they searched the apartment, looking for my stash. It didn't take them long to find what they were looking for and bounce. It took a while, but I was able to work the gag loose. I lay there for a while trying to get my hands and feet loose, but they had me tied tight. This wasn't the first time these chicks tied somebody up and robbed them, but that wasn't important now. What was important was how I was going to get out of this.

I figured that if I could make it to the phone, I could call for help. I inched my way along the floor until I got into the bedroom. When I finally made it, I look up at the phone on the night table and wondered how I was going to get to it. First, I tried to get up on my knees. Each time I tried it, I ended up back on the floor, face down. Then I started to hit the night table with my legs, hoping that the phone would come down before the lamp. Finally, the phone dropped to the floor. It just missed hitting me. I moved my body so that my face would be close to the receiver. I hit the speaker button then the redial button with my nose and hoped the last person I called would answer the phone.

"Hello," said a sleepy voice.

It took me a second to make out who it was. "Victor, this is Nina. I need—"

"I see you finally decided to call. You on your way back?" Victor asked.

"Listen to me, Victor. I just got robbed and they left me tied up on the floor in the bedroom. I need you to come and untie me."

Victor laughed. "Are you all right?"

"I'm fine. I mean they didn't hurt me."

"Do you want me to call the police?"

"No!" I said louder than I needed to. "Just come untie me, Victor. Please."

"You're not kidding, are you?"

"Victor, I wish I was."

"So, somebody robbed you and left you tied up in the bedroom?"

"Yes. Look, Victor, I know this sounds stupid, but I really am tied up, and I really do need you to come and untie me. I'll explain things when you get here."

"Okay. I'm on my way," Victor said.

"Thank you, Victor," I said and gave some thought to the fact that I couldn't hang up the phone. I had to laugh as I listened to the beeping noise and hoped that it would stop soon.

I wasn't really looking forward to explaining this whole thing to Victor. I never mentioned what I did for a living 'cause he didn't need to know. Or was it 'cause I didn't want him to know? Either way, I was glad that Victor was the last person I called and that he was coming to untie me.

But suppose he wasn't?

Suppose he thought the whole thing was my

idea of a joke and he rolled over and took his ass back to sleep? And if that were the case, how was I gonna hang up this phone so I could call somebody else? And even if I could hang up the phone, how was I planning on dialing the number? With my nose again, I guessed. *Damn, this is so fucked up.*

Time passed slowly while I lay there on the floor, thinking about where I was and what was happening to me. Those girls could have just as easily killed me after they found my stash. I was thankful to be alive, and I was happy that I didn't keep all the product I had in the apartment.

I took the opportunity to think about what I'd made of my life. I mean, this wasn't what I had in mind when I graduated from college. I was suppose to get a nice job, meet a nice man, get married and have a bunch of kids. But no. Each time I had a chance to do the right thing, I chose to take the easy route. I could have tried to do something positive after Lorenzo went to jail, but I chose to be a dancer. When that didn't work out, I chose to roll. Now look at me.

I thought I heard the door open.

"Nina!" I heard Victor yell.

"I'm back here!"

"Okay, I'm—Ahhh!"

I heard Victor cry out then I heard a loud noise. "Victor! Victor! Are you all right?" I yelled, but got no answer. I called to him again. "Victor!"

"My name ain't Victor."

"Cedric?"

He came around the bed so I could see him. He had a gun in his hand and there was blood on the barrel.

"What did you do to Victor?"

"He's all right. He's just takin' a little lie down, that's all," Cedric said as he sat down on the bed.

"Whatever, Cedric. Just untie me."

"What are y'all playin', some kinda kinky, bondage sex games?"

"No, I got robbed, okay? Now, stop fuckin' around and untie me."

"So, is that the nigga you been fuckin' around with?"

I started to say, "Hell yeah, and unlike you he fucked the shit outta me," but I figured the loud noise I heard was Victor's body hitting the floor. I had to be nice to this asshole. "Cedric, please. I barely have any feeling in my hands or feet. Please, Cedric, untie me."

"I said is that the nigga you been fuckin' around with?" Cedric yelled. He grabbed me by the hair and dragged me into the living room where Victor's body was lying. "Is this the nigga you picked to fuck wit' over me?"

"No! Please, Cedric, just untie me." Now I was really scared. There was a lot of blood on the back of Victor's head. I couldn't tell if he was breathing or not.

Cedric began wandering around the apartment like he was looking for something. Then he threw the gun on the couch and left the room. "Get up. Please, Victor, if you can hear me, you need to get up now and get us outta here," I whispered. Cedric came back in the room with the phone cord from the bedroom. "What are you doing?"

"Since he tied you up, I want him to know how it feels."

"I told you, Cedric, I got robbed and they left me tied up," I said to him, but he wasn't listening.

He picked up Victor's body from the floor and tied him to a chair. Cedric picked up the gag that had been in my mouth and put it on Victor. "Wake up!" he yelled then started slapping Victor until he opened his eyes. Cedric began punching Victor in the face.

"Stop! Stop it!" I yelled.

"Shut up!" Cedric said and hit Victor again. "Shut up, bitch."

Cedric went back in the bedroom. When he came back, he had a pair of my panties in his hand. He smelled them then he grabbed me by my hair again. I screamed, and when I did, he shoved the panties in my mouth. Cedric went back to Victor and began hitting him in the face again and again. He hit him so hard that the chair fell over, but that wasn't enough to stop him.

I cried as Cedric kept kicking Victor in the face and stomach. He turned the chair back on its legs. "You think this nigga is pretty, Nina? Well, he ain't gonna be pretty no more," Cedric said then punched Victor in the face. He hit him and hit him so many times that I know his hands must have hurt.

Cedric came over and sat down on the floor next to me. The way he was breathing was more like he had been in a fight than beating a defenseless man tied to a chair. "How you like your pretty nigga now?" Cedric asked as he snatched the panties out of my mouth.

"You didn't have to do that, Cedric. He ain't nobody. I barely know him."

"Well, if he ain't nobody, what's he doing here?"

"He just came to untie me, that's all."

"You think I'm stupid, huh? I know this the nigga you fuckin', bitch. Don't lie to me."

"I'm not lying. I barely know him," I said, knowing that I had to do something now or he was gonna kill both of us. "But it sure made me hot watchin' you beat him."

Cedric looked at me. "Really?"

"Oh, yes. It made me hot for you just like it did after I saw you jump out of that window."

"Really?"

"Yes, Cedric, just like that. You know how hot I was for you after that," I said softly. "Come on. Untie me, Cedric. Please. Untie me so you can fuck me."

"Are you serious?"

"Yes, Cedric. My pussy is throbbing for you."

"You a freak bitch, ain't you?"

"Your freak bitch. Untie me so I can fuck you."

Cedric stood and went into the kitchen. Victor still hadn't moved. I hoped he wasn't dead. When Cedric came back he had a knife in his hand.

"Untie me so I can fuck the shit outta you."

Cedric used the knife to cut the cord between my feet. It felt good. When Cedric started to pull off my jeans I said, "Not like that, baby. Not with my hands tied behind my back. Untie my hands so you can get the pussy right."

Cedric looked at me for a long moment. I turned around and held my tied hands in front of him. He cut the cord and put the knife down. As soon as he put it down, I turned around and my knee was in his nuts. He screamed and I ran for the door. I guess I didn't knee him hard enough, 'cause Cedric ran up behind me, grabbed me by my hair and slammed my face into the door. He spun me around and started punching me in the face. I couldn't run 'cause he was still holding my hair.

When he finally let me go, I ran and started throwing everything I could get my hands on at him. I made it to the kitchen where there was a pot of water on the stove. He came at me, and I hit him in the head with it. He fell back and slipped on the water. He hit the floor. Hard. I tried to run for the door again, but Cedric caught me and flung me across room. I tried to crawl away, but he was on me too quickly. He picked me up and hit me again then threw me on the couch so hard that it tipped over.

I was lying on the ground and his gun was right next to me. I picked up the gun as I saw him coming around the couch. I pointed it at him and pulled the trigger. His body fell on the floor next to me.

FOURTEEN

I didn't know how many times I shot Cedric, but he was dead. I wanted to move, wanted to get up and see about Victor, but I couldn't move. I guess one of my neighbors heard the shots and called the cops. I was never so glad to see them in my life. They found me sitting on the floor crying in between Victor and Cedric with the gun still in my hand.

One of the cops walked toward me slowly with his hand out. "Take it easy, lady, and just hand me the gun," he said. I let him take the gun out of my hand and he helped me get on my feet and to a chair in the kitchen. The other cop checked Victor. "Is he alive?" the cop asked.

"I got a pulse," the other cop said.

"What about that one?"

He looked at Cedric's body. "Judging by that pool of blood he's lying in, I'd say he's dead," he said, but checked his pulse anyway. "Yeah, he's dead."

They never did ask me what happened. I guess it was pretty obvious. I heard one of them call for an ambulance and the crime scene technicians. I don't remember too much after that. I do know that when the ambulance came, they took me and Victor to the hospital.

The next afternoon, I woke up in the hospital. The doctor told me that I was all right. "Just some cuts and bruises."

"What about the guy I came in with?"

"I don't know, but I can find out for you. What's his name?"

"His name is Victor. Victor Bell."

When the doctor came back, I could tell by the look on his face that it wasn't good. He said that Victor's condition was just upgraded from critical to stable. "He took quite a beating. He's lucky to be alive. Your friend has a concussion from some type of trauma to the back of the head. His retina was detached, his jaw was broken, as were several of his ribs, and there was quite a bit of internal bleeding," the doctor said, and I cried.

To make matters worse, two detectives came in after the doctor left. I told them my story, and they said they would have to arrest me for murder.

"You're kidding, right? He was gonna kill me, and he beat my friend almost to death. It was self defense."

"I believe that, ma'am, but that's for a court to decide if they wanna try you for it." I couldn't believe what I was hearing, but that's how I got here.

The first thing I did was call Leon and explain the situation to him. He listened to my story without interrupting then he said, "Should have called me sooner, Nina, and I would have taken care of that bitch nigga. I'll talk to you later." Then he hung up the phone. He was there that evening.

He told me not to worry; he would take care of everything. He arranged my bail and got me a lawyer, somebody he'd known since back in the day.

"Nina, this is Wanda Moore. She's an old friend and the best lawyer in the city. Wanda, this is my cousin, Nina," Leon said.

"It's good to meet you, Ms. Moore, and thank you for seeing me."

"No need to thank me. And please, call me Wanda."

After I told my story, Wanda looked at Leon then she looked back at me and stood. She walked to the window and looked out. "You should have told me that this involved drugs, Leon."

"Is this more serious than I thought?" I asked.

"Oh no, Ms. Thomas. Your case shouldn't be a problem. As long as you've told me everything, you shouldn't have anything to worry about. It was clearly a case of self defense. I'll make sure you get a good lawyer."

"No, Wanda, you gotta do this," Leon said passionately. "This is my family, Wanda. It's because it involves drugs that Nina needs you."

"You know I don't take these kind of cases anymore."

"Come on, Wanda, this is me you're talkin' to. All them drug-related cases you used to handle back in the day, now you can't get your hands a little dirty?"

"Leon, you know what Mike is gonna say about this. He'll give me that look and say, 'Drugs, Wanda?' "

"Mike Black! Didn't I hear somewhere that he married a drug dealer?" Leon laughed. Wanda did too, and I wondered why.

"What are y'all talkin' about?" I asked, but was ignored except for the *Shut up, little girl. Grown folks are talkin'* look I got from Leon.

"Look, Wanda, this is me. We go too far back and I was down for Black too many times. And when Black started talking that dead zone shit, I didn't go to war with him like everybody else. I took my business elsewhere."

"With his blessing and support, Leon. Don't forgot that," Wanda said quickly but absolutely.

"I know that, Wanda. I owe him, but I'm still asking."

After that, whatever it was, Wanda agreed to handle my defense. When Wanda left, Leon started to explain it all to me. It was some long, drawn out, back in the day stuff between the two of them and whoever this Mike Black character was.

Shay and Teena came to my trial. Leon, however, felt uncomfortable being around so many law enforcement types, so after Wanda's services were secured, Leon returned to Jacksonville. Even Victor, who had recovered nicely from the urban drama I brought into his life, came to support me.

In the end, everything worked out for me. The grand jury didn't return a murder indictment against me. I was so relieved I cried.

Now that that was behind me, I had something else on my mind—the girls who robbed me.

They didn't follow me to Jimmy's; they were waiting there for me. They had to know that I would be at Jimmy's and where I lived. I looked at Teena and wondered how they knew that.

ACKNOWLEDGMENTS

Chunichi

First and foremost, I would like to thank God. For my ability to write is not a talent, yet a gift in which He has blessed me. I credit all my success to Him, without God none of this would be possible.

Next I would like to thank Carl Weber and the Urban Books family for believing in my work and me. You have given me the opportunity of a lifetime.

To my parents thank you, thank you, thank you. I could never thank you all enough. No one has supported me as much as you all. Thanks for your patience, your understanding, your unconditional love and never ending support.

To my little brother, Vincent McZeek, aren't you proud of your big sis?

Special thanks to my girlfriends, I love you all like sisters. Toya Duncan TMD Design, your wit keeps me bright each day. Thanks for the unique designs. Sara Schaible SOZO Fashion, thanks for keeping me on top of the fashion game. Meisha

Camm, thanks for walking with me each step of the way. Chrissy Smith, thanks for introducing me to the "publication world." Lakicia Fortenberry for keeping me focused on what's important. Tracey Davis for being my big sister at heart. My lil' sis Tiffany Duncan, follow my lead. LaChele Edmonds. Melanie Camm and Deetra Foreman, thanks for simply being the ones I exhale with.

Much thanks to all those who support me. Ricardo Burress, thanks for the constant push. When I am tired and frustrated you never let me give up. Deneen Majors Major Creations Hair Studio, thanks not only for the bomb hairstyles, but also for constantly promoting the book. My coworkers, thanks for listening to all my different scenes and answering the infamous "does this sound right" question. Renee Bobb, thanks for showing me the ropes and for your endless advice.

Finally a GRAND thanks to all those who doubted me and hate the fact I made it. You have given me the strength and drive to do it over and over again. This is just the beginning!

Anyeh

CHAPTER ONE
Diablo

I circled the restaurant twice before finally parking. I was sure to have a complete view of my surroundings before making any move. I was always skeptical when meeting niggas to handle business.

Beeeeeeep. Beeeeeep. Beeeeeep. Beeeeeep. My Nextel sounded. It was Q, and he was starting to get a little impatient.

"I'm right outside, nigga," I shouted over the Direct Connect speaker. "I'm just checking out the scene before I come in."

The parking lot seemed to be clear, so I hopped out of the car and headed into the restaurant. I quickly spotted Q sitting alone in a booth near the back.

"Damn, nigga, it took you long enough. I've been sitting here the last fifteen minutes checking out shorty over there in the corner. Yo, nigga, she's fly as shit. Definitely a dime!" Q pointed in the direction of the young lady.

I turned around to see what all the excitement

was about. I recognized the female instantly. Evidently, my dick recognized her as well because it rose at the sight of her.

I'd seen this chick at all my latest parties and charity events, and she never even looked at me twice. I assured Q there was no chance in hell of them hooking up. "Man, I know that broad. I've had my eye on her for about six months now. Ain't shit jumping."

I'm not the type to approach a female because very few of them can be trusted, but that chick— I'd peeped her game, and she was one I would definitely try my luck with. I glanced at her again to see if I might be able to get her this night. She was sitting with a young lady and someone who might have been her man. They chatted and laughed as though they had a close relationship, yet they didn't show any affection. I figured the dude was either a platonic friend or a relative, but I knew I could certainly rule out a significant other. The other female sitting with them didn't look very happy. I figured she was probably a disgruntled friend. I was usually on point when analyzing any situation.

"Yo, Dee!" Q interrupted my train of thought. "Can we handle our business so I can get the fuck out of here?" I could tell Q's impatient side was coming out, so I switched my focus back to our business.

"A'ight, nigga. I got you the white girl, same weight and height," I told him.

I had been thinking about giving him some heroin along with the coke to make things a little better this time, but his impatience was just one of many telltale signs that told me it wasn't time to promote Q's status in the game just yet.

Q gave a slight expression of disappointment. "Damn, man. I've been pushing this same thing for a minute now. It's time to switch up the numbers or something. I hear you got some other niggas playing both sides of the fence, so why the hell am I only holding the white girl?" Q asked, confirming my assumption about his readiness.

There was no way in hell I was going against my instincts. Q was impatient, which meant he would rush when it came to making money. Rushing leads to carelessness; carelessness leads to getting locked up, getting robbed, or getting killed. I wanted no parts of any of those things. There was no way I was going to lose my freedom or my empire at the hands of a sloppy associate. I was careful to choose the correct words when explaining this to Q. I wanted to be firm without insulting him.

"Q, the game is very tricky. You have to read into every person and every situation you encounter. You have to predict the outcome of every situation. I think we should just chill with what we're doing right now. You know, not rush things. It's enough dough for everybody, and the white girl and heroin are good and plenty, so just relax."

He seemed to understand my point, but he wasn't willing to give in so easily.

"Dee, I've been your right hand man for nearly five years now. I was there before there was an empire. What more is it gonna take for me to prove myself to you? Maybe it just ain't no winning with you, man. You don't trust nobody. I mean, you holding me down. I'm trying to step my game up. Other niggas be hollering at me every day trying to get me on their team, but I stay faithful to you. And now you bullshitting me."

I glanced back to see if the young lady was still sitting in the same spot before turning my attention back to Q. "You're not my right hand man. I'm a one-man army. You know that shit." I began to tune him out because I already knew where this conversation was headed.

Like every hungry nigga in the drug game, he felt like it was time for a promotion, but he hadn't proven shit to me, and I refused to put my empire on the line for some starving, careless nigga.

Q continued blabbing as I checked out shorty. This time when I looked, I caught her eye. She gave me a seductive smile then continued to watch me from the corner of her eye as she talked with her friends. That was all the confirmation I needed. Tonight would be the night I would holla at her.

"Diablo! You hear me, man?" Q interrupted my thoughts once again.

"I feel you, man," I responded. That was the safest response I could give considering the fact that I wasn't listening to anything he'd been saying for the last two minutes.

"So, what's it gonna be, man?" Q demanded an answer.

I had no idea he had given me an ultimatum.

Now, how the hell am I supposed to respond this time? I can't ask the man to repeat himself. I had to think fast. Just as I looked up, I saw the young lady walking toward the restroom with the other chick from the table. That was my chance. Saved by the bell!

"I'll be right back, Q. Let me run to the restroom real quick, man."

I jumped from the booth and headed toward the restroom right behind her. The other chick from the table noticed me. She gave me an evil glare.

That shit threw me off, but I kept following them, trying to figure out what the fuck that look was about. The closer I got, the more doubtful I became. I wasn't sure if shorty would be down with the program, and I wasn't willing to risk blowing up my spot. So, instead of speaking to her, I just went into the men's restroom wondering what move I should make.

I know this chick is hot. I've wanted her for about six months now. This is the perfect opportunity. What the hell am I waiting for? But that bitch she's with is throwing shade. Maybe that dude at the table really is her man. I doubt it, but if he is, I don't need no beef to draw attention to me while I'm here doing business. What's more important?

That final question solved everything. I decided I better pass on the opportunity this time. Bitches come and go, but my empire might not be forever. "Money over bitches," I reminded myself as I looked at the display on my phone. I had programmed the letters MOB underneath the time so that I would always remember to keep my priorities straight.

I walked out of the restroom prepared to finish up things with Q, but he was nowhere to be found. I returned to the empty booth and called him on his phone. There was no response. I found that pretty peculiar, but I wasn't wasting no time figuring that shit out. I figured if he wanted to dip out without taking the coke I brought him, then that was on him. I left fifty dollars on the table, which was more than enough to cover the check, and headed toward the exit. As I rushed out the door, I nearly knocked over the young lady standing there.

"I'm sorry," I said before realizing it was the one I'd been checking out at the other table.

"Looks like you're in a hurry. I guess you better take my number down quickly then, huh?"

She caught me totally off guard. I was surprised at her aggressiveness.

"A woman that likes to take charge. I like your style. Let me put your number in my phone." I pulled out my personal cell and flipped it open. "What's your name, beautiful?"

"Cookie," she responded with a beautiful smile and beautiful African accent to match.

Cookie. I knew that wasn't her government name, and I never dealt with nicknames, but I would save that conversation for another time.

"Okay, *Cookie*. What's the number?" I was sure to put emphasis on the name to let her know she wasn't fooling anyone with her bullshit nickname. She gave me the number and I promised to give her a call the next day.

I looked around the parking lot for Q's car as I headed to my whip. There was no sign of him any-place. I started up my car and pulled out of the parking lot just as carefully as I pulled in. Within minutes I was on I-95 heading south. I had no idea what happened with Q, but pulling a stunt like that had certainly placed him number one on the "suspicious niggas" list. I set the cruise control and rode home in silence, thinking about Cookie the entire way.

CHAPTER TWO
Anyeh

I knew it would be hard to get someone like Diablo. He was a big player in the game, so he was careful about who he associated with. From my research, I knew that chicks headed number one on his shit list. Supposedly, he'd never had a girlfriend; he felt they were greedy, and he definitely wasn't looking for no baby mommas. But like every man, no matter how wise or careful, he was still attracted to pussy, and that was exactly what I planned to use to get my hands on him. I was certain that with patience and very careful moves, I would eventually reel him in.

I'd waited a long time for an opportunity to grab this guy. Diablo James was not the average man. He was really low key and dealt with very few people. In order to get in his circle, I would have to lay low and just go with the flow. I knew if I seemed too anxious it would only run him away. But I'd been waiting long enough. When I saw the way he was watching me in the restaurant, I knew it was the night to make my move.

Diablo assured me he would be calling me the next day, so I was anticipating his call. It was common knowledge that he was a man of his word. Of course, before he called he would probably ask as many people as he could about "Cookie." Little did he know that I was just as smart as he was, if not smarter. I gave him that phony nickname intentionally. No one knew me by Cookie, so he'd never find out anything. Whatever he would learn about me, I wanted to tell him myself. I wanted to create my own image before he could get a false image of me from someone who barely knew me at all. I refused to let anyone ruin this for me.

I'd worked long and hard to get Diablo within my reach. I'd been back and forth from Philly to Virginia continuously for the past year trying to get Diablo. Although my baby made sure I had living arrangements in Virginia, I flew back to Philly on a regular basis to keep my baby updated with the latest reports.

Ring, ring, ring. My baby was calling me on the cell phone I kept especially for those calls.

"Yes, my baby," I answered, anxious to report the good news.

"What is the status?" my baby inquired.

"Well, last night I gave Diablo my number, and I'm expecting a call from him some time today. He's usually a man of his word, so I'm sure I'll get a call," I explained.

"Okay. Well, keep me posted."

"Will do," I said, and quickly wrapped up the phone call.

Calls between my baby and me were usually brief. We never talked about anything except my progress with Diablo.

I became anxious as I waited for his call. I decided to browse through the many resources I'd collected on Diablo. I had everything from newspaper articles to radio interviews to newscast videotapes. Diablo was a favorite of the media, who constantly ran stories about his accomplishments. He'd gone from a "dead-end orphan" to a "great entrepreneur." His foundation, From the Ground Up, raised money for the poor. He was like a black savior to them, offering hope to many people in the ghetto. They felt that if he could rise up, maybe they could too.

Little did they know he'd accepted his title under false pretenses. No one had any idea that Diablo was a huge drug lord. He had done very well convincing the general public that he was an entrepreneur. He owned a chain of what he liked to call "your one stop shop," a combination barbershop, beauty salon, nail shop and car wash. The media reported that he had started the successful business with a small inheritance from one of his foster parents, but that wasn't the true story. When he got his inheritance, he actually used it to start his drug empire. In no time, he had made enough money to get his shops up and running so he could have a legitimate front for his illegal activities. He was always sure to keep the drugs separate from his businesses, so he was able to maintain his image for the media. The rest is history.

My cell rang while I was reading the newspaper articles I'd collected. I glanced at the caller ID and saw that it was a blocked number. It could only be one person—Diablo James. I didn't hesitate to answer.

"Hello," I answered in my sweetest voice.

"Cookie?"

"Yes, this is Cookie. Whom am I speaking with, please?" I played as though I had no clue it was him.

"How you doing, Cookie? This is Diablo. I met you—"

"I know who you are, Dee," I quickly interrupted.

"Dee? I don't recall telling you my name was Dee." He immediately sounded uneasy.

Damn. I was fucking up, moving a little too fast. I couldn't let Diablo know exactly how much I knew about him. He would either write me off as a stalker or someone trying to get a baby momma status. I had to slow down my pace and not seem too anxious.

"Oh, I'm sorry, Diablo. I'm just more comfortable using nicknames. You don't mind Dee as a nickname do you?" I tried my best to clean up my mistake.

Diablo was not moved by the sweet talk. "Let's just stick to Diablo for now. But I am glad you brought that up, Ms. Cookie. What's your real name, sweetheart?"

"Well, if you must know, my name is Anyeh," I gave him my real name as an attempt to gain a little trust.

"Your name is just as beautiful as you are. You should be proud to tell people your name," he stated.

We continued our conversation for another thirty minutes. Diablo was intrigued by my accent and wanted to know all about my African heritage. I told him the little I could. Although I spent my childhood years in Africa, I'd lived in the United States since my preteen years. I did share the few things I could. It was just enough to satisfy Diablo's curiosity.

It took some work, but I finally earned enough trust for Diablo to set up a date. We decided to have dinner the next day at a quiet restaurant at the portside area of downtown Portsmouth.

As soon as we ended our conversation, I wasted no time calling my baby. I picked up the designated cell phone and called right away.

"What's the report?" my baby asked after answering on the first ring.

"I have some great news." I was excited to share the details of my conversation with Diablo.

I told my baby everything from start to finish, making sure not to leave out one single detail. I ended the conversation with the great news about the date.

"Okay, good. First step accomplished. Call me when you have more news."

Although showing little enthusiasm, I knew in the end my baby would be pleased and so would I. My baby was aware of my sexual influence on men. We both knew that if I could just get an hour alone with Diablo, he would be mine to keep.

Now that I'd updated my baby, it was time to call the love of my life, Tiara. I'd met her in Norfolk at one of Diablo's many events. He'd sponsored everything from celebrity basketball games to car shows to auctions, raising money for his foundation. Of course, I'd attended every function since I started my mission to get Diablo.

"What's up, momma?" Tiara said as soon as she picked up the phone.

Just hearing her voice excited me. With my constant trips back and forth to Philly, we hadn't been able to see each other often.

"Nothing much. Just got back in town and wanted to come through if it's okay."

"Of course you can come through and check me. Hell, you better! It's been days since I've seen you, and you know how I feel about that." It always upset Tiara when she didn't see me or at least hear from me.

I wasted no time preparing myself. I packed an overnight bag then glanced through my closet, wondering what I would wear on my date with Diablo the next day. I wanted to choose an outfit that was classy, yet sexy enough to complement my voluptuous breasts and ass.

I decided I would wear my locks back in a perfect little bun on the ride side of my head to reveal my beautiful, round African face. As far as panties and a bra were concerned, there was no need to choose any because I had no intention of wearing them. Diablo was definitely a challenge, so I decided to use everything from charm to sex appeal to get him in my arms. I knew my hustle had to be tight and I had to come at him from a totally different angle than I was used to. There were no limits. To Diablo I would bow down, be submissive, and wait on him hand and foot. I would do things that no woman would ever dream of. He would be a true test of the powers of the pussy.

I laid my clothes on the bed, turned out the lights and jumped in the car. I turned off my baby's cell phone on the way. I wanted no disturbance or drama during my quality time with Tiara. I was sure there would be hell to pay if my baby knew I was with Tiara; the jealousy toward anyone I had relations with was ridiculous.

Tiara met me at the door. Standing at the front door, I could smell the spaghetti cooking. Tiara's spaghetti was my favorite.

"Hey, baby." She greeted me with a smack on the lips.

I smiled as I headed to the bedroom to leave my bags. While we ate dinner, I told her all about Diablo. Luckily, she wasn't the jealous type. And even if she was, I would just assure her that no one could ever take her place.

After dinner we prepared for bed. As I showered, I thought about how close I was to getting Diablo in my arms. I became moist as I imagined certain benefits of getting this fine man. There was only one thing left to do to ease my lustful desires—the same thing I'd been doing since I was a teen. If I wanted some sleep, I had to please myself.

I jumped out of the shower and slipped into the bed where Tiara lay sleeping. I closed my eyes and placed my hands between my thighs. It wasn't long before my moans of pleasure woke Tiara. She grabbed my hand. Interrupting the love I made alone, she gave me a gentle kiss on my neck and caressed my nipple. I removed my hand slowly. There was no doubt what I wanted, and I knew Tiara would please me. She slid her hand across my stomach to my vagina and began a continuous motion on my clit until my body shivered with pleasure. I moaned as my vagina pushed out the moisture of ecstasy onto Tiara's fingers. The wetness she felt along with the shiver of my body was a definite indication I was satisfied. Without saying a word, Tiara removed her hand, licked her fingers clean to savor the taste, and kissed me. Now it was time for me to return the favor. I treated her with the same passion she had given me. She reached her peak quickly, and minutes later we were off to sleep.

CHAPTER THREE
Keysha

Ring, ring! My house phone rang, nearly scaring me out of my skin.

I hesitantly rolled over to check the caller ID. I figured it could only be my social worker or bill collectors calling this early in the damn morning. The caller ID read TONY MONTANA.

To my surprise it was my big bro, Diablo. I laughed each time I saw that name appear across my caller ID. Dee was definitely the Tony Montana of the Tidewater area of Virginia.

"What's up, big bro?" I was always happy to hear from him.

"Hey, Keysh, I got some good news for you."

I wondered what the hell Dee would have to say that was so good he had to call me first thing in the morning. I figured he was either opening a new store or buying a new car. I knew it wouldn't be what I dreamed of hearing though. I always waited for the day Dee would say he was going to get my son back.

"What it is, Dee?" I asked with little enthusiasm.

"I got a girl that I'm interested in and I'm gonna take her out today."

I didn't know if this was good or bad. I mean, I knew Dee needed someone in his life, so if this chick turned out to be someone who could make him happy, that was a good thing. On the other hand, since he didn't trust women enough to keep one by his side, I was always able to remain his number one. How would things change if there was someone else in his life?

"Hello? Keysha? So, what do you think?"

I wanted to be honest, but my real reason for keeping everyone away from him was selfish. Instead of admitting this, I just pointed out what my brother always noted as most important.

"Well, Dee, I guess it's nice that you've finally found someone that's a possible candidate, but how do you know that you can trust her? You know how these females are these days. She probably just want you for your money."

I tried my best to convince my brother he was better off alone. Shit, if he wanted someone, I could have hooked him up with my girl, Kita. At least we knew all there was to know about her.

"Come on, sis. You should know me better than that. I've been peeping out this girl for six months now. She's harmless. Hell, I had to get at her. She wasn't even interested in my game at first."

Dee was obviously starting to get irritated, so I tried to lighten things up a little.

"Okay. Well, I'm happy for you, but if that bitch makes one false move, her ass is mine. Anyway, what's the hooker's name so I can have my girls check her out?"

Dee happily gave up her information. "Her name is Anyeh. She's from Africa, and she goes by the nickname Cookie." I guess he was confident I wouldn't find no dirt on her ass. Little did he know my girls out in the projects were better than Wavy News 10, and they were definitely on my side.

"A'ight, Dee. Enjoy, and be sure to call me and tell me all the details of your date. I'm sure by the end of the night you would have changed your mind about her anyway. Holla, you little faggot!" I laughed as I hung up on him.

The more I thought about it, the more the realization set in. *Right now I'm Dee's one and only. I can get anything from him, and no one comes before me. If he finds someone else, I may lose my crown.*

There was no way I was losing my place at the top to some money-hungry ho. I knew that bitch only wanted one thing from my brother, and I'd be damned if I was going to let her get it. I wasted no time calling my girls and putting out a ghetto APB on her African ass. It was now nine o'clock in the morning, and my brother's date wasn't until that evening. I figured that would give me more than enough time to gather the info and blow up that little hussie's spot.

I wanted all the information possible on her; from her place of work to the location of her dentist. Hell, I even requested a copy of the bitch's green card. With my tainted background and the title of Diablo James' little sister, anything was possible.

Half the day had passed and I still had no info. I was beginning to get a little worried. There was no way I was letting that date go down. It was sad and desperate, but I even thought about faking a little trip to the emergency room if I had to. Hey, desperate times call for desperate measures. The time was ticking and my palms began to sweat. Just as seven o'clock hit, my phone rang.

"Hello?" I answered urgently.

"Hey, girl," Kita said.

From her unenthusiastic tone, it sounded like bad news.

"Please tell me you have some info," I begged desperately.

"Yeah, girl! Shit, you think I'd be calling if I didn't? Videos is on, and I don't be trying to miss my videos for nobody, okay? Anyway, I was at the African braiding shop today, and they said they ain't never heard of no African chick by the name of Cookie. And you know those minorities stick together, girl. They know every damn African in the area. They pray together, play together, and stay together. And get this—you know that name you told me? Well, the girl up there told me it means *bad* in their language, so you know the bitch is sheisty. Don't nobody be naming they child no shit like that! So, I don't even know if the bitch exists for real. Girl, she a fake, a phony, a got-damn fagazy!"

That was all I needed to hear. I quickly ended the phone call with Kita and got dressed. It was too late to stop the date, but nothing said I couldn't end it in the middle. Better late than never. I hopped in my Honda and pressed the pedal to the floor, headed to the restaurant Diablo told me he was taking her to. I'd never forced my little car to go so fast, but if the engine blew, so be it. It would be well worth it. I flew over the bridge and through the tunnel and arrived at the restaurant in seven minutes flat.

Once inside, I instantly spotted Dee and the chick at the bar, sipping on some bubbly.

Play it cool, Keysha. Play it cool, I reminded myself. I didn't want to just run up and start blabbing off at the mouth. I wanted to handle this in a professional way, but the ghetto in me always had a tendency to come out somewhere down the line. I vowed to make an honest attempt to keep that side of me restrained.

As I got closer to the bar and saw this wench giggling and sipping Cristal in my brother's face, I became angry. That was it. My ghetto side was in full force now.

"You fake, you phony, you got-damn fagazy!" I repeated Kita's words from earlier.

Dee looked at me in astonishment, but quickly looked to Cookie for an explanation. I folded my arms across my chest and waited to see how the bitch would try to talk her way out of this.

"Ha, ha, ha. How comical. You all are looking at me as if I owe someone an explanation. I think the explanation is owed by you, young lady," she stated calmly, holding her champagne glass and pointing her pinky finger at me.

I was infuriated that this chick was actually trying a make a fool out of me. My first instinct was to break that damn finger of hers right off, but instead, I snatched her glass and threw Cristal all over her. Dee jumped up and grabbed me, which pissed me off even more. I couldn't believe he was protecting her.

"Now I owe you an explanation, bitch," I shouted as Dee pulled me out of the restaurant.

"Keysha, what the fuck is wrong with you?" Dee demanded an answer.

I explained to him all the information Kita had shared with me. To my surprise, Dee seemed un-moved. In fact, he gave me the same ridiculous laugh as the African bitch inside.

"Come on, now. How many times have I told you not to listen to Kita and her bullshit? You know they call her the mouth of the South. Half the time her information ain't even correct."

"But, Dee," I protested, "I think she's right. This African bitch is sheisty."

"I tell you what—let's go in and ask her about what you just told me." Dee escorted me back in-side the restaurant lobby where Cookie waited.

"Anyeh, let me start by apologizing for my sis-ter's behavior."

I rolled my eyes and sucked my teeth loudly. I did not need to be apologizing to that bitch. Sooner or later, Diablo would know my feeling about her was right.

"There are a few things I need you to clear up for me, though," Diablo continued.

He turned to me and said, "Keysha, tell Anyeh everything you just told me outside."

I let her have it with my best in-your-face, head turning, finger-snapping attitude. I broke down all the evidence I had as though I was Virginia's best commonwealth attorney. And again the bitch laughed.

"No, no darling. It is true that when pronounced with a long A my name means bad in the Twi lan-guage, but my name is pronounced An-yah, not An-yay. And as far as those in the African community not knowing me, you are right. They may not know of me because I never participate in any of the African festivities. I have been in America living with an American family since I was eleven, so I embrace the American culture. Aside from my accent, I have very little in common with the people in the African community." She finished her explanation and gave me a smirk like she thought she had just won.

"Fine," I stated as I gathered myself to walk away. This was not over. I would just have to get my girls to dig a little deeper for information.

"Hold up!" Dee grabbed my arm before I could leave. "Don't you owe her an apology?"

I looked at him like he'd lost his ever-loving mind. *I know this nigga ain't tripping.*

Cookie must have known the deal because she grabbed his hand and stated, "No, it's quite alright. It was just a big misunderstanding. Let her go."

Dee released his firm grip and I left in a hurry. I gave that deceitful bitch one last evil stare to let her know the battle was not over. I was the queen and she would never wear my crown.

CHAPTER FOUR
Anyeh

"Whew, what a night!" I sighed as I flopped on the bed.

I wasted no time calling my baby to give the latest update. "My baby!" I shouted into the phone, full of excitement.

"What is the report?" my baby firmly responded.

"Everything went great. I can tell he's feeling me, but I'm gonna have one problem. I'm not sure just how major yet, but she's definitely gonna be a thorn in my side."

"Oh yeah? Which one is it, the infamous baby momma drama or fatal attraction?"

"Neither," I replied. "Diablo would never stand for either of those."

"Oh, I guess I forgot who we were dealing with for a moment," my baby responded, full of sarcasm. "This is Mr. High and Mighty, Diablo James."

I ignored my baby's response. I was sure it was spoken out of jealousy. I expected my baby to get to this point, only not so soon.

"Anyway, it's his jealous-ass sister, Keysha. The bitch tried to sabotage me tonight at the restaurant. Luckily, she's an ignorant ghetto bitch and it wasn't too hard to outsmart her, but I can tell she's not gonna give up easily. She's the only female Diablo has ever let get close to him. In fact, she's the only person in his family that he really deals with. It's going to be hard to compete with her because she's his everything. She's the only one that's been on his side from the start. Even when he was dead broke she was there. No matter what he does, good or bad, she's got his back. For now, she's the love of his life, but not for long. I plan to change that real soon," I assured my baby.

My doorbell chimed unexpectedly. I walked to the door cautiously as I continued talking with my baby. I had no idea who could possibly be at my door this late. Tiara would never just pop up. I grabbed the nine my baby had given me, just in case it was an unwanted guest. I peeped out the window and to my surprise, it was Diablo. I opened the door without hesitation, forgetting all about my baby still listening on the phone.

"What are you doing back here?" I questioned since he'd just dropped me off less than twenty minutes ago.

He didn't respond. He wrapped his arms around me and pulled me close. He placed his wet, warm tongue in my mouth, engulfing my small frame in his towering body. I shivered with excitement as he took my hands and wrapped them around his waist. I wanted him just as much as he wanted me, so I didn't resist. I gave myself to him. I dropped the phone and my clothes right behind it. We didn't even make it up the stairs to the bedroom. In fact, we didn't make it any farther than the mini-bar in the living room before Diablo was undressed as well.

My heart raced and my body trembled as I realized what was about to take place. After fantasizing for years about what it would be like to be penetrated by a man, I was about to lose my virginity to Diablo. My mind screamed "no"; my body begged "yes." The moisture between my legs was a true signal that my body was overpowering my mind. I could no longer fight it. The purity I'd held for so long was about to leave me forever. Diablo bent me over the sink and firmly gripped my waist.

"No." I grabbed his hand and turned around in an attempt to stop him.

"You don't want me to stop," he assured me, looking at me seductively.

He was right; I didn't want him to stop. I wanted every inch of him, but I couldn't proceed without warning him of my inexperience.

"Diablo, I want you just as much as you want me, but there's something I think you should know." I paused and put my head down.

"What is it, Anyeh?" he asked while lifting my head.

I exhaled then quickly forced out the words. "I'm a virgin."

He smiled at me. "That's nothing to be ashamed of, baby girl. I'm honored to be your first." He kissed me gently.

I took a deep breath as he turned me back around and inserted what seemed like the penis of a Mandingo.

"Aaaahhhh! Diablo, please be gentle with me," I begged.

Diablo became even more careful, with each stroke turning the pain to pleasure. My head fell back as I enjoyed the ecstasy. This was the moment I'd longed for. For twenty years I'd lived as virgin, reaching orgasms by masturbation and female tongue penetration only. I wanted to finally experience sex so badly that I willingly gave myself to Diablo, not thinking about the consequences.

"Diablo," I whispered his name. He'd truly taken me to another land, to places I'd never been before.

"Yes, baby," he responded while slowly kissing my neck.

My body collapsed with paralyzing pleasure. I couldn't say anything more. I couldn't force out another word, so I just panted with full enjoyment. The more I panted, the more he gave it to me. He placed his hand in my locks and grabbed them firmly, forcing my head up. Then he squeezed my waist, forcing himself deeper inside me. The pleasure quickly switched to pain as he neared his peak. I noticed our reflection in the mirror of the mini-bar. Behind me stood the most untouchable man in the Tidewater area, and I had him to myself.

As I stared at my image, I didn't see a worthy woman; instead, I saw a deceitful bitch. I closed my eyes rather than face the true me. My stomach turned as I thought about what I had been planning for so many months. I could feel the moisture between my legs slowly disappear.

I'd taken note of all the moves and words from the numerous pornographic DVDs Tiara and I had watched together. I had to do something fast before he noticed the change, and things turned into a disaster. "Cum for me, Diablo. Cum for me. This is yours, baby," I whispered.

"Ahhh! Ahhh! Ahhh!" I screamed in pain as he finally reached his peak.

With both exhilaration and exhaustion I opened my eyes once again, hoping the previous image would not appear before me. Instead of the deceitful image, it was Diablo's beautiful frame I saw. It wasn't until that point I noticed he was holding my gun. I couldn't help but notice the firm grip he had on it.

"What's wrong? You're just now noticing this?" he asked while holding up my gun.

"Yes," I reluctantly admitted.

"Damn, baby. You gotta be more observant than that. I've been holding onto this since the first kiss when I walked through the door."

"So, you've had it in your hand the entire time, through sex and everything?" I was disappointed in my oblivion.

"Never once put it down," he responded as he gathered his clothes. "Which way is the bathroom?"

How could I have been so stupid? I wondered as I led him to the bathroom in a daze. *Right now he has one up one me, and that's not good. He probably thinks he's smarter than I am, but I will definitely prove him wrong. I shall prevail in the end.*

Five minutes later, Diablo was out of the restroom and heading for the door.

"You're not going to stay awhile? It's late. Why don't you just sleep here?" I asked, hoping to convince Diablo to spend a little more time with me, so I might redeem myself.

"Sorry, baby girl, but I've got a lot to do in the

morning. I've gotta get outta here. Maybe next time." He kissed me on my cheek and headed for the door. I followed behind to let him out.

My phone rang as we approached the door. Diablo looked down at the phone, still on the floor where I had dropped it.

"Your baby is calling. Must be important he's calling this late," he stated. Obviously, he had seen the caller ID screen.

I froze for a second, unsure of what to do.

"Well, aren't you gonna answer it?" Diablo asked with sarcasm as the phone continued to ring.

As much as I didn't want to, I had to answer it or Diablo would become more suspicious. I picked up the phone and flipped it open, planning to simply tell my baby to wait for me to call back later.

"Hel—"

"What the fuck was that?" My baby was shouting before I could even finish a word.

I quickly flipped the phone shut and prayed Diablo hadn't heard anything.

"Okay, well, I guess I'll talk to you tomorrow," I said, trying to hide my nervousness. I was anxious for him to leave before my baby called back.

"Yeah," he responded. His expression made it clear that he didn't like what had just happened. I breathed a sigh of relief, though, when he left without asking me any questions about the call.

Once Diablo was out of sight, I called my baby back.

"What the hell is wrong with you?" I yelled into the phone.

"Who the hell are you yelling at?" My baby wasted no time putting me back in my place. "I heard everything. Seems to me that you're losing focus. Don't get too lost. It could be a major downfall," my baby threatened.

I didn't know exactly what my baby heard, so I tried to play stupid.

"What are you talking about, my baby?"

"Anyeh, I heard everything. I knew you were gonna be weak, but I already made provisions for that. So, do your thing. Just don't forget how much you have on the line."

I was frightened because I knew my baby meant business. I had to get Diablo or I would never be able to free myself of my baby's fixed grip.

"What do you mean?" I asked, trying to act like I didn't know.

"Don't insult me, Anyeh. You just dropped the phone on the floor. You didn't even bother to hang it up. I listened to your whole escapade, and you know damn well what I mean. You know our agreement, so I'll let you make the decisions. I'm giving you just enough rope to hang yourself."

"Please just trust me. I've got everything under control. Maybe I shouldn't involve you as much. I'll keep you posted on what's important. May I go now?"

With my baby's permission, I hung up the phone, angry at the truth that I was just faced with. My baby was right; there were a lot of things I did wrong when Diablo was here. I had to stay focused or I would fuck things up in a major way.

I started a hot shower. I thought about all the events of the night as I washed the mixture of blood and semen from my inner thighs. My stomach turned as I reminisced about the first time I experienced semen dripping down my legs.

* * *

"Never, never, speak to strangers while fetching water. And especially men!" I vividly remembered my grandmother warning the girls of the village.

It wasn't long before I understood why. Daily, my developing young body would draw the attention of all the men of the village. Each morning they would come to the riverside and fetch water just so they could see me. Young and ignorant, I loved the attention and began to flirt. Flirting, I eventually found out, was a deadly decision.

One quiet morning I sat at the riverside fetching water. The man that I'd flirted with for so many days came near me. This day was unusual because instead of the many people who regularly fetched water at the riverside, it was only he and I. The man grabbed me, knocking my bucket from my hand. I knew exactly what was about to happen. I screamed for help, only for no one to hear. He continued to hold me as he forced himself on top of me, his hands exploring my body. I could feel his penis rise once he felt my clitoris.

"I knew you were one with a clit." The words of the man pierced my heart. My village believed in keeping a female's purity through circumcision of the clitoris. This was believed to deter a woman from any sexual desire, insuring that she would remain a virgin until marriage. I happened to be one of the very few women who were not circumcised. The fact that I had a clitoris instantly aroused the old man.

I cried as he continued to violate me by caressing my clitoris. He licked my nipples and fondled my vagina. It wasn't long before I felt moisture run down my legs. He had reached his peak, and his semen dripped down my legs. I jumped up when he released me, and ran back to the village, never looking back. I never shared my experience with anyone.

It wasn't long before I began to wonder what was so

intriguing about the clitoris between my legs. One night I moved my hands between my legs as the old man had done. A paralyzing rush came over my body. This was my first orgasm, and it wasn't long before I yearned to have an orgasm daily. Each night it became a custom for me to masturbate alone before I was off to sleep.

To this man, I owed my sexual addiction. Still, his assault had scarred me emotionally. I was unable to trust men, and even after I left Africa and came to Philly, I stayed away from them as much as possible. When I met Tiara, she was enough to satisfy my sexual appetite, at least until I started watching Diablo. There was something about his strength and power that just made me want to know the feeling of penetration. I was a virgin until I met him, but now everything had changed.

I quickly turned my thoughts elsewhere once I noticed tears running down the side of my face.

What could I have done differently today? I wondered. Sadly, there were many options. I fucked up and I had to face it. I came to grips with the realization and just accepted it as I prepared for sleep. Ashamed at the mistakes and events of the day as well as my past, I didn't even have the guts to call Tiara before going to bed.

"Tomorrow will be a new day," I said as I dozed off to sleep.

CHAPTER FIVE
Diablo

*A*nyeh *is everything a man could dream,* I thought as I watched her sleep as peacefully as an angel. The past few weeks had been perfect. In fact, it seemed too perfect. I'd never had an experience with a woman go so smoothly. To be honest, it kinda made me worry. Most women that had gotten this far always had a hidden agenda, but so far I hadn't been able to find one flaw in Anyeh. She waited on me hand and foot, she gave me her virginity, and all she wanted was for me to be happy. Either she had a hell of a game or I was pussy whipped. Hell, I was only expecting to fuck, but now I was seriously thinking about making Anyeh my girl.

I planned to take Anyeh to Philly to my family reunion. Although I never really had a true family, the Johnsons showed much respect while I lived with them as a foster child, so when they invited me to their family reunion, there was no way I could decline. Besides, I needed Ma Dea's approval of

Anyeh. Ma Dea was the strictest grandmother a kid could have. I knew she would tell all and keep nothing back if she didn't approve. That would be the final determination. If Anyeh could get Ma Dea's approval, she was definitely the woman for me.

"Wake up, baby," I whispered in her ear as I gently kissed her neck.

She opened her eyes and gave me that loving smile.

"How could Keysha ever think someone this precious could be conniving?" I wondered aloud.

"Interesting you mentioned that, Diablo." Anyeh sat up in the bed and grabbed my hands.

"I've asked myself over and over again what your sister could possibly have against me, and I've only been able to come up with one answer." She lowered her head and inhaled deeply as if she were troubled.

"Diablo, Keysha is jealous of me. Before I came along, she was your everything, your one and only. And now that I am here, it's sad to say, but she looks at me as competition. She's no longer your everything because you have me now."

"Nah, everything's cool," I lied, hoping to avoid a long conversation about this. Anyeh was not letting the subject go so easily.

"Diablo, I know she hates me. Each time she calls the house she says rude things to me if I answer the phone."

I listened attentively as she continued to talk about all the drama Keysha had caused in the past weeks and the truth began to sink in. I had the same thoughts many times before, but I didn't want to face them. I found myself in a constant struggle trying to decide whom to trust.

"I feel ya. It seems like the closer you and I get, the further apart me and Keysha grow. I can't even call my li'l sis and tell her how happy I am with you. Every day it's an argument with her over you. It's gotten to the point that I barely speak to her at all. Before we would speak at least three times a day. You both just need to realize there ain't no competition. There's enough of me for the both of you." I smiled, trying to blow things off easily, although I was still bothered by the subject.

Would Keysha go to such extents just to stay on top or was there something really sheisty about Anyeh? I mean, Keysha had never lied to me before, but Anyeh had shown nothing but love and respect for me as well.

This was an inner struggle I was faced with every day, but each time I was with Anyeh, I felt she was the one for me. I changed the subject before our discussion got too deep.

"I don't know, baby, but no need to worry. Go home and get your things packed. We're heading to Philly for my foster family's reunion this weekend."

Her face lit up with excitement.

"Really? You're really taking me to your family reunion?"

"Yeah. I wouldn't bullshit you. Get your things together," I responded nonchalantly.

I laughed as Anyeh stood on the bed, dancing in circles, twirling her arms as though she were a little league cheerleader.

"I'm going to the reunion. I'm going to the reunion," she sang as she danced.

Plop! Her ass jiggled after I gave her a gentle smack to the buttocks.

"Get down and get dressed before I leave your ass here," I stated as I headed for the door.

She quickly got off the bed and hurried to the bathroom, begging me not to leave her.

"I ain't leaving you. Now, get ready. I'm stepping out for a few, but I'll be by to get you at noon, so be ready."

I headed to each of the seven cities to holla at my team. I had contacts set up in each city. I was president of the empire, and these contacts were my mayors who watched over each city for me. Each mayor had delegates beneath him. My shit was very organized, and that was why I was able to lock things down like I did.

I hollered at each mayor, letting them know I was about to make some moves. Sure, the trip to Philly was for the family reunion, but I was also going there for business purposes. I had a chick up there who was supposed to be heavy in the game. She'd been trying to get at me for a minute to buy some major shit. I figured I might as well take full advantage of the trip and get up with her while I was there.

Now that all my niggas were aware of what was to come, it was time to holla at my li'l sis. Without Keysha, nothing would be going down. She was the only one I could trust to come with me to Philly and handle my package. I knew she always had my back no matter what.

"Keeeeeysh!" I hollered as I unlocked the front door and let myself in.

There was no response. That was odd because her car was parked out front. I figured she might have been next door at her girl Kita's house.

I went into the kitchen and found a letter from Social Services on the table. I scanned it briefly. My heart saddened as I realized it was a rejection letter for the return of her son, Davion. Her request was rejected due to "lack of progress," so the letter stated. It had been months since he was taken from her care.

Keysha owed the loss of Davion to her bitch-ass baby father, Pooky. That nigga had her involved in all types of shit from using drugs to selling them. I truly thought I was going to lose her to the same life as we lost our mother, but when the courts took li'l Davion, that was all the wake up call she needed. She was instructed to attend some rehab classes, see a shrink, and go to some parenting classes and work and shit.

To be honest, I thought that things were going well, but this letter told me different. It was a shame that I'd been so consumed with my own life that I hadn't taken the time to see what was up with my li'l sis getting my nephew back.

"Is there a reason you all in my shit?" Keysha asked as she walked up behind me and snatched the letter from my hand.

I didn't respond, I just looked at her in amazement. Her appearance was horrible. Her hair stood on top of her head, her clothes were dingy and torn, and her body reeked of alcohol and cigarette smoke.

"What's wrong? You see somethin' you don't like?" Her words were slurred.

Keysha was obviously intoxicated and there was no way I was talking business with her like that.

"What's wrong with you, Keysh? It's shit like this

that got you in the predicament you're in. You're heading down the same path as Mommy," I scolded her out of anger.

I was pissed at the condition my sister was in. Our mother had been doing drugs as long as I could remember. My sister and I were taken from her and placed in foster care. Separated and struggling to keep in touch, we were in and out foster homes until age eighteen.

As a kid, I could remember my mom rolling joints at least three times a day. Smoking joints turned into sniffing cocaine, and it wasn't long before I saw her sucking the glass pipe and even shooting heroin into her veins. I saw my mother at her weakest points. There were times she would suck dick right in front of me just to get a hit. My sister and I went without food many times because my mother sold our food stamps for drugs. Christmas, birthdays and school clothes were all non-existent. She couldn't even save ten dollars from her monthly welfare check to make sure we had the necessities. I hated to think Keysha was following her footsteps.

"What the fuck do you care? What the fuck does Social Services care? What the fuck does anyone care?" she rambled. "I've been going to school every-day, working everyday, seeing that stupid-ass head doctor every week, and how has it helped me? It hasn't! I still don't have my son and nobody gives a damn. Not even you!" Keysha was on a rampage.

"Well, getting drunk and feeling sorry for yourself ain't gonna get Davion back!" I shouted at her in disgust.

"Fuck you, Diablo James! That's easy for you to say in your perfect little world. You don't know what it's like. If you were so concerned, you would have helped me get Davion back. You do everything else you want to do, but you haven't helped me with what's most important—my fucking son!" She forced the words out between tears.

I had no response. Keysha was right. I did get anything I wanted, big or small, and I hadn't even thought to help her with the one thing that meant the most. I looked at my sister's tired, feeble body and guilt overwhelmed me.

How could I have been so selfish?

I could feel my eyes welling up with tears so I grabbed my keys and headed for the door, avoiding eye contact with Keysha on the way out. I ran to my car and jumped in. Keysha came behind me.

"Yeah, run from the truth, you little pussy! Run!" she shouted out the front door.

Well that's a wrap on any business I was planning to handle this weekend, I thought as I headed home. No one else was trustworthy. If my li'l sis couldn't do it, no one would.

I arrived at my house fifteen minutes later, hoping Anyeh would be back and ready to head out. The morning was stressful enough, and I knew if she wasn't ready it would only frustrate me more. To my surprise, she was not only there, she had my bags packed and the house was spotless as well.

"Hi, baby. Ready to go?" She greeted me with a kiss as I entered the front door.

I was so dumbfounded by her preparedness, I stood there in shock.

"You okay?" she asked.

"Sure, baby. You just caught me off guard. I wasn't expecting you to be ready, that's all. And you packed my bags and cleaned my house too. Baby, you are too good to be true."

"You're my man, and I'm here to serve you, baby. Whatever you need I shall supply," she answered.

As we gathered our things, she handed me four pink slips with phone messages she had taken while I was out. There were four calls: two that weren't even worth wasting the paper, one from Keysha, and one that worried me a whole lot.

Anyeh noticed the uneasy look on my face. "Is everything okay, Dee—I mean, Diablo?"

"No need to worry, baby. And it's okay if you call me Dee."

I started the car and pulled out. During the first thirty minutes of our travel we rode in silence. My brain was racing as I thought about the last phone message. It was from Q, saying to call him ASAP.

What the hell could this nigga possibly want? I haven't heard from this nigga in over a month. He just disappeared off the face of the earth and then decides to call me out of nowhere. This nigga gotta either be up to some grimy shit or be the police. There's no way he'll be hearin' from me. I've seen everything from niggas getting snitched on by envious niggas, to cats getting robbed by niggas that wanted to rise up on someone else's behalf. I don't know where Q stands, but I ain't wasting no time finding out. All contact is cut off. Game over, Q!

Hooooonk! Hoooooonk!

"Baby!" Anyeh yelled in a panic.

"Where the fuck you get your license?" an old lady yelled out the window as she passed us.

"You nearly ran her off the road. What's bothering you?" Anyeh asked nervously.

I never wanted to involve Anyeh in my business, but I was starting to feel like she earned the right to know at least what she was dealing with. I decided to tell her general information about my involvement in the game—just enough to give her an idea. I figured it was best to leave out any in-depth details until much later during our relationship. I spent the rest of the trip telling her mostly about my past, and what led up to the start of my empire.

"My mother was a junkie, so I learned about drugs early in life. I watched her progress from the small stuff to a serious addiction. She was so bad that she would neglect me and my sister just to get a hit. We ended up in foster care before we were ten years old.

"I jumped from one foster family to the next until I was eighteen. By that time I knew the streets in and out, and I learned everything there was to know about drugs. The more time I spent on the streets, the more knowledge I gained. I eventually learned the different costs of drugs, and the jail time given for each charge if I was caught with the drug.

"I knew so much, and I figured I was smarter than most of the niggas out there sellin', so when one of my foster parent left me a little money in her will, I bought me a little somethin' to sell and flipped it over real quick. The rest, as they say, is history."

Anyeh listened quietly as I told her my story. After a while she said, "Damn, so your mother was a drug addict? That must have been terrible for you as a child."

"Yeah," I answered, "but whatever. I really don't resent her for it. I mean, maybe she has a lot to do with how I feel about women now, but hell, it only made me a tougher person, a better businessman. So fuck it. Hats off to her."

"What do you mean how you feel about women?" she asked.

"I don't trust women. I mean, other than Keysha, you're the first one I've really let get close to me. I had some good foster mothers, but a lot of bad ones too, so I ain't tryin' to trust no women now."

"I see," she said, sounding uncomfortable.

I smiled at her. "It's cool, though, Anyeh. You know you my girl. You don't have the same issues some of them other chicks out there have."

She didn't answer, so I continued to pass the time by telling her stories about people I'd met and shit that had happened to me dealing with the game. She seemed pretty interested in what I had to say. That's one thing I liked about her—she was a good listener.

CHAPTER SIX
Anyeh

It had been over a month, and I was speaking to my baby less and less. It had been difficult joggling myself between my baby, Tiara, and Dee, so I decided to do things the way Anyeh wanted them done. I'd finally gained Dee's full trust, and I'd be damned if I would risk losing that for anyone. At this point, I was even evaluating my relationship with Tiara. Dee had told me all about his empire, I made a wonderful impression on his foster family, and I'd practically moved into his place. A few more weeks and he would be eating out of the palm of my hand, then things with my baby could come to an end.

"Good morning, sweetie," I greeted him while serving him breakfast in bed.

I turned the television to his favorite channel and brought him the newspaper before returning to the kitchen to clean up. I checked back with him twenty minutes later. I brought him warm water dashed with fresh lemons and a paper towel to rinse his fingers. This was a daily ritual. I made sure he received royal treatment at all times.

"You ready for your bath?" I asked him.

He confirmed he was ready and I filled the tub with hot water, turned on the jets, and laid his towel nearby. While he was bathing, I cleaned the bedroom and pressed his clothes.

As I cleaned the room I searched for Diablo's stash. I had plans to see my baby and I wanted to bring a little gift. I knew my baby was doubting my ability to complete my task, so I had to bring something back to assure my baby the plan was going accordingly.

I had a good idea where the stash was. I studied the first places he would go each night when he returned home after a long day's work or after a business trip. I'd narrowed it down to a few key places. So far, two out of the three places were empty. Knowing Dee, he'd probably switched his spot every few days. I quickly searched the third spot.

"Jackpot." I whispered as I found what I was looking for.

I grabbed a handful of money and drugs, dropped them in my Gucci pouch, and tossed it behind the dresser as a temporary hiding place.

Bang, bang, bang, bang! There was a loud knock on the front door, nearly scaring the hell out of me. I rushed to see who would be knocking so loudly.

"Hello. How can I help you?" I asked as I opened the door to a strange looking woman who appeared to be in her late forties.

"How can you help me? Who the hell are you?" she asked as she stumbled toward me, trying to force her way through the door.

I was sure this was one of Dee's stray fiends who had followed him home. The bitch was out of line, so I wasted no time straightening her high ass out.

"Excuse me, but you're not coming in here. I don't know if you're sick right now or what, but Dee doesn't allow any—"

Smack!

My sentence was interrupted by a smack in the face and a forceful shove, then the crazy woman was in the house.

"Diaaablooooo!" I shouted at the top of my lungs as I ran toward the bedroom behind the strange woman.

We both met Dee at the bedroom door. He stood soaking wet with a towel wrapped around his waist.

"Mom, what the hell are you doing here?" he asked.

"Mom? You mean—"

"That's right, bitch," his mother slurred the words as she continued toward the kitchen.

"You got something to eat in here, son?" she asked while searching through the cabinets and refrigerator.

I stood motionless as everything that had just happened registered.

This fiend is Dee's mom? You mean I cursed his mother out? I may have just destroyed all the respect and trust I worked so hard to gain.

I walked into the bedroom and sat on the bed as I gathered my thoughts.

"You okay, baby girl?" Dee asked as he walked into the room.

I had to explain myself before his mom had the opportunity to tell her version of things. I apologized and explained the entire situation, sure not to leave out a single detail. To my surprise, Dee was quite understanding. In fact, *he* ended up apologizing to *me* for his mother's actions.

I guess I've got this guy eating out the palm of my hand sooner than I expected. I gave myself a small pat on the back before kissing Dee.

"Thanks for being so understanding."

"No. Thank you," he responded as he hugged me tight.

I watched Dee as he brushed his teeth in the bathroom mirror. My body lusted, forcing my temperature to rise. Since I'd lost my virginity to Dee, I'd lusted for his sexy body every night. He'd replaced the oral sex and masturbation ritual that I'd become so accustomed to. He was so sexy as he stood before me with his tall, masculine body. His waist was wrapped in a huge towel. I wanted so badly to rip off the wrapping and expose the gift underneath.

I could no longer resist. I walked toward the bathroom, taking off an article of clothing each step of the way. Without a word, I pulled off his towel and hopped on the counter in front of him. Just as I'd predicted, Dee wasted no time taking my body into his arms and giving me every inch of the present I so badly wanted. I felt helpless as he blessed me with his paralyzing love.

Bang, bang, bang, bang! His mother knocked on the bathroom door with that same obnoxious pounding as earlier.

"Yeah, Ma," he responded while holding my ass tight, refusing to pull his erect penis out.

I gave him a look of death as an indication that he'd better finish sexing me. I didn't care if the ghost of Ronald Reagan was knocking on the bathroom door. I wanted my orgasm, and by all means, I was going to get it!

"I need to talk to you, boy. Now, come on outta there!" she shouted from the other side of the bathroom door.

"Give me a minute." He forced out the words as I rotated my waist, stimulating his penis even more.

I needed an orgasm, and there was no way I was letting his crack fiend mom ruin it for me. I grabbed his back and sucked his neck as he grabbed my ass and pulled me forward, forcing his penis deep inside me. We both gave a long grunt as we reached our peaks.

"I love you, Dee." The words slipped out of my mouth as tears rolled from my eyes.

Dee froze, grabbed my chin to lift my head, and looked me dead in the eyes.

"I never thought I would say these words to a female, but I love you too, Anyeh." He gently kissed my lips. "But it's no sad occasion, so why the tears, baby girl?" He wiped the tears from my cheeks.

I didn't respond. I just held down my head and shrugged my shoulders. The truth was I didn't know the answer.

Why did I even say I love you? Do I love him? And why am I crying? Is it the passion or is it the sad truth that we could never truly be together?

Dee turned on the shower and we both hopped in. I hoped that all the terrible guilt I had inside would wash away along with the soap from my body.

Bang, bang, bang, bang! His mother pounded on the door again, as a reminder she was still waiting.

Dee rushed out of the shower and got dressed. I came out shortly after him. As I got dressed, I could hear him speaking with his mother in the living room.

"I need some money," she demanded.

"I don't have any money, Momma," I heard Dee lie.

That must have really infuriated her, because she began yelling uncontrollably.

"Keysha already told me about you and that little bitch, Dee. Maybe if you weren't so damn pussy whipped by that gold-digging ho, you would have some damn money! If anybody should be getting money it's your family."

"She has nothing to do with this. It's your drug habit that's keeping me from giving you money. I refuse to support your habit," Dee explained calmly.

"What the hell do you know about my habit? I've been clean for over six months now!" she swore.

"Ma, I'm not buying that bullshit. You're high right now!"

I could tell Dee was fed up, so I had to intervene. I walked in the living room as she screamed in his face.

"You're so fucking selfish. You're out buying this, buying that, and doing whatever Dee wants to do, while your mother is struggling just to put food on the table. And you claim you love Keysha. Well, guess what, Mr. Perfect? Keysha hates you! You're the reason she's drinking and smoking every day. She dropped out of school, stopped working, and is even back with that baby daddy of hers. If you won't support her and help her get her son back, then someone else will. Keysha don't need you, Davion don't need you, and I sure as hell don't need you. We all hate you and we hope you die, Diablo!" She spat in his face and walked off.

"Who the hell do you think you are?" I yelled before jumping up after her.

Diablo grabbed my arm and stopped me in my tracks.

"Let her go, Anyeh. It's not worth it. Let her go," he said full of hurt. "This ain't shit new. Family only cares as long as I'm putting out loot. Otherwise, they could give a damn if I was dead or alive."

We both watched as she walked out the front door with no remorse.

CHAPTER SEVEN
Keysha

*F*uck *this, Keysha. Nobody can get Davion back but you. Who cares about Dee? He hasn't helped you get your son back. You're in this alone, baby girl, so fuck it! Get on your feet and do the damn thang.*

I opened my eyes with yet another terrible hangover. I'd spent the last few weeks drinking, getting high and wasting life away. And you know what? That's why Davion was still not with me.

"Hey, Keysha! Bring me that rim cleaner!" Pooky yelled from the front door.

I slowly rose from the bed and searched for the cleaner.

"Keysha!" Pooky continued to yell.

I didn't have the strength or energy to respond, so I didn't. I continued searching for the cleaner he'd requested. I wasn't sure why I'd even gotten back with Pooky—probably sex and drugs—but his constant yelling was definitely a reminder of why I left his tired ass.

"Keysha!"

Before I could find the cleaner, Pooky was in the house, yelling in my face again.

"I know you fuckin' hear me talking to you, bitch!"

I wasn't in the mood for Pooky or his shit, so I remained silent.

Pop! Splat!

I saw stars before my eyes as I tried to focus. My lip stung with an aching pain as blood trickled from my lip. I took a deep breath as my nostrils flared with anger.

"What the fuck you gon' do, Keysha? Huh? What you gon' do?" Pooky asked while pushing the side of my head.

I tried to walk away peacefully. I headed to the kitchen to gather some ice for my swollen lip. Of course, Pooky followed, still yelling.

"You can't call that bitch-ass brother of yours 'cause he don't give a fuck about you. That's why Davion ain't here now. Dee got the power to do anything he wants, but he can't do something as simple as get your son back. Humph! That nigga ain't shit!"

That was it! This nigga had truly fucked up. One, this had nothing to do with Dee and two, he was saying my son like he ain't have no parts in Davion's conception. I'd had it. I grabbed the butcher knife that sat in the sink beside me, closed my eyes, turned around and swung it with all my strength.

"Ahhhhhhh! You bitch!" was all I heard before opening my eyes.

Pooky stood slumped over, holding his stomach. I watched as he stumbled toward the door. I knew if he made it to the car that just might be the end of my life. I was sure he would shoot me if he could only get the gun in his hands. There was only one thing left to do; it was either him or me.

I ran to the bedroom and lifted the mattress to grab the gun Dee had given me for emergencies. I never thought the day would come when I would actually have to use it, and I definitely never thought it would be my baby daddy I'd shoot. I gripped the gun tightly and walked up behind Pooky. Tears filled my eyes, nearly blinding me. I could no longer see detail; just a blurred figured stood before me.

Crack! A terrible pain raced through my head, forcing me to the floor.

Pop, pop, pop, pop, pop, pop, pop, pop, pop . . . click, click, click. I held down the trigger until the clip was empty.

I lay on the floor motionless as I tried to regain my focus. The room was silent. I opened my eyes to a terrible mess. I realized it was a lamp that Pooky had hit me with. The front door was wide open and the neighbors stood all around. Kita was front and center, but Pooky was nowhere in sight.

"Girl, what the hell is going on?" Kita asked with her ghetto twang.

"Nothing, Kita. Just me and Pooky into it again, that's all."

I tried to keep it simple since I really didn't want to talk, but there was no way the ghetto news anchor was settling for that.

"Whatchu mean y'all into it? I mean, you firing shots and shit and you just gon' say 'y'all into it'? Naw, girl. It's more to it than that, so come wit' it," Kita said while lighting a cigarette.

Luckily the police were on their way. I could hear the sirens from afar, and it gave me an excuse to end the conversation with Kita. I promised her I'd tell her all about it later. I had more important things to do, like trying to think of something to tell the police.

Now how the hell am I going to explain this one? I'm never getting my son back now.

Just as I expected, the police were present in a matter of minutes.

"How you doing, officer? It's amazing the difference in time it takes for y'all to arrive here. A few years back when I lived out the park, it could take half an hour for y'all to arrive, and the crazy thing is y'all had a precinct out the park."

"Enough sarcasm, ma'am. Could you explain what happened here?" the officer asked, his voice full annoyance.

I gave them some bullshit attempted burglary story, enough to keep me in the clear and to get them off my back. I refused medical attention, and minutes later they were off. I walked back into my house, which was a total mess, and made myself a drink. I was truly tired, not only from the events of the day, but tired of life in general. I was ready to throw the towel in on everything.

I rolled myself a blunt as I sipped on my glass of Hennessy straight. Mixed drinks were no longer strong enough. I wondered how much longer I had before weed wasn't strong enough either. I owed much thanks to my mother for those addictions and this wonderful life.

As soon as my nerves were calm and I was starting to feel the effects of the Hen rock and ganja, my doorbell rang. I rushed to reload the gun. I knew it was Pooky and he was back to finish off the brawl. I flung the door open and hid behind the corner, gun aimed like I was the narcotics kicking in the door of a weed house.

"Jesus, help me!" the old lady from next door shrieked, holding her chest as though she was going have a heart attack.

"I'm sorry, Ms. Mary," I said as I withdrew the gun and welcomed her into my chaotic home.

I cleared a spot for us to sit on the couch. I had no idea what Ms. Mary wanted, but I prayed whatever it was she'd be quick. She grabbed my hands and looked me in my eyes.

"Sweetie, I feel the pain that you have." She spoke as though she was inside me.

"I don't have any pain, Ms. Mary. What are you talking about?" I lied, trying to hide my true feelings and rush things along.

"Honey, I am one of God's anointed, and I feel your pain each day in my soul. In fact, that's why I'm here today. I couldn't go to sleep last night because the presence of the demon was so strong."

The words Ms. Mary spoke pierced my heart so very deeply. I struggled to hold back the tears as she continued to speak to me.

"That demon of depression the devil has sent down has no power over you. You must rebuke that evil spirit in Jesus' name." Ms. Mary began to pray for me.

I tried turning away from her, attempting to fight the affects of her prayers. No matter how hard I tried I could no longer hold back the tears. I was no match for the Greater Being. Within seconds, the battle was over. My heart was heavy with pain. I fell to my knees and begged God for forgiveness.

"Please, God. Have mercy on me! Free me, Lord.

Release me from the evil grips of the devil. Free me, Lord. Free me!" I screamed as Ms. Mary held me tight.

I cried all the pain away as Ms. Mary continued to hold me. She rocked me slowly back and forth, repeating the words, "Yes, Jesus. Yes, Jesus."

She rocked me right into a deep sleep. This was the rest my body longed for. I slept peacefully for the first time in weeks.

The next morning, I opened my eyes, my body fully refreshed. Now my motivational speech had a new tune.

Okay, Keysha. This is a new day. Nobody can get Davion back but you and God. Who cares about Dee, your mom, or Pooky? You've got someone much stronger in your corner now, girl. You're not alone, baby girl. This battle is not yours, so do it! Get on your feet and do the darn thang.

This time when I got up, there was no one yelling my name, no alcohol, and no drugs. I got in the shower and washed away all the memories from my terrible past. It was a new day and a new beginning.

CHAPTER EIGHT
Diablo

"One, two, three, four . . . ten, eleven twelve . . . seventeen, eighteen." I counted aloud for the fifth time.

I was sure I had twenty thousand-dollar stacks, and I was never wrong about my calculations. I thought about all the moves I'd made in the past week. There were only two people in my home during that time—my mother and Anyeh—and I would hate to even think either of them would steal from me. I checked all my other stash spots to be sure I hadn't left the other two stacks in one of those places.

"Nope. Empty," I said to myself, puzzled at my loss.

Two grand was nothing, but the thought of someone close stealing from me made me frantic. I searched the room up and down, flipping over the mattress, emptying dresser drawers, and turning over furniture. Hell, I even removed the loose panel in the closet, and still no money was recovered.

"Anyeh!" I yelled at the top of my lungs.

She didn't respond to my desperate call, so I called again.

"Anyeh!"

Still there was no response. I wondered what the hell could be so damn important that she wouldn't answer. I walked all over the house looking for her, and she was nowhere to be found. I knew she couldn't be far because her Gucci purse was sitting on the kitchen counter. I decided to look in the garage to see if her car was in there. As I got closer to the door I could hear Anyeh yelling.

"I understand what you are saying, my baby, but I don't know what you expect me to do!"

I flung open the door, startling her. She quickly ended her telephone conversation.

"My baby, I have to go." She whispered the words as though I wasn't standing directly in front of her and couldn't hear every word she was saying.

An overpowering rage came over me and I knocked her cell phone out of her hand.

"Who the fuck is my baby?" I yelled in her face.

"Baby, please calm down. Let me explain," she begged, trying to hug me at the same time.

I wasn't moved by her phony-ass plea. I forcefully grabbed her arms, throwing them from around my neck. I headed back in the house.

I'm through dealing with this "my baby" person. All the fucking phone calls at all times of the night. She even has a special phone for this mothafucka! And what the fuck is so important that she needed to go in the garage to speak to this person? This shit is crazy! Any other bitch would have been out the door. I knew I should have just fucked this broad and bucked on her ass!

The more I thought about the phone calls, the angrier I got. I knew if I said anything at the moment I'd end up smacking the shit out her ass, so I decided to watch a little TV until I calmed down a bit. Before I could even get comfortable, Anyeh came and stood directly over me.

"What's wrong, Dee? And why is the bedroom all tore up?" She started throwing questions at me like a dartboard.

Who the fuck is she to be questioning me? If anybody should be answering to somebody, it's her ass answering to me.

I didn't speak. I just looked at her and hoped my thoughts would be written all over my face. Evidently it worked, because after reading my expression, she stated, "You're obviously upset over something I did, so let me start over. What did I do to upset you, Dee?"

I could no longer restrain myself, so I let her have it. I figured if the bitch couldn't respect me and do as I ask, fuck her.

"Look, Anyeh. I don't know who the fuck this 'my baby' person is, but I'm sick of the secret phone calls. I tried to trust you and believe you're not fucking with no one else, but things are getting more and more suspicious. I figured this person is someone you were dealing with before me and you would eventually end it, but it doesn't seem like that's gonna happen. So, now I have to give you an ultimatum. It's either 'my baby' or me. What's it gonna be?" I demanded.

"Dee, you're the only person I'm interested in, and I will do anything to save our relationship. I've told my baby about you, but I just can't get away. I'm afraid of what might happen if I cut things off with my baby on a bad note. But for you, I'm willing to take that risk. Just tell me what you want me to do and I will do it. As you know, I will sacrifice anything for you," she stated sincerely.

"Well, since you're so willing to save our relationship, get rid of that damn phone. I want you to call and turn that shit off right now," I demanded, just to see how genuine she was.

"Okay," she said as though I was asking no big favor.

She dialed customer service and disconnected the phone just as I'd requested. I was satisfied, but there was still the original issue—my missing money. I opted not to bring it up at the moment because we'd just gotten past one dispute. She was definitely not off the hook, though. I would have to start watching her little ass like a hawk. I should have been on her anyway, but I started catching feelings and now I was slipping.

I walked back to the room and started cleaning things up. Anyeh walked in shortly after me.

"Baby, what happened here?" she asked cautiously. I could tell she was afraid to ask again, since the first time I responded so negatively.

"I was trying to find something." I didn't go into much detail, since I'd already decided we weren't going to have that conversation at the time.

"Oh. Did you find it?" she asked with a very concerned expression.

"Naw, but it's cool, though," I responded, still trying to read her unusual expression.

Anyeh continued to ask question after question in reference to my loss. Once she realized I wasn't going to tell her much about it, she left the issue alone, but she did insist on cleaning the room up.

"Baby, your morning has been stressful enough. Let me clean for you. Just go watch a little television and relax." She took the clothes from my hand and led me to the living room.

The more I sat alone in the living room, the more I began to think.

Why did she look so shocked when I told her I lost something? And why is she so anxious to clean up the room for me? Is she afraid I might find it when I clean up? Is she a suspect? But I give her everything a woman could dream of, so why would she need to steal from me?

I was no psychologist, but I was pretty good at picking out suspicious behavior, and Anyeh's behavior was definitely making her a suspect. I quietly rose from the couch and gently walked to the bedroom. I stood at the door and peeped around the corner. I watched minute after minute as Anyeh cleaned the room. Ten minutes had passed, and she was nearly finished cleaning up, and still I hadn't observed any peculiar behavior. I took one last glance before walking off, and that's when something caught my eye.

Anyeh was no longer cleaning. Instead, she was reading a small piece of paper. After reading it, she quickly balled up the paper and put it in her pocket.

What was on that paper that she didn't want anyone to see? I wondered as I sneaked back to the living room and positioned myself on the couch as though I'd been sitting there the entire time. I had to figure out a way to get that paper from her pocket. A part of me just wanted to go in there and tell her I was watching her the entire time and to give me the paper, but I wasn't ready to let her know that I was watching her. I had to think of a different route and fast. I came up with a plan that would get me what I needed, and had an added benefit: make- up sex!

I rushed into the room, grabbed Anyeh, and passionately kissed her body all over. Just as I'd predicted, she submissively removed her clothes and lay on bed. I got on my knees at the edge of the bed and propped her legs on my shoulders. I pushed my head between her legs and sent her out of this world. I did my best tricks to get her so gone that she would never notice my hand rummaging through her pants on the bedroom floor.

It didn't take long for me to find the paper and put it in my pocket. It didn't take long for her to reach her peak either. The events occurred nearly simultaneously. Her body shook with her explosive orgasm. She lay motionless on the bed. I covered her with a light blanket and she was off to sleep in no time.

I went to the bathroom to wash up. While I was in there, I opened the wrinkled paper. It read: *Miss you, baby! My new number is 422-1234.*

There was no name listed on it; just a message and number. I was bewildered by the note before me. I blocked my number and dialed the number on the paper.

"You have reached 422—" the computer generated voice began.

I hung up. Sooner or later I would find a way to get the name of the person at that number. Things were becoming more and more suspicious. I sat on the toilet, silent in deep thought as I planned my next move.

CHAPTER NINE
Anyeh

It was a hard two days, but I was finally able to get the Gucci pouch I stashed behind the dresser, out of the house. Dee had been watching me with a hawk's eye. Once I got the stash back to my apartment, I counted two thousand dollars in cash. I called my baby from the house phone.

"Why the hell is your phone off?" my baby yelled furiously.

I didn't have a suitable excuse, but I tried explaining. "Things were starting to get tough and Dee was on my ass, so I had to do whatever it took to make him happy. Trust me. I know things aren't moving as fast as you want, but in the end it will all be worth it."

Although upset with my actions, my baby agreed to give me the benefit of the doubt and be patient a little longer. I promised to travel to Philly and bring along proof of my commitment to our project.

After speaking with my baby, I had one more

call to make. I searched for Tiara's new number, but I was not able to find the paper I had stuffed in my pocket at Diablo's house. I emptied the contents of my pockets and my pouch, but it wasn't in either place. I thought long and hard as I traced all my steps, but I couldn't recover the number, so I gave up. I knew Tiara would eventually call me.

My stomach ached as I prepared to meet with my baby. I'd planned to use some of the money I stole from Diablo to get a flight to Philly. I hoped to return before Dee even noticed I was gone. I booked a flight for later in the evening and a return flight for the next afternoon. I called my baby once again to give an update on my flight information. I packed an overnight bag, grabbed the drugs and money, and headed to my car. The compressed heroin was packed into a balloon, which I swallowed before I pulled off. If time were on my side, the balloon would exit my body before my return to Norfolk the next day.

After a short flight, I arrived in Philly. I walked out of the airport and found the driver waiting for my arrival. He quickly grabbed my bags and escorted me to the back door of the car. My stomach ached the entire ride to my baby's home. I didn't know if it was fear, an ailment, or the balloon passing, but it was getting worse by the minute.

I knew it would not be an easy visit. My baby was displeased with my behavior over the past couple of weeks. The frequency of my calls had become less and less, until I cut off the cell phone completely. My heartbeat rose as we entered the gates of my baby's huge home.

"It seemed like a bitch blew up and fucked up, all in the same night," I said to myself as I reflected on the events that had gotten me into my predicament.

At the sweet age of sixteen, me and my girl Gina started off as beggars at the strip club, shaking our asses all night just to leave with a hundred damn dollars in our pockets. That shit wasn't nearly enough to make up for the bullshit we had to deal with from a bunch of disrespectful niggas while we danced. Shit had to change and fast.

Me and Gina decided to pair up and start throwing private parties at hotels for those horny-ass niggas. They loved to see two chicks sexing each other right before their eyes—up close and personal. Each night at the club we would pick out a different baller and offer to give him a little private show for the right amount of money. It wasn't long before niggas was coming up to the strip club just to get a private show from us. In the blink of an eye, we were no longer dancing in the clubs; we were only doing private parties. But like everything else, things got old, and that money just wouldn't suffice any longer.

Always on the grind, me and Gina were forever looking for something bigger and better to get into. We combined the power I had to attract men, with the experience Gina had in sex tricks, to pull in any man we wanted. We had enough flava to fulfill every taste a man could desire, and even though I remained a virgin and never slept with any of these dudes, they always came back for more shows.

We found drug dealers had the biggest appetites and the deepest pockets to fill their hunger, so they became our preferred targets. We had these niggas dropping all guards just to get a little freak show, and that's when we would catch them butt-ass naked with their hands in the air, getting fucked over by two stickup broads. They never knew what hit them. Because niggas was too embarrassed to tell anyone they got hit by two bitches, our shit stayed on the low and we were able to hit the entire East Coast from Florida to New York in two months flat.

Growing bigger by the minute, it was time to switch up the game. From the jump we had big dreams, and they were finally in view. We had the brains, the loot, and definitely the hustle to make it happen. We started off with small weight—weed, heroin, coke or whatever we could get our hands on. With a little time and lots of work, we were able to build a small female empire of our own. Our shit was blowing up and taking over the streets of Philly faster than most niggas. Then the problems started.

As we all know, money breeds jealousy. Our problem was that the jealousy lay within. With every empire there is a throne. Unfortunately, it only seats one; somebody has to sit and somebody has to bow down. Needless to say, Gina demanded to sit and I refused to bow. Although the empire was built off the sweat, blood, and tears of both of us, it just wasn't enough room for two rulers. I decided to pull out, but not without a deserving severance package.

This was a decision that all niggas in the game know could cost you your life, but I took the risk. One day after completing a transaction, I dipped to Atlanta, taking all the drugs with me and leaving Gina dry. It wasn't long before she caught up with me and paid me a personal visit. In a desperate attempt to keep my heart pumping, I offered a settlement that I knew she couldn't refuse.

Gina had heard of this big drug dealer in Virginia who went by the name of Diablo. She tried many times to do business with him, but Diablo always refused. I knew if I could get Gina Diablo's empire, she would be more than pleased. I told Gina that I would come up with a plan to get her Diablo's empire, then my debt to her would be dissolved. She agreed, but warned me that if I failed, I would pay with my life.

Gina's one demand before she would agree to the plan was that her name would never be connected to it. From that point on, I was to refer to her only as "my baby." She set me up in an apartment in Virginia, and I lived there for months, studying Diablo's every move and plotting a way to gain access to his empire. I knew this would be the hardest mission I would ever be faced with, but no matter the circumstances, I would deliver. My life depended on it. There was no way around it—it was ride or die.

"We have arrived," the driver stated as he opened the car door.

My brain raced and my stomach filled with knots the closer I got to the front door. Her new flunky replacement greeted me at the door. The house was quiet as I headed to the living room to meet Gina.

"Have a seat. I'm sure there's a lot you must tell me," Gina stated without even turning around to greet me.

I sat nervously, waiting to hear what more Gina

would say. She came over and sat beside me, placing her hands between my legs.

"I brought some drugs to show you that I'm making progress. I'm waiting for the balloon to pass." I forced the words out.

She pulled her hands away and gave me a disgusted look then motioned for the flunky. "Take her to her room," she told the flunky. To me she said, "Come see me when you have the drugs."

I ate dinner alone in the room and fell asleep without any further contact from Gina. The next morning, a terrible pain in my stomach woke me. I rushed to the restroom, hoping it was time for the balloon to pass. Luckily, it was. I retrieved the balloon, emptied the drugs from it, and gathered my things. I headed to Gina's room to deliver the raw heroin to her. The flunky stopped me at the door as she waited for Gina's approval to let me enter.

"I came to deliver the drugs and to say good-bye. I'm scheduled to fly out in two hours." I placed the drugs in Gina's hand and waited for her response.

Without even examining the drugs, she gave them to the flunky to be discarded.

"If you don't get your shit together and bring me something better than this, the deal is off," she stated nonchalantly.

I stood motionless as she approached me.

"How's things with your lover boy?" she asked while forcing her hands down my pants.

I knew Gina still cared for me, and the thought of me having sex with Dee probably infuriated her.

"Things are fine, Gina. I'm just using my sex appeal to get him where I want him. Isn't that why you had so much confidence in our plan from the beginning?" I asked, hoping to boost her confidence in me.

"Sure, Anyeh. Just get the job done, okay?" She placed her finger under my chin and lifted my face to hers. I closed my eyes and held my breath as she forced her tongue down my throat.

"You may go now." She smiled and smacked my ass as I walked away.

Without hesitation, I grabbed my things and headed to the airport. During the entire flight I thought about revenge. I was not giving up. By all means I would settle my debt and be free from Gina's hands.

CHAPTER TEN
Keysha

I hesitantly put my key in Diablo's front door and turned the knob. I took a deep breath as I walked in. It had been weeks since I spoke to my big brother and I said some hateful things. It was now time for us to reconcile our differences.

"Hello." I spoke softly as I walked toward the kitchen.

I could smell the spices of the evil bitch lurking in the air. I peeped in the boiling pot over the stove to see what was brewing. It seemed to be some sort of rice and hash mixture.

Umph. I guess she's still around. I can't believe Dee hasn't learned yet. Well, I'm back now, and I'm still on a mission to destroy the African beast, I thought as I headed toward Dee's bedroom. To my surprise, Dee wasn't in there, but Miss Anyeh was, and I caught her in the act. She was searching through Dee's dresser drawers.

"What the hell are you doing?" I asked, scaring the hell out of her conniving ass.

"Oh, my. You scared me," she responded, attempting to quickly close the drawer.

"Where's my brother?" I asked, eager to tell Dee what I just caught his little princess doing.

"He's in the shower. He'll be out in a minute."

I took a seat on the chair and flipped through the channels on the television as I waited for Dee. The African bitch gave me a dirty look and stormed out of the bedroom. Five minutes later, Dee was out of the shower. Steam rushed out of the bathroom as he opened the door and headed into the bedroom.

"Keysh, what the hell you doing here?" He smiled at my arrival.

I was surprised at his excitement. I expected him to still be upset over our last conversation.

"Hey, big bro," I said while giving him a huge hug.

"How's life been treating you?" he asked while getting dressed.

I told Dee about all the great things I'd done to improve my life in the past few weeks, starting with the fact that I'd found God. I told him how I was on my last leg, but with the help of Ms. Mary and God, I was able to do a complete turn around and send my life in a new direction. The courts were granting me a reconsideration hearing to get Davion back. I wanted all my family to attend so that the courts could see Davion had a family and a support system.

Dee seemed really impressed with all my efforts and he assured me he would do anything he could to help. He did make me promise one thing, though. He wanted Pooky out of my life. He believed Pooky was the cause of my downfall, and if he was going to stand behind me, Pooky had to be out of the picture. I assured him Pooky was no longer around, but I failed to mention the big fight I had with Pooky. If I told Dee about the fight, he would surely have Pooky killed—if he wasn't already dead, that is.

After briefing Dee on my life, I asked him about his life. "I see Anyeh is still around. So, how's everything in the relationship world?" I asked, hoping he would tell me it was hell and he wanted out.

She must have been listening outside the bedroom door the whole time, because as soon as she heard her name, the bitch was right in the room.

"Hey, baby," Diablo said. "Why don't you give us a few minutes to talk alone, okay?"

She rolled her eyes and stormed out of the room again, slamming the door behind her. I grinned at her little hissy fit.

"To be honest with you, Keysh, I don't know what's up with her right now. It seems like every day there's a new situation between us. At times I feel like I don't trust her."

He told me about the missing money, the "my baby" calls, and the paper with the strange number. I assured Dee he could rule out mommy stealing from him. She had been clean for several months. Dee was sure she was high when she came over, but if anybody knew mommy it was me, and I was sure that she was no longer using. Now, drinking was a different story, but using—no way. So, I told him that only could leave Anyeh as the thief.

Dee was reluctant to accept my theory. He felt my opinion was biased. My brother was even more pussy whipped than I thought. I could see there was no convincing him that she stole the money, so we moved to the next issue, the strange number. I figured that was easy to solve.

"Have you tried calling the number?" I asked Dee the obvious.

"Yeah, I called from the house and pressed star sixty-seven to block my number, but I never got an answer, just a damn computer voice."

"Give me your phone." I grabbed Dee's cell from his hand.

I pressed star sixty-seven and dialed the number. To my amazement, there was an answer.

"Hello?" a female answered.

"Hello. This is Yolanda Jones. I'm calling in reference to Anyeh. Is she there?" I imitated the tone of the social workers who often called my home.

"No, she's not. Is there something wrong?" The young lady seemed to be very concerned.

"Unfortunately, this is a private matter, so I'm unable to discuss it with anyone other than Anyeh—"

Anyeh walked in on our conversation.

"Thank you. I'll try back later," I said, trying to end the call before Anyeh caught on.

"What's going on in here?" she demanded.

Dee didn't respond to Anyeh. He looked at me with a *told you so* expression on his face.

"I heard Keysha on the phone inquiring about me. What is going on?" I could tell Anyeh was very angry and I was loving it.

I knew Dee wasn't going to say anything, so I gladly stepped in.

"Dee found this number and he knew it wasn't his. Well, you're the only other person staying here, so it has to be yours. He didn't want to call the number, so I did," I said to her with no remorse.

"Dee, all you had to do was ask, honey," she said, looking at Dee with disappointment.

"And that's not the only thing. He also knows you stole his money," I stated, adding fuel to the fire.

Dee hadn't actually said he believed it was Anyeh who stole the money. I figured I was on a roll, so I might as well put it all out there. Anyeh turned to Dee with amazement.

"I would never steal from you. Maybe it was your mother. You know she was left alone in the bedroom for a long time, and she wasn't in her right state of mind that day, either. She was begging for money and was very upset when you wouldn't give it to her. You said it yourself; she was high and she probably wanted another fix." Anyeh stated her case as though she were on trial in front of the Supreme Court.

Dee ignored what she said about our mother and started to ask Anyeh questions about the money. I joined in, and eventually she became very flustered.

"I didn't take your two thousand dollars!" she screamed hysterically as tears rolled down her face. She sobbed heavily as she grabbed her things and headed for the door.

"Diablo, you're going to lose the one woman that ever cared for you because of your jealous little sister. When she wasn't around we were happy, and now she's back in your life and our relationship is going to hell," she shouted before slamming the door behind her.

When she left, I brought a few things to Dee's

attention. "Dee, how does she know it was two thousand dollars missing?"

Dee was sure he never mentioned the dollar amount that was missing. Just to add a final touch, I decided to tell Dee about how I discovered Anyeh searching through his dresser drawers. That was the final straw. Dee was fed up. He was on a mission. He wanted to know everything there was to know about Anyeh, and he was appointing me leader of the pack. I finally had Dee's approval to destroy the African bitch, and I couldn't wait to get started. I didn't know if I was tripping or if he was, but I didn't care; things were looking on the bright side.

CHAPTER ELEVEN
Diablo

This was just the beginning of a nationwide search I had out for information on Anyeh. I was stupid not to do that in the beginning anyway.

Two days had passed and I hadn't spoken to Anyeh. To be honest, I missed her a lot, but things just didn't seem right with her. I had to get to the bottom of things. I could no longer sit around and wait for the reports. I decided to call her and invite her over to talk the situation through.

"Hello?" She answered on the first ring.

I didn't respond. I sat on the phone quietly as I listened to the chatter in the background.

"Hellooooo?" she sang into the phone again.

Again, I didn't respond. I just listened. I could hear a female speaking to her in the background. She seemed to be encouraging Anyeh to get off the phone. Anyeh laughed as the female influenced her to hang up. She disconnected the call before I could gather any additional information.

Should I call back? Is it even worth it? She's probably still not gonna tell me truth.

My phone rang before I could decide. The caller ID read COOKIE.

"Yo," I answered, trying to sound calm.

"Hey, did you just call?" she asked sweetly.

Just the sound of her voice was enough to make me crumble. There was no denying that I loved Anyeh.

"Yeah, my phone wasn't getting good service," I lied, ashamed to admit I was actually eavesdropping.

"So, what's up?" she asked, full of energy as if we didn't have a huge argument a few days ago.

I decided that was enough of the games and invited her over. She eagerly accepted the invitation and asked if she could bring a friend. I was kinda thrown by that question, but I wanted to see her so bad I would agree to almost anything. I quickly straightened up the house then jumped in the shower. A few hours later Anyeh was at the front door.

She came in and greeted me with huge hug and kiss. Like always, my manhood rose to the occasion. Evidently, he missed her just as much as me.

"I see you're not the only one that missed me," she said while rubbing my erect penis.

I grinned, trying the hide the embarrassment I felt since she'd called me out in front of her girlfriend.

"How you doing? I'm Diablo." I introduced myself, hoping to change the subject.

"Nice to meet you, Diablo. I'm Tiara," she said, extending her hand.

I shook her hand as I sized her up.

Impressive! I thought as I checked out her small

Spanish frame. She was very shapely. Her tiny waist accented her round ass perfectly. Her skin was flawless; however, it was apparent that she tanned on a regular basis.

"So, when do I get to meet him?" she asked, pointing toward my now relaxed dick.

I didn't know what to say. I just raised one eyebrow and looked at Anyeh as if to say, "What's up with your girl?"

"Dee. She asked you a question," Anyeh stated, looking me dead in the eyes.

I looked at Tiara and she was doing the exact same thing. I didn't know what to say, so I played it safe. "Y'all tripping. Come on in here and make yourself comfortable."

I led them to the living room and started making drinks. I don't know if I needed the drinks more or they did, but none of us wasted any time getting fucked up. Anyeh had thrown salt all up in my game. I'd planned to speak to her about the missing money and the other issues we were having, but this whole sexual shit had me tripping.

With the combination of the sexual tension and liquor, it wasn't long before our clothes were off and Tiara and Anyeh were giving me the massage of a lifetime. I knew the events that were about to come. Each area they massaged was followed by a gentle kiss. It was only a matter of time before there was less massaging and more kissing and caressing. I was in heaven as they took turns giving me brain. I'd had plenty of chicks in my day, but nothing was comparable to the shit they were doing. While Anyeh sucked me off, Tiara licked me in places that I wouldn't even fuck with.

These bitches are freaks! I took a moment to think

before instructing Tiara to give Anyeh the same treatment. I watched as Anyeh lay across the couch with her legs propped. Tiara moved as gently and precisely as a surgeon. I didn't know what the fuck that bitch was doing, but it was sending my girl to the moon.

Oh, hell no! This bitch ain't making my girl cum.

I went behind Tiara and turned her over. I'd planned to fuck the shit out of her little ass. I threw her legs on my shoulders and dove right in. She moaned with each pump.

"Sit on my face," she said to Anyeh between moans.

She grabbed Anyeh by the waist. Again I watched as my girl's eyes began to roll to the back of her head.

What the fuck!

The more I watched, the more pissed off I became. All sorts of shit started running through my head.

This bitch has probably been fucking my girl on the regular! Hell, they may even be doing these threesomes with other niggas too!

I pulled out, grabbed Anyeh's waist and bent her over the leather sectional, leaving Tiara alone. I slowly inserted my penis to savor each moment of Anyeh's tight pussy. She gripped the back of the couch while taking my penis inch by inch. She screamed "I love you" with every other pump. I looked at Tiara to make sure she heard those words. I wanted her to understand I was the one Anyeh loved.

Tiara grinned sarcastically then slid beneath Anyeh and started to kiss her. She pushed Anyeh's head toward her vagina. Anyeh got on her knees so that she could continue pleasing me doggie style and please Tiara at the same time. I became infuriated. I was surprised my dick was still hard. It had to be the liquor because I wasn't even feeling this shit anymore. Out of fury, I grabbed her waist forcefully, piercing her sides with my nails. I pulled my penis out, and with one powerful push I shoved my penis in her ass.

"Aaaaahhhhhh! Dee, please. I can't take it. You're hurting me." She begged me to stop.

That was enough to make her get her face out of Tiara's pussy. I ignored her plea and continued to pound her harder and harder as I ejaculated inside her. She lay motionless as she sobbed silently. Tears rolled down her cheeks as she looked at me with disappointment. Tiara held Anyeh tight while cutting her eyes at me. I glared back, daring her to say one fucking word. Anyeh noticed our tension.

"I deserved it. I've deceived you in many ways," she said to me as she gathered her things and headed to the bedroom. Tiara followed close behind.

Anyeh caught me totally off guard. I didn't know how to respond, so I didn't. I just stood there butt-ass naked and looked at her in disbelief. I'd plan to ask her about things, but I never thought she would just come out and willingly admit to deceiving me. I wondered just how many things she'd done. Her statement had me fucked up. I didn't know if I should smack her ass or console her.

Once I gathered my thoughts, I followed her to the bedroom. I grabbed her by the arm and sat her on my lap.

"Yo, give us a minute alone." I directed Tiara to leave before I continued.

"Anyeh, why would you lie to me?" I asked.

She started out by admitting that she had stolen the money from me because she needed to fly to Philly. This was only the beginning, though. I was definitely not expecting the rest of the story she told.

She sobbed heavily as she told me about this chick, Gina, who used to be her partner. I couldn't believe it—my precious little virgin was actually a big-time drug dealer at one time. Now she was trying to save her own life by setting me up.

When I first heard her confession, I wanted to smack the shit out of her. Anybody else who admitted to crossing me like that would have been dead in the blink of an eye. Something inside wouldn't let me do that to Anyeh, though. Even after learning that she had been planning to take me down, I still couldn't deny my feelings for her. And she admitted that she, too, had fallen in love with me.

It crossed my mind that maybe her saying she was in love with me was all just part of her plan, but then I thought about everything else that had happened. When I had told her to cut off her cell phone and stop talking to this "my baby" person, she did it without hesitating. Now that I knew the whole story, I knew she had taken a big risk by shutting out Gina like that. I watched Anyeh sobbing next to me and realized that this girl was truly scared for her life now.

After listening to the horrible things she told me, I had no choice but to forgive her. I had to help Anyeh, so together we devised a little plan to put all things to rest.

I told Anyeh that I had connections with Gina.

She'd tried to contact me a few times for work, but I'd never hooked up with her. I assured Anyeh we would settle the debt, but she had to follow my lead and work with Keysha as well. Although I believed every word Anyeh was saying this time, I still needed my li'l sis on the scene just in case Anyeh decided to play both sides of the fence.

Once we'd set our plan, I prepared a nice bath for Anyeh to calm her. I filled the tub with hot water and bubbles then turned on the jets, just the way Anyeh did for me each day. I watched her meditate with relaxation candles lit all around her. She was beautiful. While she soaked, I went to the living room to have a little talk with Tiara.

I asked her all about the relationship she and Anyeh had. She assured me this was the first time either of them had ever done such a thing. She was confident Anyeh loved me. In fact, she loved me so much she wanted to do something special for me. Anyeh had been planning this night for a while. There was nothing more I could say. I was shocked at the extent she would go to prove her love to me.

I called everyone to tell them I no longer needed information on Anyeh. I ended with Keysha, though I knew she would be most disappointed.

"Hey, Keysh."

"What's up, Dee? I got some news for ya." She sounded eager.

"Hate to disappoint ya, Keysha, but I don't need it." I braced myself because I knew my little sister was about to snap on me.

"What? Why the change?" she asked angrily.

"Man, this girl loves me. She admitted to stealing the money and even explained why."

I knew Keysha still wasn't buying it. She said, "Oh yeah? And what was her excuse, Dee?"

I told Keysha all about the story Anyeh had shared with me about her debt to Gina. Before I could even finish, Keysha busted out laughing.

"Ha! I didn't know my big brother was so damn green."

"What the hell do you mean?"

"Nothing, Dee. Do you, big bro. I gotcha back when you really find out the true Anyeh."

"Baby!" Anyeh yelled, interrupting my conversation.

"Keysha, I'll call you back." I rushed off the phone as I heard Anyeh yelling in a panic.

"Yes, baby?" I ran to the bathroom to see Anyeh slumped over, holding her stomach.

"I'm having really bad cramps. Could you help me out the tub? Maybe it's the hot water causing them."

I helped her from the tub and covered her with a robe. She lay on the bed in pain. I wondered if I'd caused injury to her with that agonizing sex.

"You think we should go to the hospital?" I began to worry as I watched her pain progress.

"No!" she shouted as she pushed away from my comforting grip.

Even though she had kept secrets from me, she was still my girl and I still loved her with all my heart. There was no way I was going to stand by helplessly and watch her suffer. I grabbed her, threw her slim body over my shoulder and headed to the car. She screamed and kicked the entire way, but there was no changing my mind. Anyeh was having unbearable pain and I was taking her to the hospital. I directed Tiara to take Anyeh's car and go home.

I promised to keep her posted. Once in the car I locked the doors and sped out of the driveway. She begged me to turn around. I couldn't understand why she was so afraid of going to the hospital. Then she finally explained.

"Please. I am an illegal immigrant. They must not know I'm here," she said with a weak voice.

I sat silently in the car in front of the emergency room entrance.

"Please," she begged again while grabbing my hand with the little strength she had left.

Not wanting to risk Anyeh being deported, I reluctantly turned around. It wasn't until that moment I realized just how much she meant to me. It was a rule of mine to never go down at the hands of a bitch, and housing an illegal immigrant was a true way of going down. But for Anyeh, I was willing to take the risk.

The ride home was silent. While Anyeh slept, I drove home in deep thought, examining the decision I'd just made. I had no choice but to accept the true love I felt for Anyeh. No doubt about it, she had me gone. She'd truly taken me places I'd never been with any other woman and had no desire to be. I just hoped it didn't turn into the biggest mistake of my life.

CHAPTER TWELVE
Anyeh

The next morning I didn't feel any better. The pain I felt the previous night was much too familiar. I was worried about what I suspected was the true source of the pain. I turned over to see my king sleeping peacefully.

"Good morning," I said after kissing him on the cheek.

He opened his eyes slowly and ran his fingers through my dreads.

"Good morning, baby. How do you feel?"

"I'm fine, honey." Honestly I felt awful, but I didn't want Dee to be troubled.

I forced myself out of the bed so I could prepare breakfast. As I washed my face and brushed my teeth, I noticed Dee staring at me. I could tell he was trying to analyze something.

"What's wrong, baby?" I asked.

I'd just revealed everything to Dee so that I could regain his trust. I didn't want him wondering about anything more. It was total honesty from this point on.

"Nothing, baby. I love you, that's all," he stated.

I knew that wasn't what he was thinking, but my stomach ached so badly I didn't have the strength to discuss anything deep with him. I walked out of the bathroom and headed toward the kitchen, stomach still aching. I stood over the stove cooking for Dee. Like each morning, I brought him breakfast in bed.

Dee finished eating and I prepared his bath and laid out his clothes. He had a little business to take care of that day. Although he was reluctant to leave me, I assured him I would be fine. He promised it wouldn't be long and instructed me to start executing the plan he and I discussed about Gina.

After Dee left, I tolerated the continuous pains in my stomach while I tried to mentally prepare myself for what I had to do that day. The phone rang. I checked the caller ID before answering; it was Tiara. I knew she would be worried about my condition after seeing me in so much pain the night before. I assured her I was okay then explained she might not hear from me in a while. Tired of our back and forth relationship, she demanded an explanation. I was tired of lying to everyone, so I admitted to her about my debt to Gina and the plan Dee and I devised to settle the score. Although uneasy about the entire situation, Tiara understood and agreed to be tolerant.

After speaking to Tiara, it was time to call Gina. It had been nearly a week since we'd last talked. I was in no hurry to speak with her again, but as part of Dee's plan, I had to call Gina and convince her that the plan was going perfectly. I was to tell her I'd convinced Dee's connects to try her out on a small business transaction. Once the transaction was complete, we would knock Dee off so Gina would become their only heavy client, which would ultimately leave Gina in control of Dee's empire.

"Hello?" Gina answered in an annoyed tone.

"I fulfilled your original request, and if you're still interested, I would like to make arrangements to start the process of handing over Diablo's empire to you," I said in my most respectful, bow-down-to-the-master tone.

"So, you completed the task even with all those mistakes. Good for you. When will you hand over my new empire?"

I arranged a time and place for us to meet that night. I was excited yet nervous. I knew Gina was never to be trusted, but I also knew how passionately she wanted Dee's empire.

After making my phone calls, my first task of the day was resolved. Now it was time to deal with issue number two. I headed to the African market to gather a few things. Even though I was possibly carrying Dee's first born, I knew I could not keep the child. If the things I had been told as a young girl in Africa were true, then the terrible pains I'd experienced could only mean I was carrying a cursed child. I'd done so many evil things, and this was my punishment.

Once at the market, I told the old African woman of my pains. She told me how African women abort their children. She gave me a list of instructions and ingredients. I purchased Florida water, Guinness, sugar, and a few other items.

I wasted no time boiling the Guinness when I

got home. I knew Dee would be home soon and I wanted this done before he arrived. Once the Guinness heated to the right temperature, I poured a cup, added lots of sugar and began to drink. Tears rolled down my cheeks as I forced down the hot substance. I hated the thought of killing Dee's child, but I knew that was the only way out. I took the final swallow and lay down to sleep.

When I awoke, my pains were less, but I was disappointed that there was no blood on my sheets. There was no way to know if the remedy had worked to end my pregnancy. I would have to buy a pregnancy test later, then I could decide if I needed to take further action to prevent the birth of a child.

When I looked at the clock, I was surprised. It was already 9 p.m. and Dee had not returned home. That was very strange. Dee never spent the entire day out without at least calling to check in. I began pacing, and as it got even later, I started worrying. All sorts of things went through my mind.

What if he's hurt or in jail? What if Gina was one step ahead of me and had plans to get Dee on her own?

It was now 10 o'clock and I knew there was definitely something wrong. I never disturbed Dee when he was working, but this was an exception. There was no way Dee would just disappear without calling me, especially since I was ill.

I called his cell a few times, but got his voicemail each time. I began to panic. I didn't know what to do. I tried to pace my breathing so that I could think rationally.

Okay, Anyeh, think. Who can you call? Finally, an idea came to me. *Keysha!*

As much as I hated to call the wicked bitch of

the west, I knew she was my only option. I took a deep breath as I scrolled through the caller ID until I found her number.

You can take a bitch out the ghetto, but you can't take the ghetto out the bitch, I thought as the phone rang.

"What up, Dee? You come to your senses yet?" she answered, assuming it was her brother on the phone.

I knew what she meant by that statement, but I had bigger issues to handle.

"This is not your brother, Keysha. This is Any—"

"And what the fuck do you want?" she asked before I could finish.

I knew I had to be patient if I wanted to get anywhere with her, so I answered calmly. "Look, Keysha, I don't want to argue. I called you because I believe Dee is missing."

I finally had her attention. I explained to her the plan Dee and I had to destroy Gina. I told her the last time I saw Dee and how I worried Gina might have something to do with Dee's disappearance. Keysha didn't seem really worried.

"He's probably out with one of his other hoes. Let me call him and see if he answers. If he doesn't then we may need to worry, because he would never avoid a call from his number one," she said before hanging up in my ear.

Thirty minutes passed as I waited for a return call from Keysha. I couldn't wait any longer. I called her back, but only got her voice mail message.

Now she was no longer answering her phone. I had no one else to call; I had no place I could check. It wasn't until that point I realized I really didn't know that much about Dee. I sat in silence as I dialed his number and Keysha's over and over again. When 11 o'clock rolled around, I still hadn't reached anyone, and it was almost time to meet Gina at our prearranged spot. I had no choice but to go there myself. My instinct was telling me that Gina had something to do with Diablo's disappearance. I hoped that if I went to the spot to meet her, I could find out where he was. As far as protecting myself from Gina, I would just have to take my chances. The only thing I cared about was finding Diablo.

CHAPTER THIRTEEN
Keysha

"Kita!" I yelled as soon as she picked up.

"Yeah, Keysha," she stated in an irritated tone. "Something's up with this bitch Anyeh. She's up to something and I think Dee is involved. Can you check shit out and call me back?" I begged, ignoring the aggravation in Kita's voice.

"Yeah," she stated before hanging up in my ear.

Normally I would have been snapping over the shade Kita was throwing me, but I had no time to figure out what her issue was. My brother was missing and that was my only concern.

When Anyeh initially called to tell me that Dee hadn't been home, I knew something had to be wrong. As much as I hated to admit it, I knew how much Dee loved Anyeh. There was no way he would run out on her like that. When I called his business phone and there was no answer, I knew there was definitely a problem. I wasted no time calling Kita. If there was any current gossip on the street she would know it, and if not, she had the sources to find it.

It didn't take Kita long to call me back with the scoop. "Anyeh's a sheisty little bitch!" she yelled into the phone.

"So, what's up?" I was eager to know any information she had to help me find my brother.

"She's a stick-up broad! She's been hitting niggas all up and down the East Coast. And from what I hear, she's fucking wit' dis chick from P-town named Tiara. Tiara goes both ways and she's fucking everybody and their man, which includes Anyeh and your brother. From what I hear, she's supposed to be a stick-up broad on the low too. Now, if you want my opinion, I figure they've paired up and Dee's probably next on their list."

When she told me the tricks Anyeh had up her sleeve, I became infuriated. Again, I found myself flying across town full speed. I was going to my brother's house to fuck that bitch up. I arrived there in a record-breaking five minutes.

"Where the fuck you at, you sheisty little bitch?" I yelled as I busted through Dee's front door and ran through the house looking for Anyeh.

This was the moment I'd been waiting for. I couldn't wait for the opportunity to kick her African ass. I ran through each room, including the bathrooms, but I still didn't see her.

Where the hell could she have gone so quickly? I wondered as I searched around the house for any clue I could find to lead me to the conniving little bitch. I looked up and down and all around the house, but there was nothing that seemed unusual. I checked the phone's caller ID as one last hopeless attempt.

"Hot damn!" I said as I looked at the number of the last call. The name under the number was Tiara Smith.

So she spoke to her. Maybe she is planning to set Dee up, I thought as I continued my phone search. I pressed redial to see the last number dialed.

"Philadelphia!" I shouted as I looked at the number and recognized the area code. I was sure this was the number for that woman Gina she had told me about.

What the fuck is going on? Why is she calling this bitch when she told me that her and Dee was gonna destroy Gina? Maybe Anyeh called her to tell her where Dee was at so they could knock him off. Maybe all these bitches is in on this.

I wasted no time calling the number. The phone rang continuously with no answer.

"Hello, this is Gina," the voicemail said each time I called.

I called Kita right away.

"Kita!" I yelled as soon as she picked up.

"Yeah, girl?"

"I need info on a dealer named Gina from Philly." I gave her the little info I had, including the number I had just found on the redial.

"Naw, girl. Not until you tell me what the hell is going on now. I be giving you all this info, but you don't never give a bitch the lowdown on shit. I ain't telling you a damn thang. Hell, you still ain't even told me what was up with Pooky that day. I had to do my own research on that one."

I explained the whole situation to Kita so that I could get her help.

"Daaaaaaaamn, girl! You gotta come pick me up for dis one. I need to see this go down with my own eyes. By the time you get here, I'll have the info on that Gina chick for you."

I had no choice but to agree. If I was going to save Dee, I needed all the details. I got to Kita's house in no time.

I blew the horn to let her know I was outside. She ran out of the bootlegger's house next to hers. Kita started blabbing as soon as she opened the car door.

"Gina is a ho that transformed herself into a drug lord. Her and Anyeh used to be lovers/stick-up broads, but somewhere along the line, Anyeh built dis huge debt with Gina and now her life is on the line. If you want my opinion, Anyeh was probably gonna team up wit' Tiara to hit your brother to pay Gina off. Da hit's probably going down soon, and dat's why Gina was contacted. I'm no detective, but I am a gossip queen, and I know my shit!" Kita looked at me for a reaction.

I had no choice but to go on her assumptions for now.

"Okay, sounds about right," I said, giving her an approving nod of the head.

"Good. I'm glad you're convinced. Now, here's where they always meet. Luckily I stopped at the bootlegger's to see if it was any other word on da street I ain't know 'bout. Da fiend out Park Place gave me dat bit of info. He said he sees Tiara out there meeting with different people every other Friday around eleven at night."

Kita handed me a piece of paper with an address on it. I entered it in my navigation system and we headed there. We were only ten miles way.

"You have arrived," the navigation system announced as we pulled up to a church.

"Why the hell are we here?" I asked, doubting Kita's accuracy on her notes.

"You don't know?" she asked.

"No, I don't."

"Well, let me tell ya. Dis is a Catholic Church, which means it's open all night. And what cops do you know that watch the church for sheisty shit to go down? It's the safest place you could go, girl."

Again, I knew Kita had the answers to everything.

I scanned the parking lot as Kita hopped out of the car and headed to the church entrance. I didn't see Anyeh's car anywhere. I prayed that I hadn't gone on the wrong hunch. I didn't have much time. I had to find Dee, and that bitch Anyeh was my only hope. A few minutes passed and I saw her car pull up. *I guess meeting at the church wasn't a bad idea after all,* I thought, relieved that God had heard my prayer.

I watched as Anyeh tiptoed into the church. I rushed over and slit the tires on her car just in case that bitch decided to flee the scene before I got to her ass. I followed a short distance behind her as she entered the church. I watched as Anyeh walked over to Tiara, who was already sitting in a pew. Anyeh kissed her on the lips.

"What are you doing here?" I could hear Anyeh ask Tiara.

"I couldn't let you come here alone. It's not safe," Tiara responded.

I didn't see Kita anywhere. I was sure she had a good hidden seat so that she could capture all of the action without being part of it.

Patience, Keysha. Patience, I constantly reminded

myself as I sat observing the two deceitful devils. I listened closely to hear what they would reveal.

"So, when are you going through with the plan?" Tiara asked.

I couldn't believe what I was hearing. It seemed like Kita's assumptions were proving true. It took all I had to stay calm. I couldn't believe that bitch was actually planning to set my brother up.

"You know I'm planning to meet Gina here, Tiara. You have to go. We'll talk later," Anyeh insisted.

This confused me. Why was she telling Tiara to leave? Furthermore, where did Gina fit in? I thought about my next move as I watched Tiara gathered her things to leave the church.

If she is sheisty like Kita says, I need to stop this bitch. Maybe if I hold her hostage it would show Anyeh I'm not playing and force her to tell me where my brother is.

That was it. My plan was final. It was time to execute. I unzipped my handbag to grab my gun. I reached deep in my bag but recovered nothing. My heart raced. When I left the house after I heard Diablo was missing, I was frantic. Had I really been so upset that I forgot to bring my gun?

I prayed that in all the commotion I'd just forgotten to slip it in my purse, and that it was in the car outside the church. The only problem was getting back to the car without Tiara or Anyeh noticing me. It was risky, but I had no choice. I quietly left my secure spot and headed to the exit.

Ugh! My breathing was cut off by an enormous pressure to my windpipe as I crossed the grass to get to my car.

"Where you headed?" Tiara asked. I felt something pressed to my back.

I struggled to loosen her grip around my throat, gasping for air with the little strength that remained.

"I knew yo' bitch ass would show up. Anyeh always said you were trouble," Tiara said right before pistol-whipping me in the face.

Pain ripped through my head, forcing me to the ground. Tiara stood over me, pointing the gun, but I was released from her grip and now able to speak. Knowing that I had a small chance, I quickly made my next move. There was no way I was giving up so easily. I would try to bend her trust and make Tiara turn on Anyeh.

"Anyeh doesn't love you," I said. "She's sheisty. She's using you just like she was using my brother. She probably gonna try to make your ass disappear just like she did to Diablo."

"Oh, please. Anyeh couldn't pull off a plan like that. And as far as her loving me, I couldn't care less. I have my own agenda."

Tiara's answer shocked the hell out of me and confused me. Now what was I supposed to say to get that gun out of my face?

"Tiara?" I heard Anyeh yelling as she came near the doors of the church.

Tiara was startled. "Oh, shit," she mumbled, shoving the gun in her waistband under her shirt. She didn't even look in my direction as she headed toward the entrance to meet Anyeh before she could come outside and see us on the dark lawn. In that brief moment, I got up and ran to hide behind a car.

I watched as Tiara and Anyeh headed back to the sanctuary. Tiara looked over her shoulder, but didn't make a move to come find me. *That's right, bitch,* I thought. *Look out for my return. I'm out to get you.*

I wondered why Tiara led Anyeh back into the church. If they were working together, they would have been out there searching for my ass instead of heading back inside. After what Tiara had just said, I was starting to think that maybe she had something in store for Anyeh like what she had just done to me.

I jumped into the car I had been hiding behind. When I got to the church, the street had been deserted except for this car, so I figured it must be Tiara's. I figured a stick-up broad would always have a backup in the car, so I searched for a gun. I found one in no time, silencer and all. Now strapped, I ran back into the church.

"Anyeh, I don't think she's gonna show. I think you should just go back to your crib and wait for Dee's call," Tiara was saying as I entered and hid behind a pew.

"But what if she does show? I need to know where Dee is, Tiara," Anyeh protested. "I need to wait here for Gina." Anyeh was doubled over, holding her stomach as she spoke.

"No, Anyeh, you need to be home in case Dee tries to contact you. Besides, look how weak you are. You're still sick. Go home and wait for Dee. If Gina shows up and sees you're not here, she won't stay anyway. I can hide outside then follow her car. I'll call you as soon as something happens."

"No, Tiara, I can't let you do that," Anyeh insisted. "This is my mess, and I have to take care of it."

Tiara stood up slowly and reached into her waistband. "Damn it, Anyeh. I didn't want to have to do this, but you leave me no choice." She pulled out her gun and pointed it at Anyeh, who looked like she was about to pass out.

"Tiara, what are you doing?" she asked.

"I'm doing what I should have done a long time ago. Gina wanted me to kill your ass as soon as she figured out you were falling in love with Diablo. If it wasn't for the good sex you were giving me, I would have done it, too. I was trying to convince you to get out of here to save your own life, but you just wouldn't listen, would you?"

Anyeh looked totally confused. "What the hell are you talking about?" she asked through her tears.

"You are such a stupid bitch, Anyeh. You think it was a coincidence that we met as soon as you came to Virginia? Gina knew all along that you weren't strong enough to get Diablo on your own. Shit, she even predicted you'd fall in love with his stupid ass. You were only useful to get information, then you and Diablo were both supposed to die.

"I was hired to keep an eye on you while you gathered whatever information you could on Diablo and his connects. That way, if you ever fucked up and gave Diablo the wrong information, I would be there to take care of you."

Anyeh only sobbed in response.

"Then today you told me that you confessed everything to Diablo, so I reported it to Gina. She got down here in a flash, and now your precious man is with her."

"No!" Anyeh cried out.

From my hiding spot, I wanted to jump up and strangle Tiara, but I needed to know if she had any more information that would help me find my brother.

"Yes, I'm afraid so, Anyeh. Your precious fucking Diablo is probably one step away from dead now, and you're not far behind. Gina is on her way here to finish you herself."

I felt a small glimmer of hope. If Diablo was still alive, he might be on his way to the church now with Gina. As I plotted my next move, a thought came to me. As much as I hated Anyeh, I knew that my brother loved her. If Tiara was serious, Anyeh might not be alive much longer, and if Diablo survived, his broken heart might just do him in. I had no choice but to try to save Anyeh.

I stood from behind the pew and raised the gun to aim it at Tiara. Anyeh's sobs echoed so loudly in the church that I went unnoticed. As Tiara continued to tell Anyeh about Gina's plans for her, I steadied my arm and pulled the trigger.

Pop! Pop! The silencer did the job, and two shots to Tiara's head and neck knocked her to the floor with almost no sound. Anyeh screamed as I raced toward her. I looked down at Tiara's body. There was not much left of her face, and I knew we wouldn't have to worry about her anymore.

"Anyeh," I said forcefully as I grabbed her arms. "Get up! We need to get out of here before Gina shows up."

Anyeh was clearly confused and wouldn't move.

"Shit, Anyeh, I ain't gonna shoot you. Get up and get outta here or I'm gonna leave your ass here to deal with Gina on your own. We need to get outside and hide if you wanna have any chance of saving Diablo when they show up."

She stood up and followed me, still crying. I ran to the exit, dragging her with me, but stopped dead in my tracks when I heard a car pull up outside the church. I retreated back to my hiding place in the pews and spoke to Anyeh. I needed her to calm down if we wanted to survive.

"Anyeh!" We heard a woman yelling outside.

I grabbed Anyeh's shoulders and asked, "Is that Gina?"

She nodded.

"Look, Anyeh. You have got to calm the fuck down. You are our only chance of getting out of here right now. You gotta go out there and face her before she comes in here and finds us."

"I can't," she answered.

"I'll be right behind you with my gun, but you gotta do it. If you can distract her then I can come out shooting."

"Anyeh!" We heard another shout and then a car door slamming.

"Shit! She's coming! You gotta get out there now!" I commanded.

Anyeh wiped her tears and stood up. She looked over her shoulder at me one last time as she headed to the door.

"I got your back," I whispered as she exited the church.

CHAPTER FOURTEEN
Diablo

I was restrained in the back seat of Gina's car with blood trickling down my face from a nasty blow to the nose. Hell, in a situation like this I would take a blow anytime. That was a sure ticket for a longer ride. If they wanted me dead, I wouldn't be in the back seat.

We had pulled up to a church in Norfolk, and I saw Anyeh's car parked on the street. Gina started yelling for Anyeh to come outside. She got out of the car followed by her male sidekick, who had beat the shit out of me when they jumped me after I went to talk to one of my mayors. I still couldn't believe I had let myself get caught out there like that.

My heart lurched when I saw Anyeh coming out of the church. She looked so scared, and there was nothing I could do about it.

Gina approached Anyeh and smacked her, knocking her to the ground. Anyeh just sat there, not even attempting to get up. Gina proceeded to hit her with blow after blow. I couldn't stand to watch the beating she was receiving. The muscle-bound sidekick just stood there and watched as Gina threw Anyeh around like a rag doll.

It looked like Anyeh's only hope of surviving was if I could get out of the car and help her. Gina definitely had every intention of beating her until she was dead. I started squirming in the back seat, trying to loosen my restraints. The black Hercules looked over to the car and saw what I was doing. He alerted Gina, who paused only long enough to laugh at me.

"Oh, so your ass want to come out here and save her, huh?" she asked. "Okay, Calvin, go get his ass and bring him out here. These two lovebirds should die together anyway, don't you think?"

He came near the car, and though I had managed to loosen the cords around my wrists a little, I couldn't get my hands out. Calvin pulled open the door and hit me in the face. My head snapped back and the blood running down my forehead, momentarily blinded me.

I felt Calvin dragging me across the grass. He dropped me on the ground next to Anyeh. I could hear her whimpering. Gina laughed at us.

"Look at you two bitches down there on the grass. Shit, Anyeh, I don't know how you coulda fallen in love with his bitch ass anyway. If only you woulda stayed with me, we coulda had everything. Too bad you had to go and get greedy on me. Now both y'all gonna die."

I heard Anyeh grunt as Gina kicked her in the stomach. Even if I could have untied myself, I was in no position to save her. I was no match for Calvin and his steroid-filled muscles as he delivered blow after blow to my weakening body. Sadly, I couldn't provide any defense for myself or help for Anyeh. The muscle-bound monster towered over me and pressed his shoe into my neck. It wasn't long before the pressure began to cut off my breathing. I knew this was it. I prayed silently as the life left my body.

Again I looked at Anyeh. I could read the hurt and despair in her eyes. Realizing I was defeated, I laid down my flag. Gina had won the battle. I knew I was going to die, but I was still a man, so I would die looking my killer in the eyes. I fixed my gaze on his face, and that's when I heard the pop and saw him fall.

His body lay limp on the ground. I didn't know where the shot came from, but it came right on time. I jumped up and looked around for my savior. I saw Keysha running toward us. Gina, who was still looking at her dead bodyguard, didn't see her coming, so Keysha was able to knock her out with a single blow to the head.

"Dee!" Keysha yelled as she jumped in my arms and hugged me tight.

"What the fuck took you so long? At first I was confident 'cause I knew I had Rambo for a sister, but damn, you had me worried!" I said while I squeezed her.

"Yeah well," she answered, "Anyeh here was supposed to come out and distract Gina so I could get a clear shot. I didn't think Gina would jump on her that fast. I couldn't do anything until one of them stopped beating y'all long enough to stand still."

Somehow, I suspected Keysha had waited a little longer than she had to. Knowing her, she was sitting in that church enjoying the show as Anyeh was beaten. What Keysha did next, though, changed my mind.

"We still have a little unfinished business," Keysha stated. I watched in shock as she walked over to Anyeh and hugged her.

"I'm sorry for all the hell I've put you through, but I was only protecting my big bro."

"Why the sudden change?" I asked.

My sister cried as she told me what she'd heard in the church before she shot Tiara. "I thought these chicks were all in this together to take you down, Dee, but after hearing what Tiara had to say, I believe Anyeh really did come over to your side. She was waiting in this church for Gina to bring you. No gun or nothing, but she was gonna try to help you, even if it meant losing her own life. Dee, I hate to admit it, but Anyeh really loves you."

Clap, clap, clap, clap!

We heard a noise coming from the church. I snatched the gun from Keysha's hand and aimed to shoot.

"That was wonderful. Better than the soaps. I ain't neva witnessed nuttin' like dis up close and personal," Kita said as she exited the church.

I dropped the gun to my side and we all let out a sigh of relief.

"Bitch, you ain't shit!" Keysha yelled at her. "You sat and watched all this shit that was about to go down and you ain't once try to help."

"Hell, if I got killed then who the hell was gon' report shit? I'm just a spectator, not a participator!" Kita stated as serious as could be.

"But Dee, I do know one got-damn thang. That

damn girl love you, boy. I don't know if you got the sweet dick or what, but the bitch love you!"

That was all I needed to hear. Confirmation from Kita and Keysha—you couldn't get any better than that! It was a wrap. I called my boys and gave specific cleanup instructions as well as business instructions. I made sure they dealt with Gina so that no one else would ever have to again. I sent Kita, the big mouth of the South, home with some hush money. Finally, I had one mission left, and this one was especially for Keysha.

CHAPTER FIFTEEN
Keysha

The continuous ringing of my house phone had become a part of my dream. I don't know how long it was ringing before I finally woke up. I forced myself from the bed to check the caller ID. I figured it could only be my social worker or bill collectors calling this early in the damn morning. The caller ID read TONY MONTANA.

I felt as though I was having déjà vu as I picked up to speak to Dee. I just prayed this time he wouldn't tell me there was another female he was interested in. There was no way I could repeat the same drama that I'd just experienced over Anyeh.

"What's up, big bro?" As always, I was excited to speak with him.

"Hey, Keysh. I got some good news for you," Dee stated, full of excitement.

"Oh no, not again. This is exactly how the last conversation started," I said aloud, confusing Dee.

"Huh? What you mean?" he asked.

"Never mind, Dee. What's up?"

Just like the last time Dee called me in the wee hours of the morning, I wondered what the hell he had to say that was so good it couldn't wait. And again, I knew it wouldn't be what I only dreamed of hearing. I was wrong.

"Keysh," he said, his voice full of excitement. "I pulled a few strings and convinced the Department of Social Services to release Davion into my custody."

I almost dropped the phone. "What did you just say?" I asked to be sure I wasn't still dreaming.

"When we were fighting, you told me some things about myself that were true. I was too wrapped up in my own shit to do what was most important. You risked your life to help me out of that shit with Gina, and you reminded me of what's really important—family, someone who truly has your back. So, to redeem myself, I made a few calls and pulled a few strings. They agreed to let Davion stay with me until your reconsideration hearing, which I have also worked on."

"You did?"

"Yeah. Instead of waiting another month for your court date, I got it pushed up on the docket to next week. I spoke to a few key people and they got your back, so it's pretty much a given that you're gonna get him back, Keysh."

I couldn't speak. I could only cry tears of joy as I realized I would finally be getting my son back.

"I'm coming to get you now, Keysh. I have to sign some paperwork and then we can go pick him up."

"Thank you, Diablo," was all I could manage to whisper through my tears.

"Anything for you, sis," he said before hanging up the phone.

I wasted no time getting dressed and preparing for Davion's arrival. I paused for one moment before getting in the shower. This day came not because of Dee, but because of someone much more powerful, and I had to give thanks.

"Thank you, Jesus. Thank you," I said aloud.

CHAPTER SIXTEEN
Anyeh

I sat on the balcony of the resort over the private beach where Dee had taken me, Keysha and her son for a vacation. I was reflecting on the recent events that had occurred, grateful that Diablo had forgiven me for everything. He told me he understood that I only did what I did to save my own life. He had faith that I loved him and would never betray him again, and he was right. I would do whatever I could to make our relationship work.

In order to do that, I felt like I had one more thing to confess to Diablo. We had a new beginning, and I wanted to be open and honest with him about everything. It took all my courage to tell him about the most hurtful situation. I had to tell him about the child I had tried to abort.

I could see the hurt in Dee's face as I admitted to him about the African concoction I had drunk. "But I don't know if it worked," I explained, hoping to encourage him.

Dee gave me a long lecture about his views on

abortion, then made me promise to never keep anything from him again, no matter what the situation. That wasn't much to ask. We agreed to be nothing but honest from now on. And of course, we made plans to visit a clinic for a pregnancy test as soon as we returned home to Virginia.

"Dee, do you love me?" I asked while looking in his eyes.

"Yes, I do," he answered without hesitation.

"Well, why don't we marry?" I asked.

I knew I loved Dee and he was the man I'd lost my purity with. It was only right for us to have a lifetime bond.

"I would love to marry you, Anyeh. Hell, no other woman has ever taken me the places you have, and I've never shared the feelings I have for you with another woman. The thing is, I think you and my sister need to be sure everything's cool between you before we take that next step."

I had no choice but to respect that. I went to Keysha's room in my most humble manner. I needed to formally apologize for all the events that had taken place, and give an explanation for my actions. I didn't know how to start. I thought about a story my grandmother would share with the children of the village. I started by telling Keysha this folktale.

"The mouth blabs cautiously; the nose tells it to keep quiet. The mouth never listens. The eyes tell the ears to tell the mouth to shut up, but the ear responds, 'it's none of your business,' so the mouth continues to blab until the face is slapped. Then the ear feels the pain of the slap, the eyes water, the nose runs, and mouth screams."

Keysha looked at me like I was crazy. I explained, "You see, Keysha, I was the mouth. I caused all the problems. Even though I had numerous warnings and signs that I was going down the wrong path, I ignored them because I had my mind set on what was important to me. I fell in love with your brother and would never want to hurt him, but because of all my bad choices, I ended up doing just that. You all never should have been involved. There is no excuse, but I would like to apologize. I love Dee and I know there is no him without you, so I ask for your approval, Keysha. I would love to be Dee's wife and your sister-in-law."

Keysha didn't say a word. She just walked over and hugged me tight as tears rolled down her cheeks. Dee smiled with consent. I knew he finally felt whole. Keysha looked at him and returned the smile.

"Looks like we're gonna be one big, happy family," Dee said to us.

"But you're still not getting my crown, bitch," Keysha responded and we all laughed.

"I love you, Diablo James," I whispered in his ear.

"I love you too, Anyeh James."

His response was music to my ears.

Something special and erotic
from

Carl Weber
#1 national best selling author
and the publisher of
Urban Books

HE MAKES LOVE
LIKE A WOMAN

I'd had a hard life to be so young. I'd been raped as a child, thrown into foster care, and run away by the time I was twelve. The only stable thing in my life was my grandma, and she died of cancer before I could tell her how much I loved her. My mother, God bless her soul, was on crack so bad I had to become a stripper just to feed my brothers and sisters.

When I was sixteen I ran into this nigga named Black who I really cared about. He was real smooth and told me everything I wanted to hear. Like most sistahs in the life, I confused good sex with love and he ended up pimping me. I didn't mind turnin' tricks for Black, though. Especially since he kept tellin' me how much he loved me and that he planned on marrying me when we had enough money. After a while, though, he started beating on me, and when the beatings got real bad I had to cut his ass loose.

Well I'd *tried* to be with guys and that didn't

work, so I looked to chicks. I'd been attracted to females ever since I was a kid and experimented with my neighbor next door, so chicks weren't a real problem. To be honest they turned me on. There is nothin' in the world like a sexy sistah, not to mention the fact that they're not trying to shove something hard into you every time they get the chance.

Don't get me wrong; I like guys too, but if I had to choose, I'd take a woman over a man any day. Women are soft, sensual and sexy, and the way they make love is so completely different from the roughness of a man. Just the thought of being with a woman gets me moist. There is nothing in the world like the gentle touch of a woman when she kisses your breasts, or the expertise she has when she goes down on you. Try as hard as you want, some things you just can't teach a man. That's 'cause only a woman knows what another woman really wants.

By the time I was eighteen, my younger sister had joined me in the clubs. I don't know why she didn't learn from my mistakes, but six months later she was pregnant and being pimped. After she had her baby, I left the streets and came home permanently. I was still turning out chicks left and right, but I wasn't stripping as much. For some reason, it just wasn't in my heart anymore. Plus, I'd made my fair share of enemies in the clubs and although I loved fighting, things were getting a little too hot. Not that I was scared of the girls, but Black was back in town and I was sick of fucking niggas just to protect me from him. He'd been popping up talking a lot of shit lately, and although I didn't wanna admit it, I was more than a little scared.

When I got home, my mom was still on that crack shit, so I felt obligated to take care of my little brother and nephew. My sister was just straight up out there, and the truth is I was more of a mother to her child than she was. I guess inside I really wanted a baby of my own. Someone I could take care of and be that family I'd always wanted. At that point in my life, the only thing I really had was my nephew, my little brother and my singing.

I loved to sing more than anything in the world. Shit, I was good at it. I could sing my ass off, and that's what I did every chance I had. I belonged to two churches and was a member of both of choirs. I know it sounds fucked up, a stripper going to church, but God knows the deal. I was doing what I had to do.

My life wasn't great, but it wasn't terrible either. My nephew really brought a lot of joy into my life. He was starting to fill that lonely void I had. That is until I ran into *him*.

He wasn't all that. Short, dark-skinned with dreads and a beard. Truth is, I really don't know why I stopped to talk to him in the first place . . . Let me stop lyin'. It was his eyes and the way he looked at me. That's why I talked to him. From the second he laid eyes on me, that nigga thought he knew me. I remember him asking me for my phone number. I smiled right in his face as I gave him some bogus shit. Then I walked away, never expecting to see him again, until something inside of me made me go back and get *his* number.

He wrote his number on the back of some poetry he was writing and I read it before leaving. It was *real* good. So I told him about my singing. He was the first person I'd ever met who was really interested in my singing. That's when he asked me for a kiss. Would you believe I almost gave it to him, too? And I honestly have no idea why.

I went home that night and thought about him. There was something about that brother. I didn't know what it was, but I couldn't get him out of my head. I didn't even know what kind of car he drove. The nigga could have been a broke ass, but it didn't matter. He got to me that fast.

The next day, I called him at work and set up a date. I knew it wasn't gonna be anything more than a slam-bam-thank-you-ma'am, but that was okay. If I wanted to be truly intimate, I woulda called a girl. I was just horny as hell and needed something warm inside of me. Every once in a while everyone needs something warm inside. Know what I mean?

When he picked me up, I didn't invite him inside. I was too embarrassed. My moms was home and she was high as shit. I just came down and got in his little car. He asked me if I wanted to go to the movies or to dinner, but I jut told him to take me to a hotel.

When we got inside the hotel, homeboy took off his clothes and got into bed. He propped a pillow behind his head as he watched me undress. He was smiling like he was really looking forward to getting some. When I got all my clothes off, it was cold and I couldn't wait to get under the covers. The sex was gonna have to wait 'til I warmed up a bit.

To my surprise, the bed was real warm, and when he wrapped his arms around me, so was he. He stared at me with those bedroom eyes and I didn't know whether to laugh or cry. He was making me feel like they do in the love stories.

He kissed me. I'm not into kissing, but it was nice. Then he began to gently kiss my neck the way I like it. I closed my eyes and it was almost as if I was with a woman. I rolled my neck around so that he could kiss the other side, and he did. I couldn't help myself. I let out few moans. He took his time alternating between my ears and my neck, and not once did he touch any other part of my body.

I was getting moist and my nipples were begging to be touched. He must have read my mind because his fingers oh-so-gently rubbed up against them. I was in heaven, and when we made eye contact, I tried to let him know how much I appreciated his touch.

His lips moved down to my breasts, and the way he licked them made my womanhood gush with moisture. Those sexy lips around my nipple were driving me crazy. I started slowly grinding my hips. He was moving back and forth between my titties like it was the last time he'd ever see them.

I softly stroked his hair and neck. I'd never been with a man who was so attentive. Hell, I'd only been with a few women who were this intent on pleasing me.

After he'd given both my titties proper attention he surprised me by kissing his way down to my womanhood. He didn't shove his tongue inside me or use his hand and try to open me up like most men. No, he knew exactly what he was doing. His tongue ran down my pubic hair and found its way right to my clit.

When he touched it, I tensed up because it felt

so good. I looked down at him and he smiled before licking me again. My toes curled, that shit felt so good. His tongue was soft on the up stroke and hard on the down stroke.

I glanced down at him, and he was into it—I mean *really* into it. I just prayed he wasn't gonna stop. If he did, I would have begged him to continue. He was doing things to me that no man had a right to do, and my body was tensing up for something I rarely felt. I was so close to exploding it scared me, and what was pleasure was becoming overwhelming.

He wrapped his lips around my clit, sucking on it gently as his tongue danced on the tip. It was so good I couldn't take it anymore. I tried to get away, but he held on, and when I moved, his face went right with me. Tears of pleasure were falling from my eyes and I felt like I was gonna pass out.

He eased up, smiling. He knew exactly what he was doing to me. I wanted to say something but I couldn't. I was still confused by what he had done to me. He made his way up my body until his face was directly over mine. He didn't say a word. He just kissed me and I savored the taste of myself on his lips.

I don't know why, but I felt compelled to say something. I looked him in the eyes and said, "I love you."

He smiled, almost laughed, then rolled over on his back. I didn't know what he was thinking, but I didn't care. I was feeling something. Maybe it wasn't love, but it was something. When I was with Black and them I had to say "I love you." It was just part of that pimp game. But with this brother, I *wanted* to say it.

I pulled back the covers and looked at his body. It wasn't anything special, but it had done special things to me. God, what had I gotten myself into?

I slid down between his legs and looked at his penis. It wasn't huge, but it wasn't little either. What I did like about it was that it was smooth and didn't have a lot of bumps like some brothers I'd been with. I wasn't really into giving head, but I knew men liked it, so I licked him, hoping to return the favor he'd given me. He jumped when the ball from my pierced tongue touched him. I did it again and he moaned.

I wasn't thrilled about what I was doing, but I wasn't upset either. I could tell he was enjoying himself, but he was a real gentleman about it. He wasn't like most guys who tried to shove their things down my throat and hold my head. He let me do what I had to do. I liked that. After a few minutes he stopped me, pulling me up to his chest as he whispered, "Ride me."

I looked down at him in amazement. How the hell could he know that was my favorite position? I gently took his thing and slid down on it. Damn, that shit felt good. All my life I heard girls talk about how they wanted big-ass dicks to fuck, but this brother was the perfect fit for me.

As I rode him, he sucked on my breasts, and I have to admit things were getting kinda hot. I was wetter than I can ever remember being, and I felt the urge to move faster and faster on top of him. I felt like I was almost there, and the faster I went the closer I was. He was doing a masterful job on my breasts. When I closed my eyes, things started to happen.

My entire body became rigid and my lower half

went into convulsions. I felt so good as all the blood in my body rushed between my legs, sending me to a place I'd never been before.

I collapsed on his chest with a contented smile. I kissed him passionately, something I rarely never did, then looked into his eyes.

"I love you," I told him.

"Sure you do." He smiled, wrapping his arms around me. "Sure you do."

He rolled me on my back, and the only thing I could think of was that I wanted to give him the same pleasure he'd given me. Wrapping my arms around him, I massaged the muscles in his shoulders as his hips began to slowly move his manhood inside of me. As he moved faster, a wave of pleasure hit me. It became hard to concentrate on his pleasure when mine was so great. He was doing it to me again, and this time I was going to be ready. This time I was going to savor the moment.

The faster he went the more I concentrated on that feeling, and when the time came, our lips were pressed against each other. Again my upper body became rigid and my lower half went into convulsions, but this time was even better because his body went rigid also. When he looked at me with his bedroom eyes, I could feel the warmth he was splashing into my womb, and at that moment I knew I was in *love*.

We left that hotel that night a couple. He may not have known we were a couple, but we definitely were. When he pulled up in front of my house, I refused to get out. No way was I letting go of what had just happened to me. I needed some reassurance. I needed to know he was mine.

"You got a girl?" I asked.

"No."

"You got a wife?" I checked his finger for a wedding ring.

"No."

"What do you got?"

"I got you." He smiled.

Then I smiled. I never smiled like that before in my life. He made me feel so good with just a few words. I got out of his car that night, but the next day he picked me up and took me home to his moms. She was a church woman and took me in right away like I was her daughter. It felt good to part of a real family.

Oh, yeah. Me and him? We're married now and we got three kids—Tyrell and LaShawn and my nephew J'Quan. Well, I guess that old cliché about whores has been proven wrong in my case. You can make a whore into a housewife. You just have to make love like a woman.

If you liked this short story, check out

Carl Weber's

national best selling novels:

Married Men
Lookin' for Luv
Baby Momma Drama
Player Haters
The Preacher's Son
So You Call Yourself a Man
And his new release due out January 2007
The First Lady

Anthology

A Dollar and a Dream